...ection of Titles by Sarah Harrison

* available from Severn House

THE

A Sel

THE DIVIDED HEART

Sarah Harrison

This first world edition published in Great Britain 2002 by
SEVERN HOUSE PUBLISHERS LTD of
9–15 High Street, Sutton, Surrey SM1 1DF.
This first world edition published in the USA 2002 by
SEVERN HOUSE PUBLISHERS INC of
595 Madison Avenue, New York, N.Y. 10022.

British Library Cataloguing in Publication Data

Harrison, Sarah, 1946-
   The divided heart
   1.   Love stories
   I.   Title
   823.9'14 [F]

   ISBN 0-7278-5837-8

Typeset by Palimpsest Book Production Ltd.,
Polmont, Stirlingshire, Scotland.
Printed and bound in Great Britain by
MPG Books Ltd., Bodmin, Cornwall.

Preface

The Divided Heart was my second novel, written more than thirty years ago, but not published until now. It's something of a shock to confront one's younger self, personal and professional, the more so because this was an attempt to write in that hardest of all genres to get right – the romantic novel.

There's a common but erroneous view that romantic novels are bound, by definition, to be simplistic and sentimental. These are certainly the traps of which a writer should be aware. Ideally, such a novel should be not simplistic but simple, not cloyingly sentimental but invested with honest sentiment. And it should leave the reader with the assurance that love is a benign emotion. It can be misplaced and mishandled, but one of the qualities of what we call 'true love' is that it is redemptive. In other words, a romantic novel carries a strong feel-good factor.

In spite or perhaps because of the inexperience of its author, *The Divided Heart* does, I think, fulfil these criteria. In fact reading it again after so many years, along with the inevitable winces and blushes, I was struck by its quality of innocence and a kind of emotional integrity that goes with it.

And what a time-capsule it is, too! This is a world where people still 'got engaged', where the wine-at-home revolution was still taking place, a world without the fax, let alone email and the computer, and where it was considered noteworthy for a man – even a gay one – to be a good domestic cook. And what, you may ask, does he cook? Why, moussaka! That Greek shepherd's pie, now sadly out of favour, which even then we suspected had more to do with King's Road bistros than Hellenic pastures . . .

You may find this novel quaint, a curiosity. But in all modesty you'd have to made of stone not to be touched by it. The past may be another country, but certain things don't change, and love is one of them. I do hope you enjoy *The Divided Heart*.

Sarah Harrison, 2002

One

The dress was a dream. Elvi took two steps back from the mirror and stood demurely, feet together and hands lightly folded, like a flower bud, against the smooth waterfall of white silk. But even the demure pose could not disguise the vibrancy of her youth and beauty, the crescent-shaped Tudor headdress could not crush the springy mane of auburn hair – and her eyes, glancing round for approval, were sparkling with excitement.

'Will I do?'

'Will you do!' The plump old dressmaker moved round her, adjusting a fold here, pinching a seam there, talking through a mouthful of pins. 'You know you will. You look a picture, my dear, you don't need me to tell you.'

'All thanks to you, Miss Markham.'

'Rubbish. The most beautiful dress in the world is only the frame that sets off the painting. But I grant you it's one of my better efforts.' She stepped back with a little sigh of pride. 'Yes, he's a lucky man.'

'And I'm lucky, too, you know, and so happy I could burst!' To emphasize her point she executed a series of energetic twirls across the room, the skirt swirling round her like water. Miss Markham, picturing her handiwork ruined before its grand debut, fussed after her, cornered her against the back of the chintz-covered sofa and suggested gently that it was time the dress came off again so that the final touches and alterations could be made. Reluctantly, Elvi allowed herself to be unfastened, and the wedding dress to cascade with a whisper to the floor.

'Now step out *carefully*,' Miss Markham admonished. Elvi

did so, and hauled on her sweater and jeans with her customary speed. The Tudor headdress, forgotten, hurtled off under the onslaught of the sweater and bounced on the carpets to be fielded by Miss Markham. Elvi then bustled about the room collecting up hairbrush, tote bag and fur jacket. The snug little room seemed filled with her energetic youthful presence.

'So many things to do, Miss Markham, do you think I'll get organized?'

'Of course you will, you've a full two months before the wedding.'

'Two months! What's two months when you're preparing for a lifetime? I'm sure I shall put rufflette tape on my veil and walk up the aisle wrapped in curtain material!'

'Not if I have anything to do with it, you won't. Now wait a minute, you've forgotten this—' She handed Elvi a square white box.

'Heavens, the invitations, and they've got to go out this week! I'll forget my head next. Do you want to see them? You'll be getting one, of course, though we're taking it for granted you'll be coming. But anyway, I must show you . . .'
She fought with the neatly tied string, impatiently tucking her hair behind her ear when it fell across her face. Miss Markham had to turn away for a moment to push aside the memories that crowded unasked into her head.

'Here you are, what do you think . . . ? Miss Markham . . . ? You look as though you'd seen a ghost, are you okay?'

'Yes, yes, I'm all right. But just for a moment there you looked – never mind. Let me see these invitations.' She gave a loud sniff and made a business of taking the thick white card and turning it to the light to examine it. When she handed it back, Elvi's mood had changed.

'I know what you were going to say. You were going to say I looked like her – like my mother.'

'I can't deny it.'

'You mustn't worry, you know, I like to hear about her. I can't remember her, so every little helps. Father won't mention her at all, I know it's too painful for him, but I'm out for all the information I can get. Tell me, was she as beautiful as I believe? You made her wedding dress too, didn't you?'

'Yes, I did. She was even younger than you, only eighteen when she married the Major. People said he was too old for her, perhaps a bit too stuffy as well—'

'That's all right, he can be – go on.'

'But I've never seen a girl so much in love.'

'Not even me?'

'Hmm.' Miss Markham was thoughtful. 'She was different, more serious about it. In any event, it suited her. She was a beauty, but every time she tried on that dress she looked a little lovelier, and on the day – well, people said they'd never seen a more breathtaking bride.'

'Was the dress like mine?'

'It had a tight bodice and high neck like yours – you have her slim figure and can wear that kind of thing – but the skirt was very full, all lace, "like a summer snowstorm" she used to say.'

'It sounds fabulous. What happened to it?'

'That's the sad thing. She always said she wanted her daughter to get married in it – even if it meant taking it to bits and just using the material – but after she died your father brought it back to me and asked me to cut it up and use it as quick as I could. He couldn't bear to have it hanging around the house.'

'Oh, but how could *you* bear to do it?'

'If you'd seen his face when he came round here with that dress in his arms, you'd have done anything to help.'

'I'm sorry. What's a dress, anyway?'

'That's right. And now you know what her wishes were it doesn't seem so bad somehow.'

'I shall think of her on my wedding day,' announced Elvi. 'What flowers did she have?'

'Just a posy of rosebuds.'

'I shall have the same.'

'Don't, they won't suit the dress.' Miss Markham was brusque. 'Whatever an old body like me says, you're yourself, not a carbon copy of her, and you shouldn't try to be.'

'Okay, okay.' Elvi was laughing. 'Remember you started it!'

'Well maybe I should have held my tongue. I talk too much – it's old age.'

'Nonsense, you're lovely, I won't hear a word against you. By the way, you *are* coming, aren't you?'

'Of course, I need to keep an eye on you in that dress. But don't bother with one of those—' She indicated the invitations.

'Why? Don't you like them?'

'They're fine, but it's tosh to send me one when I've said I'll come.'

'All right. Shall I see you next week, then?'

'Yes, Friday as usual, and the dress will be done.'

'It will be perfect, I know it.' Elvi planted a kiss on the dressmaker's cheek. 'See you then!'

Miss Markham closed the front door after her and seemed to feel her little house settle back into snug tranquillity after this burst of fresh spring wind. She was not altogether sure, if she was honest with herself, that she preferred the tranquillity. Still, there was work to be done. She bustled back into the sitting room.

It was a marvellous day, thought Elvi, as she swung back through the village and along the lane that led home. Only England in April could produce a day like this. There was a wonderful clear, rain-washed sunshine over everything, and yet the breeze was fresh enough to bring the pink to your cheeks, and small clouds dragged their shadows, like the tails of kites, across the patchwork of fields and woods. Elvi did a hop, skip and a jump, and then glanced hastily round to make sure no one had seen her. She began to whistle 'I feel pretty, oh so pretty, I feel witty . . .'

Major Beecham was in the garden when she got back. She dropped her bag and jacket in the hall and ran out through the kitchen to greet him. He did not at first see her and she paused for a moment to reflect what a fine-looking man he still was, tall and soldierly and handsome in his well-cut clothes – he'd always had good taste and been proud of his appearance. It was only when he caught sight of her and began to walk across the lawn to meet her that you noticed the stick, carried stiff and straight by his left leg, and the painfully slow step. He was crippled with arthritis.

To save him the dreadful limping progress which she knew he hated, she ran over to him and linked her arm through his. He pressed her hand.

'How's the haute couture going, then?'

'Swimmingly, thanks. She's an absolute treasure, Miss Markham, I'd have had to spend a small fortune in London to buy a dress like that.'

'Good, good. Your swain rang up, by the way.' The Major always referred to Alan Neilson in this manner, even if it made Elvi giggle. Alan was no 'swain' and they both knew it. One of the things she loved about him was his natural air of authority – he was older, a man of the world, a man who'd learnt hard lessons in the school of experience.

'And what did he have to say?' she asked.

'He wants to come down tonight. He can't stay the whole weekend, he's got a conference starting on Saturday evening. I told him he was welcome.'

'Of course. There's lots to talk about and I want to persuade him to come shopping with me in town next week – I've got to choose some carpet and I need his help.'

'Poor fellow.' The Major looked down at his daughter indulgently. 'He's a busy man, you know.'

'Not too busy to please me.' She smiled confidently, and her smile was immediately reflected on her father's face.

'Of course not.'

Since his wife's death Dick Beecham had concentrated all his love, care and attention on his daughter. Impervious to warnings of spoiling and over-indulgence he had given her the best of everything. To the dismay of the Cassandras it became increasingly obvious that far from being ruined by so much kindness and tender loving care, not to say material comfort,

Elvi was growing into a lovely and charming girl. She was popular with everyone in the village, and for a good reason: she carried around with her, like a charm, the aura of her own happiness. She had never known anything but gentleness, and comfort, and protection, and so she expected nothing else. Although her many friends might not have defined it in so many words, she represented the gaiety and innocence that was so often lost after earliest childhood. She was also good-natured and outgoing, free with her generous affection – people smiled when they saw her coming, and looked after her as she departed.

Her natural advantages were enhanced by the fact that she took them for granted. She paid little attention to her appearance and was universally liked for it. She trudged over the fields to the village shop clad in baggy cords, anorak and Wellingtons, her cloud of chestnut hair bobbing on her shoulders, her nose pink in the cold wind.

Dick Beecham ached with love for her. If he could have kept her forever protected and cherished among those who knew and loved her, he would have done so. But with a terrible, sad certainty, he knew he owed her to others. She would fly the nest, and every man that saw her wanted to be the one to lure her away. However, until Alan, her attitude to her admirers had remained artless, friendly and naïve and though he did not intend to, the Major quelled their ardour with his cold, defensive attitude. But Alan was different. He was thirty-five, fifteen years older than Elvi and, from the first, he won Dick Beecham's respect and admiration. Wisely and gently he won the Major's friendship first, and then his daughter's, and as he became a more and more frequent guest Elvi began to see him in a new light. Here was a man worthy of her father – a man her father liked and admired – and a man she herself could love. Alan was undeniably handsome – tall and broad, with the ash-fair hair and smoky grey eyes of his Swedish father. His manners were always impeccable and gentle, manners born of kindness and consideration rather than mere protocol. He had made his own business successful through a mixture of flare and aggression, but the latter quality was reserved strictly for work. With Elvi he was a perfect old-fashioned suitor and she was enchanted by him. She had daydreams of herself as Alan's bride, taken to London, fêted and made much of, living a life with no hardship or shadows, her father and her husband gazing down on her benignly. It was the first time she had crystallized her position in her own mind. With Alan, there need be no change, the future would stretch away like a bright sunlit summer garden, walled about with care to keep the world at bay.

When she had known Alan five months, he proposed to her and she had accepted. It was to be a June wedding. Everyone approved and admired, the whole village celebrated the engagement, Major Beecham was quietly satisfied, and more relieved than he could say to think of his little bird passing into such eminently suitable hands.

They bought an old vicarage, a romantic house hedged about with roses, and Elvi suddenly discovered the fun of planning rooms and decorations, of buying furniture and fabrics – and with no financial restrictions, for Alan was both prosperous and generous.

It was all so *right*, everyone said.

Now, Dick Beecham watched his daughter race up the stairs to her room and thought: It's not long now. I must prepare for it, stop loving her so much. But how? He sank down in his chair and dropped the stick heavily to the ground. He felt suddenly cold.

Upstairs, Elvi flung open the window and then, on an impulse, went to the dressing table and picked up the photo of Alan which stood there.

'I love you,' she said, because it sounded so good, and gave the serious face a kiss. The expression held an indefinable sadness, a world-weariness which made her sharply conscious of her own relatively short, and wholly carefree existence. She knew, every time she looked at that photograph, that Alan's decision to marry her had not been taken lightly. Any amount of time, care and thought had gone into it. And how much

7

care and thought had she put into her decision? Very little, she was bound to say. In fact it had hardly been a decision at all, more a gradual, placid acceptance of what seemed an eminently suitable situation, causing the fewest possible ripples on the calm surface of her life.

She felt a small stab of guilt. So much love and sincerity had been invested in her, and what had she given back? But she very quickly brushed the feeling aside. She was happy, happier than she'd every been. Surely that spoke for itself?

She went to the wardrobe and began to rummage through her clothes. Alan was the only person who had inspired her to make a conscious effort with her appearance – he was so obviously delighted when she wore a particularly becoming outfit. She selected some bottle-green velvet trousers and a vivid orange silk skirt, and begun to tug them on, humming softly to herself.

At half-past six Alan Neilson pulled the grey Mercedes off the main road into the forecourt of a brightly lit modern café. He knew he'd hate it, he could hear the jukebox before he even got out of the car, and the coffee would be revolting. But it would at least, God willing, be warm, and the coffee hot, and he wasn't prepared to drive around looking for somewhere more salubrious.

The girl behind the counter, who was heavy and glum, gave him a long look, first appraising, then coquettish. Definitely a cut above their usual run of customers.

'I'll have a black coffee, and a bar of that, please,' he said, selecting a packet of bitter black chocolate off the plastic shelf.

The girl giggled. 'Watching your figure?'

'Oh yes, we have to too, you know.'

'It looks all right to me.' She giggled again, and this time had the grace to blush fiercely at her own boldness.

'Thank you.' This was said with withering politeness.

The tactic worked. The girl subsided into her former sullen gloom and put his coffee in front of him with a slight push so that it slopped into the saucer.

'That'll be one pound.'

Alan paid and carried the coffee and chocolate to a table in the window. He glanced at his watch. No need to ring Elvi, he'd be there by eight and they never ate before half-past, anyway. Also, he liked to treasure the feeling of anticipation. As a child, nothing would have induced him to peep at Christmas or birthday presents before the appointed day, and now it was the same. Every moment he delayed here was making the moment of meeting more delicious. He lit a cigarette and, as he did so, caught sight of his own reflection in the rapidly darkening expanse of plate glass. God, he looked terrible. It had been a hard week and he was over-tired and subsequently chilled to the marrow by the cool April evening. His reflection stared back with great dark holes where eyes should have been, and cadaverous shadows under each cheekbone. He looked haggard and old. What would Elvi make of him tonight? He gulped at the coffee as if its warmth could regenerate him. He must not be cold, and weary and depressed. He must not be a burden. He was about to snatch the fairytale princess from her ivory tower, and now he must be worthy of her and not bring her extra cares. He knew what he had to do, what he had to be, and if it meant sacrificing a little bit of himself, he would do it – for her.

He wondered how she would greet him this evening. She was like a child, never quite the same. Sometimes she would run to him with her hair flying and he would gather her up and feel the soft curtain of that hair over his face, and her laughing mouth against his neck, and he wished it could be like that for ever. Sometimes, if she was in the garden, she didn't hear him coming, and he would seek her out, walking softly over the lawn to surprise her, fighting down the urge to run, tantalizing himself. And then there were those times when she was on her 'island' as he privately called it, when her welcome was warm, but he could catch her looking at him in a strange detached way. When their eyes met she would smile and reach out her hand but he knew that he took the hand across an abyss.

These occasions were rare, and did not worry him. He

expected her to have doubts, and even occasional moments of panic, about their marriage. After all he was many years older than her, and worlds away in experience, though even she did not yet know how far. But now he was confident of his own love – its strength, and stamina. He could and would ride the storm, he would *make* it all right, he would outface the world if it meant protecting this treasure he had thought never to find. By sheer force of love and strength of will he would keep his young bride, and in the end she would love him the more for it.

He drained the coffee, grimacing at its bitterness, stubbed out his cigarette, and rose, slipping what remained of the chocolate into his coat pocket. He felt a little better. Now all he wanted to do was see Elvi. He settled into the seat of the Mercedes, feeling with satisfaction the way it fitted to his body, and started up the engine; the pale glare of the headlights raked across the car park as he turned back for the road. He'd be there soon.

An hour later he swung into the circular gravel drive of the Beeches and pulled up in front of the porch. He switched off the hum of the engine and sat for a moment in the sudden silence, savouring his arrival. Then the door opened, and a bright beam of light poured through the car window so that he was temporarily dazzled. By the time he was bending his head to get out, Elvi was there, and as he straightened up she flung her arms round his neck.

'Hallo, hallo! Oh, it's so gorgeous that you came.'

'My darling.' He was always more touched than he could say by these naïve, enthusiastic welcomes. What girl of his acquaintance in London, engaged or not, would be so open-hearted, so uncalculating? He held her close. She was chattering something about her dress, but he did not hear, he was only conscious of her boyish thinness against him and the scent – nothing assumed, but her own – which rose from her hair, damp with the soft spring rain which was now falling.

'We must go in and see your father,' he said. 'You'll catch your death standing here in the rain.'

'Don't be silly.' She leaned away from him. 'What's a bit of rain? It's healthy. But you're right about Father. Come on, forget your case, we'll bring it in later.' She raced ahead of him to the door, turned to watch him come up the steps, then ran on again into the bright warm interior of the house. He followed more slowly, and as he closed the door behind him she re-emerged with the Major in tow.

'Alan. How are you? You look tired.'

'I am, a little. It's been a tough week, I'm afraid I've wished myself on you in a somewhat debilitated condition.'

'You know you're always welcome.'

'I'm all the better for being here, I assure you.' Alan shook the older man's hand. He had a tremendous affection for the Major, and a feeling of responsibility, too. God knows what he was about to do to this man – tear from him not just his most loved and treasured possession, but a living part of himself. It had to be – both men knew that – but it was his, Alan's, responsibility to make sure it was painless. The three of them went into the sitting room and Alan immediately went over to the hearth and stretched out his palms to the welcoming fire. He could feel light and warmth spreading through him again after the bleak greyness of the past week, like the sap rising in a tree in springtime. Elvi came to his side and slipped an arm round his waist.

'I've made a scrummy supper,' she said, giving him a squeeze.

'You always do.'

'Oh no, not always, but tonight because I did it all in a rush everything went right. But there's no hurry, you can sit about and thaw and mellow for as long as you want.'

'This is what he needs.' It was the Major, handing him a tumbler with a generous measure of Scotch.

'Thank you, just what the doctor ordered.'

'I imagine,' said Dick Beecham, quite sternly, 'that if I were a doctor confronted with such a case of overwork I should order a good holiday and plenty of rest.'

'Good Lord, there's nothing the matter with me. In fact –'

11

to change the conversation and shift it away from himself he addressed himself to Elvi – 'one of the reasons I invited myself at such short notice was to ask you if you'd like to come over to the house tomorrow. I haven't got to be at this wretched conference until six tomorrow evening, we could set off early, make a day of it and I could drop you off at about five and go on there.'

'Oh, you *know* I would! There's so much to talk about it and I don't like to think of it standing empty waiting for us. We need to get to know each other.'

'Not only that, there won't be a stick left in it if it's empty for too long.' Dick Beecham was grim.

'Father, don't be so dreary and realistic. I'm sure I'd know if someone burgled that house, I'd feel it in my bones and he'd be caught red-handed.'

'Anyway, if you'd like to go, that's enough for me.' Alan smiled down at her. Her happiness and enthusiasm washed over him. He could deny her nothing.

After dinner, Major Beecham went early to bed, leaving Alan and Elvi in a sleepy glow before the dying fire.

'Don't forget to put the guard in front of it when you come to bed. Good night,' were his last words, and then they listened to his steps, slow and irregular, ascending the stairs. Halfway up there was a pause. Elvi whispered softly, 'He always stops there.'

'Taking a breather?'

'That, and looking at mother's portrait. Saying good-night to it.'

'Of course.'

It was moving to think of that elderly man, standing in the dark before a painting, making his silent salutation. They both sat quietly until he had moved on, and across the landing to his bedroom, closing the door with a soft click behind him.

Immediately and instinctively Alan cupped Elvi's face in his hand and tilted it towards his for a kiss. Its beauty, softly dappled by the firelight, almost took his breath away.

'Elvi, I love you,' he said.

Two

The next day dawned perfect, as Elvi knew it would. When she opened her eyes she was immediately conscious of an air of expectancy in the world outside the drawn curtains. It was waiting for her quietly out there, holding its breath, keeping its beautiful secret, like a present waiting to be unwrapped. All she had to do was get up, and draw the curtains, and the happiness would begin.

Unlike her fiancé, Elvi had no taste for anticipation. She flung back her duvet and rushed over to the window, pulling back the curtains with a rattle. The garden lay in a moist, misty stillness, the lawn still veiled in its perfect newborn caul of dew – not a footprint to break the spell. The clear milky call of a cuckoo chimed across miles of English countryside. Elvi knew that she had to be first down there, she had to share the secret before it became public and tarnished.

She glanced at her watch. Seven fifteen. Her father would go down to make his cup of tea in a quarter of an hour, he'd take Alan a cup and then it would be at least another half an hour before they were down: half an hour she could have quite to herself before getting the breakfast. She pulled off her cotton nightdress and replaced it with the jeans and sweater of the afternoon before. The finery of the previous evening lay in a bright, neglected heap on the floor by her bed. Rummaging in one of her drawers, she found socks of a suitable thickness to wear under boots, tugged them on and left the room, quietly shutting the door with a click behind her. The thrill of being a fugitive made her lean down the last few stairs, run across the hall and through the kitchen to the

Sarah Harrison

back porch where she stepped into her already mud-encrusted
boots – then she was out.

She glanced up at the window of Alan's room, curtained,
like a closed eye. He was probably still fast asleep after his
hard week. He had no idea that she was out here, so near and
yet so far. She was suddenly sensible of the great separateness
of the three of them, all variously preoccupied with each
other, and for different reasons, and in varying degrees. At
this particular moment they might each have been on different
planets for the amount of contact there was between them. It
struck her that Alan – her husband to be – was almost unreal
to her at his instant. She found it hard to invest the idea of
him, and marriage to him, with any substance. But then she
remembered the trip to the house. That would be real, that
would be good. No need to worry about anything now. She
walked quickly across the grass in the direction of the gate
that led into the lane.

Alan watched her go. He seemed to have been awake for
hours in that tense, staring trance that accompanies over-
tiredness. What sleep he'd had was early on in the night
and of a thin and restless variety, full of dreams and worry.
In the small hours he had woken up feeling stiff and shivery,
filled with an irrational dread of the proposed trip to the
house. It was miles. He was going to have to get back into
the car and drive all the way there, almost straight away after
breakfast and then there'd be the journey back in the evening
and then on to this blasted conference. Something shamingly
like tears of sheer fatigue had pricked his eyelids. Why had he
suggested it? He couldn't do it, he wouldn't, it was crazy. He
was fit for nothing but sitting about with the papers, perhaps
a drink at the pub, a quiet walk over those soggy, comfortable
fields which banked about this house like pillows, insulation
against the outside world. That was all. But then there was
Elvi. He'd made the suggestion just to see the excitement and
pleasure it gave her, he'd been buying an extra bit of love in
the easiest way he could think of. Now he had to carry it
through. Predictably, as the thick darkness in the room had

14

begun to break up into a monochrome patchwork of shadows, he'd begun to feel drowsy. The awful loneliness of the night was ebbing away.

Then he'd heard the click of Elvi's door and her soft hurrying footsteps along the passage. It had occurred to him that she might – but the footsteps did not pause and he'd listened to her patter down the stairs and out of the back door. He'd waited a couple of minutes so that she should not see him, and then got out of bed and went over to the window. He'd parted the curtains and watched her as she threaded through the light morning mist towards the fields, leaving a trail of footprints on the damp grass. He thought: If she'd wanted me to go she'd have knocked on my door. I mustn't follow. But as he climbed back into bed to while away the obligatory extra twenty minutes, he comforted himself with the thought that she might, after all, just not have wanted to disturb him. For all she knew he was still deeply asleep. He smiled wryly to himself and dozed off.

When Elvi got back both men were in the kitchen, the table was laid and coffee was percolating cheerily, if a little fast, on the stove.

'Oh Lord, I'm sorry.' She heeled off her boots and beamed at Alan. 'I'm afraid I've neglected my duties.'

'You mustn't patronize us, my dear,' said the Major, 'we're both perfectly competent in the kitchen.'

'Treasures.' Alan enjoyed to the full the seconds that her cool, damp cheek brushed his, the light pressure of her arm across his shoulders. He readily recaptured those sensations that had made him suggest the visit to the house. He caught her hand as she moved away.

'I saw you setting off this morning.'

'Did you? I thought you'd be dead to the world.'

'No, I slept rather lightly last night and I was awake early.'

'But I was *so* quiet.' She was like a child seeking praise. Alan gave it readily.

'As a mouse. But then I always hear mice.'

15

'Well, you might have waved, or called or something.'

'Not worth it. You were practically out of sight by the time I got to the window. And early morning walks are best enjoyed alone.'

'Bless you.' She lifted the hand that held hers and pressed it to her cheek. 'You're much too decent. Did you get any sleep at all?'

'Enough.'

The Major slid open the warming drawer of the oven and produced a plate of sausages, bacon and fried bread.

'Look at that!' Alan enthused.

'Not bad, is it?' Dick Beecham began to straighten up slowly, the plate at a sickening angle. With practised speed and tact Elvi had relieved him of the plate, helped him up with her free hand, and was busy apportioning the food on to three smaller plates, apparently all in one movement. Her natural delicacy in dealing with her father Alan found especially appealing. She was young for her age – a mere girl compared to the women of the world that most were at twenty these days, and yet in this respect she showed enormous maturity – the ability to help smoothly and efficiently in practical ways, but with a lightness of touch which demanded no gratitude nor caused any embarrassment.

Over breakfast Elvi put forward her theory on the kind of day it was going to be, the Major consulted his paper, and Alan listened to, and agreed with, Elvi.

'Now!' she announced, when they'd finished. 'I shall wash up and make a picnic, you go and consult the map, and then we'll go. Will you be okay for lunch, Father, or shall I organize something?'

'No, no, I can fend for myself, there's plenty of food in the house. I want you two to think about nothing but your own affairs for a change.'

The Major was well aware that he said this not purely for altruistic reasons. It was a kind of stiffening of the sinews against the fast-approaching day when his daughter's attention would be directed elsewhere. Also, he feared for both her and Alan if he did not turn her more away from himself. She *had* to look out into the world and towards her husband and her married life if she was to enjoy the happiness with Alan that she did with him, her father. To cling to her now would simply hurt all of them in the end.

He stood in the mullion window, very still and straight, with one hand raised in farewell, watching them go.

The day had emerged from its veil of mist and dew, like a bride after the wedding service, all mystery gone now, beaming beneficently on everything and everyone, delightfully well-disposed to all the world. Alan had pushed back the sunroof on the Merc and Elvi stretched up her arms so that her hands fluttered like pennants from the top of the car, luxuriating in the warm wind. Her one sartorial concession to the day out was a large woollen tam-o'-shanter pulled on so that it flopped fetchingly over one eye. Alan was forcibly and surprisingly reminded of Beatrix Potter's Benjamin Bunny. He thought, how like her to remind me of something I haven't seen or thought of since I was eight years old.

She had revelled in all the minor organizational aspects of the day out, fussing happily over picnic, rugs, camera, tape measure (to measure rooms) and boiled sweets (for the drive). The latter she made a start on almost as soon as they left the Beeches, rolling a large barley sugar from one cheek to the other and making energetic sucking noises.

'I don't know how you can stand those things so soon after breakfast.' Alan smiled in case he sounded prim.

'No car journey of any distance is complete without barley sugars,' she replied, with a large swallow, 'and anyway you know how easily I feel carsick, and they do help.'

'You could take a pill.'

'I know, but they're not the *same*.' There was no refuting the logic of this.

Elvi cast a covert look at Alan from under the floppy corner of her hat. She loved to watch him drive. Driving seemed to highlight all the qualities she most admired in Alan. He was so calm, so authoritative, at once dashing yet protective. And, of course, so handsome. She admired his fine, rather sad profile, the deep lines etched between the corners of nose and mouth and his hands, very firm, but relaxed on the wheel. And I am going to marry this handsome, older man, she said to herself. She often thought such things, repeating them over and over in her mind like a mantra, soothing and reassuring. On an impulse she put out her hand and touched his cheek. He smiled and she felt the skin contract beneath her fingers. She almost wished that her every small gesture of happiness or affection did not please him quite so much, she felt it to be an almost burdensome responsibility, the more so since she was aware of a certain falling-short in her feelings for him. She admired him enormously, and loved him of course, she felt wholly safe and happy in his presence – and yet. If she made herself face up to what it was she did not feel, it was desire. Even thinking the word embarrassed her, and when it crept into her mind she would usher it out again quickly and start on another of her mental itemizings of Alan's virtues. Now he turned and gave her a quick, quizzical look.

'Penny for them.'

'They're not worth even a penny.'

'Make it a free gift, then.'

'I was thinking,' she said, truthfully but not wholly so, 'how lucky I am to be going to marry you.'

'That's nice. It's entirely mutual. I hope you feel not just lucky, Elvi, but happy.' He gave her another swift, penetrating glance.

'Of course, I'm fantastically happy, don't I look it?'

'You look wonderful, my darling, but then you usually do, it's one of your recognized talents. I just wondered if you were truly, deep-down happy – content, if you like.'

'Yes! Anyway, content's boring and stuffy, being happy is more important. I think, I've never been happier than I am right at this moment. There, you can't make me say fairer than that.'

This *was* the whole truth, for she was someone who responded readily to the immediate. The weather, the expedition, the circumstances, all combined at that moment to make her perfectly happy. The shadowy worries of a few moments

18

before were brushed away. Alan was not entirely satisfied with her answer, but chided himself for being fussy. He should be like her, live for the moment, stop worrying about what lay beneath the surface of everything.

They sped on, occasionally slowing down to admire some house, horse – anything which caught Elvi's eye or her fancy. Once they stopped outside a village church.

'That's lovely!' cried Elvi. 'Come on, we must go in.' It was indeed lovely, quiet and old, with that particular smell of silence and polished wood. There was a woman changing the flowers. She smiled at Alan and Elvi and went on with her job as they walked round. Elvi was enchanted.

'Think of all the people who've been christened, and married and buried in this church. It's solid history.' She ran her hand along the warm, gleaming back of one of the pews. 'This wood feels alive, as though it can remember all those people.'

'It is nice – peaceful.' Alan walked slowly up the centre aisle and surveyed the small altar with its two stoneware jugs of fresh daffodils.

'This is where we'll be standing soon, my love.'

'Trying to give me stage-fright?' She went over to join him and they stood side by side.

'Not at all, just the opposite.'

'It's going to be a wonderful day.' They stood for another moment and then, by mutual and silent consent, turned and walked, arms linked, back down the aisle and out through the cool, dark porch into the sunlight. Elvi's mood changed again.

'Come on, now we'll whizz the rest of the way. No more delays, I want to get there!'

She leaped into the passenger seat of the Merc and went through an energetic dumb show of starting up and revving a racing car. Alan laughed and obligingly took the car away at a good pace. Elvi rustled in her bag and popped in another barley sugar.

They reached the house at twelve and as usual Alan slowed down in the lane that approached it so that they could relish the excited anticipation that went with this final stage of the journey. Their first view of it always brought a gasp from Elvi. The house was a Victorian vicarage in mellow red brick, solid, angular and friendly, 'a house for families' Elvi called it. The garden, somewhat gone to jungle over the duration of sale and purchase, was nonetheless flourishing and the high grassy bank that bordered the lawn wore a fluttering boa of daffodils and narcissi. The tall arched windows of the house caught the midday sun as the car wound its way down the lane, and the glass beamed brightly at them as if in welcome.

Elvi was out of the car before Alan had even switched off the engine.

'I'm going to walk all round and remind myself first,' she announced, 'and then we must measure up those two rooms we didn't do that last time, and then we'll have our picnic on the lawn.'

'Lawn! Better not sit down or we'll lose each other.'

'A lovely summer just for you, Alan. I can see you now, leaning on the mower and mopping your perspiring brow while I glide towards you bearing a jug of iced lemon.'

Alan laughed aloud. 'I notice who's got the best job!'

'It'll still be better for you than being with a lot of boring business people in town. You won't want to do that when you can be here, at home, in the country air.'

'With you.'

'With me. Of course!' She laughed gaily as if it were a joke, and after a brief battle with the stiff old lock, flung open the door and began her rediscovery of the house. She was like a dog coming home after an absence, rushing here and there, picking up old trails, enthusing over every remembered delight. And there were some new ones, too, for the decorators had begun work that week and the hall shone in all its glossy new white and caramel glory.

'Doesn't it look fantastic, just how I'd hoped.'

'It's coming on.'

'It sounds silly but I'd quite forgotten Mr McReady was

starting this week, what with all the other – and Alan, look at the dining room!'

Alan followed dutifully. Interior design and decor were not his forte. A comfortable chair and a well-filled bookcase were far more important to him than the colour and texture of the walls, and these were two commodities which the house so far signally lacked. The dining room over which his fiancée was in such ecstasies filled him with gloom, not least because it was only half-finished, and the whole of the centre of the room was therefore filled with a conglomeration of work trestles, ladders, buckets and pots of paint, all covered with ghostly grey dust sheets.

The large drawing room and kitchen, at the back of the house, were to his mind far more encouraging, because they overlooked the garden and were filled with spring sunshine. He instinctively unbolted the windows and flung them open. Elvi had run upstairs, and he could hear her hurrying from room to room. Presently she galloped down the stairs again.

'Where are you?' she called from the hall.

'Here.'

'Where's here?'

'In the sitting room.' She found him leaning forward, straight-armed against the mantelpiece, gazing down as though there were a fire already in the hearth.

'What are you thinking?'

'Nothing much. It's hard for me to imagine these rooms as home. I don't have your knack of mentally decorating and furnishing them.'

'Don't *worry*, you'll see, it'll all be perfect. Could you come and give me a hand with the steel rule?'

Obediently Alan spent the next forty minutes crouching on draughty, dusty floors, his thumb pinning the end of the measure to the skirting board, while Elvi made copious notes and cross-references in a dog-eared red notebook she kept for the purpose. Periodically she gave him lightning sketches of the decor she had in mind, but no matter how vivid her descriptions, he found it impossible to imagine the house in its refurbished condition. To him it seemed full of its past, its ghosts, no matter how genial those ghosts might be. In the spare bedroom cupboard they found some wire hangers tied together and a well-worn pair of pink fluffy bedroom slippers. In the attic there was an old tin kettle and a cardboard box full of the year-before-last's Christmas cards. Elvi immediately read some out.

'"To you all with heaps of love, Auntie Dot and Uncle Patrick . . . A Happy Christmas from all in Capetown" – good lord, a cast of thousands! What's this – "So sorry to hear about Aunt Eve, hope all well soon, love Jack." The black sheep of the family perhaps?' In the end, the cards' entertainment value exhausted, she carried the box downstairs and plonked it unceremoniously in the large rusty dustbin outside the back door. Alan found her lack of sentimentality in this regard mildly shocking, but when he teased her about it she said: 'All those people have moved on, they've made a new life somewhere else. If we hang on to all the old junk we find in dark corners we'll never make this house truly ours. It'll be like a tree all choked up with fungus and ivy, it won't *grow* properly.'

It was another of her highly individual interpretations, and one which Alan was unable to argue with. They collected the picnic from the boot of the Mercedes and carried it round the side of the house into the back garden. This was divided into two main areas, the boundaries somewhat blurred now for want of care. There was a spacious lawn area, bordered on one side by the high bank overlooking the lane, and on the other by two fine chestnut trees – beyond these trees to the right of the house, was what had been the orchard and vegetable garden, now a flourishing wilderness of weeds and wild flowers; straight ahead, in the centre of a tall and tangled hedge, was a picket gate leading into an enclosed flower garden, quite small, but perfectly laid out with little circular paved paths, two rickety lichen-covered benches and a lily pond in the centre no more than four feet in diameter but sporting an important and mature-looking Victorian stone cherub in its centre. Because of the paved areas, this part of the garden had suffered least, and Elvi decided it was the best place.

They passed through the picket gate into the seclusion beyond – 'rather like that little country church,' commented Elvi. She kneeled down beside one of the benches and began to unpack the picnic – quiche lorraine, salad, crusty bread, a thermos of homemade chicken soup, fruit and a bottle of white wine.

'What a spread. You're wonderful, where did all this come from?'

'Oh, it was around, I always cook a bit before the weekends.'

Alan bent and kissed her cheek as she busily laid things out and buttered hunks of bread. She was enchanting.

'I love you,' he said, catching her face between his hands and turning it up so that the large honey-hazel eyes looked directly into his own. 'I love you, you're all I want.'

'Except your lunch, I suppose.'

'To hell with lunch.' He slipped his hands down to her shoulder and pulled her up gently so that she was kneeling against his legs, leaning slightly towards him, her face only inches from his. She dropped the butter knife with a tinkle on the paved path.

'It's you I could eat,' he said. 'I could kiss you to death.'

Elvi didn't reply, but continued to stare calmly back at him, gentle and accepting but withdrawn, like a shy young animal. She thought: it's always like this, this is the bit I can't bear. I don't know what to do, what to say, or what I should be feeling. I just know it's not right. She felt hot tears of confusion, shame, and sadness for both of them well up in her eyes and the pain that was immediately reflected in Alan's made her cover her face quickly with her hands. In an instant he was kneeling beside her, his arms round her, his mouth against her hair.

'My darling. What is it? What can I do? Tell me, I'll understand. I can't bear to see you unhappy.'

'Oh God. Oh my God . . .' It was something between a cry and a prayer.

'He's up there, I'm *here*. Tell *me*. But I beg of you, Elvi, don't shut me out. You're all that matters to me, and if I can't help you I'm no good to anybody, not even myself. You have to share it with me.'

But Elvi knew that was something she could never do. Even through her tears the practised lie slipped out readily, the lie that suited her as well as Alan.

'It's just that – you love me so much, and you're so good to me . . . it makes me feel worthless. I can't live up to you, I'm sure I'll disappoint you . . .'

'What nonsense.' A surge of relief flooded over Alan, he laughed quietly and rocked her to and fro. 'I never heard such nonsense. Love isn't a bargain that's struck, you know. I'm not looking for a certain rate of interest or a particular level of returns. My poor silly darling, haven't I said enough to convince you that I'm happy with what I feel for you? You are enough for me, all I need, just as you are. And if I can make you happy in any way at all that's a bonus. Yes?' He pushed her back from him and kissed her reddened eyes, wiping the tears from her cheeks with his finger. He felt in his pocket. 'Here. It's clean.'

She wiped her face and blew her nose noisily on the large crisp white hanky. Already the beginnings of a sheepish smile were dawning. The dreadful moment was passed. Now they were back on a footing she could cope with. That dreadful agony of guilt and confusion was being pushed back again into its black cave at the back of her mind.

'Come on –' Alan sat back on his heels – 'let's have some of that lunch.'

They spent the afternoon in the garden clearing and weeding as best they could. The exercise was therapeutic, they enjoyed themselves getting red-cheeked and muddy, and talking about the wonderful creative things they would do when they were living here. At half-past four they left. Elvi locked up the house lovingly, left a note for Mr McReady containing some esoteric instructions concerning the dining-room ceiling, and picked some early honeysuckle and daffodils to take home.

They drove in silence, Elvi with her head tipped back on the seat, eyes closed but not asleep. She had removed the Benjamin Bunny hat and her conker-coloured hair spread round her face like a child's drawing of the sun. The car hummed along smoothly between tall hedges, a little module of warmth and comfort in the chilly April evening.

'Okay?' asked Alan quietly.

She nodded, and smiled but did not open her eyes.

By the time they reached the Beeches, Alan was acutely tired, and beginning that forced build-up of nervous energy reserves which he resorted to on these occasions. The parting with Elvi, the tedious conference, the continued driving, and the necessity to throw all his energy into work once more when he had no energy left – all were trials he was used to, but which required a particular screwing up of the emotional muscles, a deliberate hardening of the heart to make them bearable. When they arrived he went straight upstairs to collect his case, took his leave of the Major and went with Elvi into the porch.

'Goodbye,' she said, 'and thank you for a lovely day.'

'Don't thank me. It was our day, we did it together, didn't we?'

'Yes, but I know it was a treat for me, really. You don't find those empty rooms very exciting.'

He kissed her lightly on the mouth to silence her and she immediately enveloped him in that wild, feverish, childish bear hug which was at once so rapturous and so strange. She clung like a limpet for a full minute, until he gently disengaged himself.

'I must go.'

'I know. Ring, won't you?'

'Of course. Goodbye, my darling.'

'Goodbye.'

He climbed into the car, tossing his small case into the back seat before settling himself in front of the wheel. She came down the steps to wave him off, but the light from the hall was behind her and she was no more than a silhouette. He couldn't see her face. As he pulled away, waving and blowing a kiss, it was like bidding farewell to a statue.

Three

The Major, seated by the fire, turned to look at his daughter. 'Hallo, again. A good day?'

'M-hm.'

'Is the house progressing?'

'Oh yes, it'll be lovely. It's slow of course—'

'Builders always are.'

'But he was *strongly* recommended to us.'

'I'm sure he's another Michelangelo.' The Major was loth to remove the gilt from that particular slice of gingerbread. She seemed to glean enormous pleasure from her plans for the house. More pleasure, he sometimes thought, than from her imminent wedding.

'I thought Alan looked very tired.'

'Yes, poor love.'

'It's tiresome for him to have to go to this conference, it would have done him good to stay here and take things easy.'

'Oh, I don't know.' She curled up in the corner of the sofa like a kitten, gazing into the fire. 'He loves his work, you know. I sometimes think he's a masochist about it.'

'You may be right,' said the Major.

Alan arrived at the conference centre at a quarter past six. It matched his darkest forebodings. The centre was in fact one of the smaller red-brick universities, and the delegates were to be accommodated in a hall of residence. With a sinking heart Alan noticed that the evening meal was about to begin at this hideously early hour – he could never bring himself

27

to contemplate a three-course meal at such a time. Still, he didn't want to eat, and it meant that he had at least half an hour's grace in which to find his room, wash, and take a breather. The porter directed him to the sleeping quarters and supplied him with a key. He knew exactly what the room would be like, and he was correct. It was small, and bright and functional, a Habitat-style prison cell, the sort of room which various well-meaning, elderly members of the intelligentsia considered to be jazzy and youthful, but not so much so as to encourage any reprehensible permissiveness. Indeed, thought Alan, dropping his case on the bed and gazing about him, it was too small for any but the most restrained Lothario. Still, he could turn the key in the lock and put his feet up for a few minutes. He drew the orange-and-red striped linen curtains, kicked off his shoes, and sank down gratefully on the orange candlewick bedspread. His mind was a blank. Within seconds he was asleep.

He awoke with a start at seven thirty, his mouth dry, his head aching from the fierce central heating, and unable to accustom his eyes to the very white overhead light which he had not turned out.

'Hell.' He went over to the basin – one of those small affairs out of which even the meanest amount of water slops over one's feet, and sluiced his face and neck. Then, as he pushed his feet into his shoes, he rummaged in his case for the timetable he had been sent a fortnight ago. Saturday evening – discussion groups. Hell again. A further scrutiny of the badly duplicated sheet revealed that he was expected to join a group headed by one Professor Dinsdale in Room 12. Shrugging on his jacket and collecting up the relevant papers, he left the room, mentally composing a few phrases of apology as he did so.

Room 12 discovered, and the phrases duly delivered, he found himself a chair and sat down with a sense of relief, ready to pick up the threads of the discussion so far as quickly as he could. But almost at once a hand tapped his shoulder from behind. Alan turned. It was the odious Cavendish from the firm's Birmingham office.

'Hallo, sir.'

'Hallo, Dick.'

'I was wondering when I'd bump into you, sir. Care for a drink after this?'

'Well, I . . . I'm a bit tired, to be honest.'

'Just a quick one. Set you up.'

'Very well, that would be nice.'

Actually there was nothing which appealed to him less than a late-night drink with Cavendish, a bright young man of the most trying sort, but it was obviously both rude and impolitic to refuse.

The discussion wound on interminably. A great many intelligent and articulate people said their pieces on the subject of industrial training schemes for school leavers, but absolutely no conclusions were reached. Alan found it dispiriting. What on earth was the point of it? Everyone would go home tomorrow night feeling virtuous but the wretched school leavers would be no better off.

Later, in the college bar, it was obvious that Dick Cavendish did not share his views.

'That was most interesting, didn't you think?'

'It was a lively argument, if that's what you mean.'

'You sound dubious.'

'It didn't lead anywhere.'

'But surely, if you don't mind my saying, sir – surely the vital thing is to get management and teachers thinking along the right lines . . .'

For the next hour Alan stood sipping his tepid Scotch and listening to Cavendish expound his theories, which were many and wide-ranging. It was only when he had begun to make his excuses that Cavendish asked:

'How is your fiancée, sir?'

'She's well, thank you.'

'Plans for the wedding going all right, are they?'

'They seem to be. I don't have a lot of say in the matter.'

'Ah, that's women for you. It was the same with my wife – still is, as a matter of fact. She's the manager and I leave her to it.'

Alan had always found this line of Cavendish's intensely irritating. He was aware of being subtly set up. Here was one area where Cavendish the married man (and, recently, father) was points up on him, the blasé voice of suburban experience. He resented this patronage, especially since he could see no parallels whatever between Cavendish's circumstances and his own. The younger man had always seemed to represent the things he admired least in modern marriage: a sort of bored materialism, plastic happiness and dreadful predictability.

'Wait till she gets going on the house,' Cavendish was saying.

'She has. She's very good at it.'

'I told you!'

Alan could see there was no point in prolonging the discussion.

'I must hit the hay. Thanks for the drink.'

'Well, I think I'll just have a nightcap. Good night, sir.'

Damn fool, Alan thought as he undressed and got into bed. What did he know of Elvi, of her specialness, her youth, her magical quality of unspoilt optimism? He had to keep her away from the Cavendishes of this world, or they'd contaminate her with their crass attitudes. Elvi was his private treasure. And private he would see she remained.

For the first time in many months he allowed himself to think of Pru, his first wife. What a long time ago that all seemed. He had been only twenty-three, impossibly over-confident, hopelessly impractical, head over heels in love. And what had it brought them? Not idyllic happiness, but misery; not understanding, but bitterness, confusion and poverty instead of security: and instead of a family, the horrors of divorce after eighteen months, and it had been his fault. He had not known how to keep what was most precious to him. And after it was all over he had put his heart away in a dark, locked cupboard deep inside himself, and worked like a slave to erase the guilt and loneliness. He had been overwhelmed with a dreadful sense of waste. With Pru, there had been all that love, and energy and passion and hope, and between them they had wrecked it all with the foolishness and selfishness of youth.

He had thought never, ever, to unlock that cupboard where his heart lay. He had almost forgotten it was there, shrunken and hard from lack of light. No fool he, not any more: all that was behind him. But then Elvi had happened. He had met her while spending a weekend with a friend in the country. She and her father had attended a Sunday morning cocktail party there, and the moment she entered the room he had felt a small shaft of light force its way into the dark cupboard inside him. He had asked to be introduced and had ended by being ensnared.

Ironically, she reminded him of Pru. At first this had inhibited him, he had instinctively held back for fear of embarking again on that particular journey of disillusionment. Her air of untarnished optimism, so like Pru's, simply underlined his own forebodings. And yet he could not resist suggesting that second meeting, and the next until he was willingly in thrall. With one difference – this time, he could cope, he knew how to make it work. He knew all too well the value and the transience of her special qualities. If she took them for granted, he would not: this time, the sparkle would stay, he would make it his particular care to keep alive the sense of wonder in their relationship.

Lying quietly, but wide-eyed in the dark, he found he could now contemplate Pru with equanimity, with gratitude even. If it were not for Pru he would never now be about to marry Elvi. Pru, he knew, had married a few years back, he'd seen it in the paper, and she was doubtless a mum several times over now. She would, he imagined, have turned into one of those amazing women of boundless energy and affection, whose children kept an army of pets and who crammed the family hatchback full of other people's progeny before and after school. It made him smile to think of her. She would probably have a good hearty laugh if she could see him now, all wound up and nervy like a lovesick teenager, about to embark on marriage with a girl almost half his age. But Pru's would be a kind laugh; he was sure she would wish him well with all the energy at her disposal.

But the problem remained, like a nagging tooth: when to tell Elvi? And how? And would it make any difference? He kept telling himself that it would not, but the longer he delayed the process the more of a shadow it cast. Suddenly she would see him in a different light. All sorts of doubts would rear their ugly heads. All too vividly Alan could imagine the effect of the word 'divorce' – no matter what he told her, there would always be the possibility that he was not telling the truth and that there was another, darker side to the story. How could he explain to Elvi that his marriage had foundered for reasons she would consider to be virtues? That it had fallen apart for lack of grit and fibre, a pinch of salt and a smattering of cynicism. He would have to tell her soon, very soon. But not at once. He turned over, pulled the bedclothes up to his chin and tried to sleep.

On Monday, Elvi went to visit the playgroup. She had been told by the senior teacher, Mrs Maynard, that the children had now completed their wedding present for her and a formal presentation was in order. As Elvi entered the lobby of the village hall and removed her coat she could hear the small, resonant, tuneless voices chanting, 'One, two, three, four, five, once I caught a fish alive . . .' Her job here was something she'd miss. Since school and a secretarial course she had elected to live at home and work locally – she loathed the idea of London, liked the country and the people she knew, and preferred to know her father was well looked after. The playgroup had helped her discover a talent she didn't know she had. The children adored her – she had the knack of creating fun while holding their interest sufficiently to prevent chaos. Her patience with them was boundless and she was able to make each child feel it had a special place in her affections, without actually showing partiality to any of them. Now, as she tried to enter the hall quietly and inconspicuously, one of the boys spotted her.

'Here's Elvi!'

'Elvi!'

She was at once surrounded by a clamouring swarm of children, each after some personal token of affection. It wasn't until Mrs Maynard called them over to collect the present that they withdrew, leaving Elvi laughing, breathless and dishevelled. They formed a shuffling circle and Mrs Maynard beckoned her over to a position in the centre. Jamie Douglas stepped forward. Elvi smiled encouragingly. He had always been a gauche, shy child, a hanger-back who needed a lot of affection to draw him out of his shell. Now he hesitated, was vociferously prompted by the others, stepped forward again and mumbled: 'Have a very happy wedding and we all send lots of love.' From behind his back he produced a small bumpy package. Elvi kissed him, thanked him, and opened her present. It was a clay model, brightly painted, knobbly and roughly X-shaped.

'Oh, *Jamie!*' she said with all the feeling she could muster. 'It's lovely, I'll treasure it.' She glanced desperately at Mrs Maynard. What was it? She knew he'd be able to tell if she didn't know. Mrs Maynard pointed vigorously at the boy himself. Suddenly it dawned on her.

'It's *you* isn't it? So I'll always remember you.'

Jamie nodded, his plump face suffused with a flush of gratified pride.

'I couldn't have asked for *anything* nicer,' added Elvi for good measure, and the flush deepened.

There was a similar figure from every child in the class. Some were very good, some less recognizable than Jamie's and one even emerged from its wrapper in several pieces: the tearful modeller had to watch it being repaired instantly. Each figure had the initial of its maker painted somewhere on it. Elvi was touched, and the delighted Mrs Maynard, practical to the last, provided a box full of wood shavings for the transportation of the present; each model was carefully

laid to rest with appreciative comments from Elvi. Now that
the tense moment of the presentation was over, the questions
came thick and fast.

'Elvi! Who are going to marry, Elvi?'

'Have you got a pretty dress? My cousin got married and
she had a *beautiful* dress!'

'Will you come back, Elvi?'

'Where are you going to live?'

'Have you got lots of presents?'

'Do you like ours best?'

Elvi bore up well under interrogation but was nevertheless
quite relieved when the church bell struck twelve and the mums
began to arrive to collect their offspring. When the hall was
eventually empty Mrs Maynard came over.

'Cup of coffee?'

'You're an angel, I'd love one.' They went out into the
chaotic small kitchen and sat down at the Formica table while
the kettle boiled.

'We'll miss you, you know that,' said Mrs Maynard.

'I'll miss you, too.'

'It's a gift you have, Elvi. Don't waste it.'

'I should like to find some kind of similar job in Sussex –
but I don't have any formal qualifications.'

'No, that's true, and in a bigger place they'd probably
take a qualified teacher over you. But you could get the
qualifications, you know.' The older woman glanced at her
quizzically as she handed her a mug of coffee. Elvi was
surprised.

'What, you mean go to college after I'm married?'

'Of course, my dear, it's a brave new world you know.'

'I hadn't even considered it . . . no, I don't really think
so . . . I couldn't, not right away.'

'If you don't do it right away you'll find it gets harder and
harder – you'll have a family of your own—'

'That's a long way off!' Elvi laughed.

'You may think so now, but it'll happen, and then there'll
be no chance of college for some time, and you'll be older, you

may not feel like being a student again. My advice is to talk to Alan about it now, I'm sure he'll understand. Otherwise you may find you're just a paint-mixer and bottle-washer for the rest of your days.'

'What a ghastly thought!'

They laughed and moved on to other subjects, the wedding and the house, but the idea had been implanted. It was something Elvi had never for a moment considered. But perhaps there was something in it, perhaps now was the moment. But the house, the garden – she'd never have the time! She pushed the notion to the back of her mind.

That evening the phone rang, and when Elvi answered it it was her godmother, Jean Anderson. Jean had been a friend as well as a godparent for as long as Elvi could remember, though she was some twenty years older, and had always had a wise and sensible head on her shoulders. She was the ideal confidante – a good and understanding listener, able to give sound advice when required, but never bossy or critical. The fact that she had lived in Scotland since her marriage six years ago had made her an even more valuable source of friendship, for she was able to view things objectively and calmly. She had always thought privately that her goddaughter had led far too protected an existence, although she conceded that in some ways it had added to her undoubted charm. The notion of Elvi's getting married had come as quite a shock – in her estimation Elvi was a child, not a woman: a loving, caring and delightful child, but a child nonetheless. She had not met Alan, but she was intrigued to know what kind of man could be letting himself in for marriage to this particular person – she longed to know what made the relationship tick.

Now she asked, in her typical straightforward way: 'Are you going to come and visit us, then?'

'Oh I'd love to, you know that, but I'm so tied up at the moment, and it's so far, and—'

'And you'll be even busier in a couple of months! Come on, it'll do you good to get away from all the ballyhoo for a bit. Just come up for a week or ten days, bring Alan along too, have a little holiday.'

'Heavens, you don't want *both* of us.'

'Why ever not? We want to meet your intended, we're bursting with curiosity, and we'd ask you together when you're a staid old married couple – I should hope!'

'Of course. But you'll see us at the wedding.' Elvi was making excuses though she herself wasn't quite sure why. She was slightly nervous of Jean's directness. She would *know*, she would see through it all. But Jean was relentless.

'Look, are you saying you don't want to come?'

'No—'

'Then come. By the way, we may not be able to make the wedding, my love. Ian's got a million things on and we'd have to make it there and back in a day which just isn't on with the kids. So there you are, one more reason why you owe us a visit. And Alasdair and Fiona are dying to see you again. You just have to come, we can have a good gossip.'

That's what I'm afraid of, thought Elvi, but there was obviously no getting out of it. 'Okay, you've talked me into it. You know I'd adore to come. I'll ask Alan when he calls tomorrow.'

'Terrific! No more now then, the phone's so hideously expensive. We'll look forward to hearing from you. Love to your father. 'Bye!'

Elvi sat in the dark hall for a moment. She was guiltily aware that if she had to face perspicacious Jean she would rather do so without Alan. She was perfectly certain that if the two of them were there together Jean would detect that hidden nameless flaw in their relationship. On an impulse she picked up the phone and dialled the number of Alan's London flat. He had said he had an evening meeting tonight and would call tomorrow, but he might well be back by now. He was.

'My darling! What a surprise. I've only just walked through the door as a matter of fact.'

'I know, you're probably tired, I know we agreed to talk tomorrow.'

'Don't be silly, it's great to hear your voice.'

'How was the conference?'

'Bloody. Bloodier than usual. A waste of time.'

'Enough said?'

'Precisely so. How are things with you?'

'We've had an invitation.'

'Really, who from?'

'Jean Anderson.'

'She's your godmother, isn't she?'

'That's right. She lives on the west coast of Scotland.'

'So it's not just dinner then?'

'No indeed, they want us to go up for about ten days. I said we were busy but she's not the sort of lady who'll take no for an answer.'

'Say yes then. I must say I'm snowed under, dearly as I'd love a holiday in Scotland, and much as I'd like to meet the Andersons. I'd suggest you go for a week or so, it'll do you good.'

'But what about you?'

'What about me? I'll take the opportunity to get a heap of work off my plate so that we can have plenty of time together when you get back. I'm really sorry I can't make it but I think it'll work out for the best. If you give me their address I'll drop them a line. But you go – definitely: I know how much you like Jean.'

'Well, if you're sure—'

'Positive.'

'Okay, I'll write this evening. You're a love. By the way, can we have lunch on Wednesday, I'm coming up to town to look at some things at Liberty's.'

'Wednesday, Wednesday . . . can't find my diary but it sounds all right. Will you come round to the office?'

'Well, I thought if we met at Liberty's—'

'I know, you want me to fritter away half my hard-earned lunch hour shopping. I'll do it, thousands wouldn't.'

'Oh marvellous. Otherwise I feel I'm spending our money and you don't even know what I'm spending it on.'

They arranged to meet outside the main entrance of Liberty's and Elvi put the phone down with a sigh of relief. Now she could look forward to meeting Jean. She was sure that on her own she could present the picture she most liked of herself, that of the radiantly happy bride-to-be. Which she almost was.

Four

Throughout the last part of her train journey, Elvi experienced a wonderful feeling of freedom. It had been increasing from the moment she had boarded the train in London, and now that she could see from the windows the grave, awe-inspiring beauty of Scotland all around she felt like a bird escaped from its cage.

It would be marvellous, she knew it. She'd go for long walks, and eat and drink too much and be able to chat her head off with Jean and Ian. Although she was too loyal to admit it, gossiping with a girlfriend was something definitely missing from her life. She had no special friends of her own age and sex in the village, since most of them preferred to move away when they left school. Her father, for all his understanding and love could not be chatted to on that special feminine level that is meat and drink to most girls, especially just before getting married. And Alan – well he idolized her, and was such a wonderful, experienced person himself, she could not imagine giggling or gossiping with Alan. She hastily put the idea of Alan out of her mind, it was too discomforting. She was here to be herself, by herself, for a while, just as he'd advised.

The train began to slow down as they approached Oban, and Elvi busied herself getting her cases down from the luggage rack and humping them out into the corridor near the door. Ian was going to meet her and drive her out to the village of Kirkmuir, where he was senior partner in the local medical practice. She looked forward to meeting Ian almost as much as Jean. He was one of those rare men who simply exuded goodness, integrity and love of his fellow man – it shone out of him, warming and illuminating everyone he came in contact with.

Now, as she leaned out of the train window, her hand already on the handle, Elvi could spot him standing halfway down the platform, towering head and shoulders above the rest of the people. The expression 'a tower of strength' might have been created to describe Ian Anderson.

As soon as the train stopped he spotted her, and was at her side in seconds, lifting her down from the train as if she were a child, enveloping her in a massive tweedy embrace.

'It's tremendous to see you again, really tremendous,' he said fervently when he had put her – and her cases – on the platform. 'I can't tell you how we've all been looking forward to your visit. We're only sorry Alan couldn't come. I was looking forward to introducing him to one or two of the local pubs!'

'I know, it's a shame, and he was disappointed, but he simply couldn't have made it this time. He's got so much on his plate.'

'He probably works too hard. I've heard about these businessmen, and I've treated their coronaries at forty, too.'

'Thanks for being so cheery!'

'I'm not saying it'll happen to him, God forbid. But you look after him, my dear, don't let him drive himself into an early grave.'

'As if I would. And anyway you're a fine one to talk about working too hard: you never stop!'

Ian made a face at her as if to suggest he'd wallop her if his hand weren't full of baggage. They passed through the ticket barrier and piled into the Andersons' Land Rover. Their dog, an amiable black labrador, was sitting in the back and greeted them both as if she had been alone for months.

'I see Donna remembers me,' laughed Elvi, fending off the enthusiastic greetings as best she could.

Ian gave the dog an affectionate, but firm, push, and she flopped down on her stomach and lay looking affable and unabashed, her red tongue lolling. He started the engine.

'I think she's one of the dumbest dogs in Scotland. That's why we love her.'

The Land Rover moved off and Elvi sat back contentedly as they drove out of town and along the winding white road towards Kirkmuir. The amazing variety and beauty of the Scottish landscape cast its never-failing spell. Every bend in the road opened up some entirely new, and equally breathtaking vista. At one moment it would be all majesty and grandeur, the purple peaks dominating the skyline, the gleaming slate-grey of the lochs lying still and mysterious between; the next they would be in a soft green valley, beside tumbling water, secluded and idyllic.

Kirkmuir was situated at the end of one of these valleys, at the point where the road turned and began to climb steeply up the lower slopes of Ben Keir. It wasn't a pretty village – the houses straggled up the side of the hill in an untidy broken string, small, plain, hardy houses, standing firmly against the elements. But Elvi loved it for its unpretentious toughness, the way it clung, tenacious as a limpet, to the great wind-scarred shoulder of the mountain. The Andersons' house was the last, and highest, in the village, a square, whitewashed building with a moss-covered grey slate roof. As they climbed the main street Elvi could see the children perched on the rough grey stone wall. As soon as they spotted the approaching Land Rover there was an explosion of activity – waving, jumping up and down, beckoning someone out from the house, plus a good deal of mutual pushing and shoving. Elvi smiled.

'They have grown. I shall hardly recognize them.'

'It's been nearly a year. Far too long.' Ian's tone was admonitory but his blue eyes twinkled. He was looking forward to taking Elvi into his home, and among his family. He believed quite unreservedly that both had enormous value, that the peace and happiness he derived from them must naturally spread to others on contact. He pulled up in the muddy drive and opened the door for Elvi, watching with quiet satisfaction as the children fell on her with shrieks of delight. He felt rather as though a third child had come home to roost. He found it hard to imagine what this homecoming would have been like if Alan had been present – indeed, he found it hard to imagine Alan at all now that Elvi was here on her own. She had always blended so easily into their family life, and she had scarcely changed at all. Smiling contentedly to himself he began to unload the bags from the back of the Land Rover, and Donna leaped down to join in the general rejoicing, her great tail waving.

Jean appeared in the doorway, paused for a moment to push her feet into boots, and ran over to hug her god-daughter.

'Elvi, my love, what fun you're here. Are you worn out?'

'What, from sitting in a train?'

'No, of course you're not, we'll all walk up the hill path after tea. Poor Alan, how can he bear not to be here?'

'He can because he doesn't know what he's missing,' said Elvi. 'He isn't under the spell yet.'

'Please, *please* –' it was five-year-old Alasdair in a frenzy of anxiety – 'can Elvi sleep in my room?'

'No, she cannot.'

'Why? That's not fair. Is she going to sleep with Fiona?'

'No, she's going to sleep in the spare room, in peace and quiet, I hope.'

'I'd let her have my pillow –' careful thought – '*and* my frogman Action Man.'

Elvi realized this was the highest accolade her young host could offer.

'Alasdair, what a kind boy you are. Tell you what. I'd better sleep in the spare room, as Mummy's gone to all the trouble to get it ready for me. But I'd love it if you'd both come and see me early in the morning—'

'Not *too* early,' interposed Jean.

'And I can bring my cloth dolly, can't I?' piped Fiona, a small but forceful figure with a cap of spikey blonde hair and plump cheeks whipped red by the wind.

'Of course you can bring your cloth dolly.'

'And my sheep pyjama case.'

Alasdair looked scornful. 'It's not a sheep, you silly thing, it's a poodle, I've told you before.' He rolled his eyes wearily at Elvi. 'She doesn't know a *thing*.'

'I *do*.'

'You don't.'

'I do. I hate you.'

'Hey!' Elvi, seeing Jean beginning to bridle and sensing a skirmish in the offing, stepped in to draw the fire. 'Will you two show me where the spare room is?'

'You know,' said Alasdair bluntly. 'You've been here before.'

'Well, I've forgotten. And anyway it's nice to be escorted when you arrive somewhere.'

This line of reasoning worked better, and the two children went ahead of her, while Ian, grinning broadly, clumped behind with the cases. Jean called: 'Come to the kitchen when you've dumped your things, love. I'll have tea ready.'

'Marvellous.'

The children led her into the room at the end of the long, narrow landing, and sat down on the bed, watching her expectantly as though she were a paid entertainer. Ian put the cases down inside the door and said: 'I'll leave you to it, then. Come when you're ready – and don't let these two be a pest.'

'They won't be.'

Elvi had not brought many things – one dress 'in case', plus a couple of pairs of jeans and plenty of sweaters. There were also two bottles of wine for Jean and Ian, and parcels for the children. The latter were instantly spotted and fallen upon.

'Can we undo them now? Can we?'

'Yes, of course.'

Elvi had solved the problem of giving each exactly the same by ordering T-shirts with the children's names on, and supplementing them with a box of crayons each. The gifts were accepted rapturously and then (predictably) discarded on top of the chest of drawers when Elvi announced her intention of going downstairs.

Jean was just pouring water into the teapot when the children rushed in. Ian, jacket on and boots off, stood in his socks before the enormous Aga, looking through some leaflets.

'Mum! Elvi brought presents. Bottles you've got.'

'And I suppose she got you something too? Elvi, you are naughty.'

'Yes! We got T-shirts with our names and coloured pencils. Can I draw after tea?'

'We're going for a walk after tea.' Jean was firm. 'I hope you said thank you to Elvi.'

'Yes.' Elvi smiled and nodded her corroboration. She put the two bottles of wine on the work surface next to the stove.

'Grog, lovely. We'll all get sloshed tonight. Thank you so much, my love, you shouldn't spend your cash on us at a time like this.'

'Time like what?'

'She means,' said Ian, 'that you should be filling your "bottom drawer", whatever that means.'

'Oh, that.' Elvi laughed and dismissed it with a wave. 'It's pretty well full. I say, that looks a smashing tea.'

The conversation duly changed they sat down to a tea consisting of homemade scones, cake, flapjacks and short-bread. Ian ate a scone, gulped a cup of tea and then excused himself.

'I'm sorry folks, you'll have to excuse me. I've got some calls to make.' He bent to kiss Jean, and blew one to Elvi. 'I shan't be late if I can help it.'

'Do your best,' said Jean. 'We've got a nice dinner for Elvi's first night, *and* decent wine for a change.'

'Don't worry, I'll try. Night, you two,' he hugged the children, who continued to munch unconcernedly. 'You'll probably be in bed when I get back.'

'Night, Dad.'

'Night, Daddy, sleep tight.'

Ian laughed. 'No sleeping for me, young lady, I'm off to work.'

After he had gone, Jean and Elvi sat over another cup of tea while the children assembled their new crayons and pieces of paper to draw pictures. Jean watched her goddaughter as she enthusiastically licked her finger and wiped it round the plate of flapjack crumbs. She is in her element, thought Jean, she's perfectly happy here. As a hostess the thought delighted her, but something about it troubled her. Elvi fitted in too well, there seemed to be nothing missing, and yet there *was* – the man she was going to marry.

When they'd finished their tea and put the plates in the sink, Jean said: 'Shall we walk? It's lovely up the hill path at this time of day, and the children will be beautifully knocked out for bedtime.'

'Wonderful.'

They put on boots and anoraks and went out through the back gate of the garden, following the narrow ribbon of green that wound upwards through the heather. The air was clean and sharp, Elvi could feel it coursing through her lungs like spring water. For a while they didn't speak, but walked vigorously, hands thrust into pockets, while the children raced ahead, their voices resounding shrilly from the mountainside.

After a while, slackening their pace, Jean asked: 'So, you're looking forward to being a married lady?'

'Oh yes, I think I'll have quite a talent for it, actually. The house is gorgeous, I'm mad about it, and it's tremendous fun planning the way I want it. I'm really rather a domestic body—'

'Tell me about Alan.' Jean was abrupt. She gave Elvi one of her most penetrating looks.

'Well – what do you want to know?'

'Everything. What does he look like?'

'Very handsome.' Elvi was on safe ground here. 'His mother was Swedish and he can look quite Hereward-the-Wakish at times. You know blue-eyed and blond-haired. Going a little grey, actually.'

'And he loves you to distraction.'

'He's very good to me. Too good to me – I don't deserve him.' Elvi laughed gaily but Jean sensed more than a grain of truth in the last remark.

'We were so sorry he couldn't make it, it would have been lovely to meet him, especially as we may not make the wedding.'

'There's always next time. It's just so marvellous to *be* here.'

With or without him, Jean added mentally. In fact it struck her that Elvi was happier here on her own. She seemed quite complete, quite satisfied just to become one of their children. It wasn't right. Jean tried again.

'He's quite a bit older than you, isn't he?'

'Yes, a lot. He's older than you and Ian, actually. But it doesn't make any difference.'

It should, thought Jean, it should. What she actually said was: 'It must be flattering to know that a much older man, with so much more experience, loves you enough to marry you. And a bit frightening, too.'

'Frightening? Good heavens, no, Alan is the most *un*frightening man you could wish to meet.'

'I mean a responsibility. You're almost from different generations. You surely both have to make a special effort to understand, to see each other's point of view.'

'I suppose so . . .' Elvi was thoughtful for a moment but then grinned. 'He certainly understands me. Where have the children disappeared to?'

'They're all right—' But Jean's words were snatched away by the wind and Elvi was off, racing up the hill; shouting and waving to the children, who were perched on a pile of rocks further up. She escaped from me, thought Jean, she ran away because she didn't like my asking about Alan. She's not entirely happy, but she won't face up to it.

This worried Jean. She was a sensible, good-hearted person and she was genuinely devoted to Elvi. The last thing she wanted to do, she reflected, was to upset the apple cart, but at the same time could she sit by and watch something happen which she sensed not to be right? Perhaps she was wrong, perhaps Elvi simply thought she was being nosy. After all, she *was* nosy. She smiled to herself. Mustn't jump to conclusions, the poor girl had only just arrived, it would probably do her good to be one of the family again. And yet . . . Jean could remember so clearly how she had felt in those months before she married Ian . . . it wasn't so different now, except that they were slightly older and more peaceful. She had lived only for him, through him. She had felt only half a person when they were apart, she had longed more than anything to be seen with him to show him off and bask in reflected glory. She had never been so unselfishly happy, for her happiness had consisted in her man. And Elvi did not seem like that.

She trudged on, wrapped in thought, and would have walked straight past Elvi and the children if they hadn't hailed her.

'Mum!' Alasdair was mortified. 'We're here! Where are you going?'

'I'm sorry, I was in another world.' She laughed and clambered up the rocks to join them.

'Isn't it beautiful?' Elvi sat with Fiona on her knee, drinking in the view.

'You get used to it.' Jean was down-to-earth. 'There are times when I curse it, in the winter.'

'But you could never settle for anything less.'

'Probably not. I certainly don't think Ian could.'

'And where he goes, you go.'

'Of course.' Jean glanced at her sharply. 'I'm no docile little woman, you know that, it's simply that there's nowhere I'd rather be than with him, even if it does mean getting snowed up and never seeing a decent dress shop, and not being able to get back to work.'

'You don't fool me, you're no martyr.'

'Exactly. I'm as happy as Larry.'

'Well, I think you're terribly lucky,' said Elvi, addressing Fiona and giving her a smacking kiss on the cheek. 'You're the happiest, nicest family I know and I adore you.'

'Come on.' Jean stood up with a shiver, and pulled the hood of her anorak up. 'It's beginning to get cold and it's bath night. We'd better start back down.'

Alasdair, who had been exploring the summit of the cairn,

was summoned, and set off helter skelter down the hill, his arms flapping at his sides to help him balance. Fiona demanded a lift from Elvi.

'Now come on, darling,' said Jean, 'you're too heavy these days, and it's all downhill anyway.'

'I want to ride with Elvi.' Fiona was adamant, turning away and putting both arms round Elvi's neck.

'Honestly, it's a pleasure, let me.'

'Very well, but you're too soft.'

'I'll be firm tomorrow.'

Yes, thought Jean, always tomorrow. That was Elvi all over, treasuring the happiness of the moment, never wanting to hurt anyone's feelings, always wanting to love and be loved – but at what expense? She felt the anxiety creeping back. She could not let Elvi, with all that she had to give, sacrifice herself and Alan for the sake of a quiet life. She wished again that she had met Alan, that she could see and evaluate for herself the other side of this strange coin.

That night as she and Ian undressed for bed, their breath steaming in the unheated bedroom, she broached the subject with him.

'How do you think Elvi seems?'

'I think she *seems* fine.' Ian jumped into bed and drew the quilt up under his chin. 'That has to be a trick question. What do you mean by *seems*. She *is* fine, isn't she? Never better.'

'I don't know . . .' Jean climbed in more slowly and leaned her head back on her linked hands. 'I mean she's well, she looks marvellous, but I don't think she's happy.'

'Away with you, woman, Elvi's always happy. She's got the greatest capacity for happiness of anyone I know. And surely now more than ever—'

'That's just it, she *should* be happier now than she's ever been, but she's not. And she's closing her mind to it. Didn't you notice the way she didn't want to discuss Alan at dinner—'

'I was a bit tight at dinner.'

'—and when we suggested she give him a ring at our expense she just said he was bound to be working late? She

The Divided Heart

didn't *want* to talk to him. It worries me. All's not well.'

'You're suffering from inflamed intuitions.' Ian slipped an arm round her shoulders and drew her towards him. 'It's not your style to worry. Let the girl live her life. She may well be worried at a time like this. Marriage is a big step. She's very young, he's a good deal older, there are bound to be things giving her pause for thought. She can't live in toyland forever you know.'

Jean had to laugh at his choice of words.

'But if that were so, I'm sure she'd discuss it with me. She's always been so open with me before. If there *were* a few natural worries, then I think she'd be talking about them. It's not like her to shut us out.'

'Or like you to shut me out.' Ian stretched across to switch off the light and placed his mouth firmly on hers. When he removed it his arms were round her. 'Now, who are you going to concentrate on, her or me?'

Five

The days drifted by idyllically for Elvi. The sheer physical distance between her and the complications of her life at home was a relief. She ate with the gusto of a child, walked for miles and played with the children. She sat for hours in the kitchen watching Jean at work – she was an excellent cook – and chatting, her mind flitting from one topic to another with complete unpredictability. Jean observed her gradual rallying, but noticed that it brought with it no unfolding on the subject of Alan. They talked a great deal about the wedding.

'All the flowers are going to be white!'

'At a summer wedding?' Jean put a drop of water into the mixing bowl and began to knead vigorously. 'Wouldn't you like some colour?'

'Of course! The *people* will be the colour – all those lovely friends, and aunts and children in their best bibs and tuckers. They'll be the colour, and the flowers will really stand out – sparkling white.'

'And you, of course.'

'And me what?'

'You'll stand out. The star of the show.'

'Well, yes, I hadn't thought of it that way, but then the bride always does stand out, doesn't she?'

'Yes, of course. Are you having bridesmaids?'

'No, I'm not, because I haven't got any relations the right age, and if I'd asked one of the playgroup I'd have hurt the feelings of all the others. So it'll just be me.'

'You and Alan.'

'That's right.'

'You were both all for a white wedding?'

'Yes – at least, I don't think we discussed it that much . . . I'd always imagined it that way, it seemed perfectly natural. Why do you ask?'

'I don't know really – So many people these days take a practical view: that it would be more sensible to spend the money on a house or a car or something.'

'Yes.' Elvi took a small lump of dough from the bowl and began rolling it on the scrubbed wooden table top. 'There's a lot to be said for that, I can see. But I know it sounds awful put so bluntly—'

'You're going to say that you and Alan have no money worries?'

'That's right. Does it sound terrible?'

'Sounds marvellous! We've had money worries all our married life and no sign of them ending, either. Just be grateful, my girl. Enjoy it, don't be guilty, but be grateful.'

'Believe me, I am. I know I'm very spoilt.'

'You are. You've put flour all over your face, too.' Jean grinned and brushed off the offending white stuff. 'Give me back that dough, or I shan't have enough.'

'Sorry.'

'So –' Jean began deftly rolling out the pastry with quick, economical movements – 'not a cloud in the sky, eh?'

'Not really. No, not one.'

'Clouds are Alan's province anyway, I imagine.'

'That's right – I mean, no, what are you trying to make me say? That's unfair of you.'

'Is it?' Jean finished pressing the pastry into the dish and crimping the sides with finger and thumb. She sat down and looked at Elvi with her most astute expression, half-smiling, half-accusing.

'Elvi, love, there is something I want to say to you.'

'What? Are you going to be terribly godmotherly and reproving? What have I done?'

'You've done nothing, silly. Just take what I'm going to say

51

as a piece of general advice from a friend. Or don't take it, it's up to you, I shall say it anyway.'

'Go on then.' Elvi clasped her hands on the table and deliberately composed her features into a look of grave attention. Her stomach churned with anxiety.

'All I want to say,' said Jean, 'is that you mustn't look on marriage, especially marriage to Alan, as a present. Happy marriage doesn't come in a big beautiful box tied with a satin ribbon and labelled "To Elvi from Alan". You're getting his love, and his promise. And he gets yours. And all the years to come are the time it takes to keep those promises.'

'You're talking to me as if I were a child.' Elvi sounded genuinely hurt. 'Do you think I'm not grown up enough to bring something to my marriage?'

'Oh my love, I didn't mean it unkindly, and I don't mean to patronize you. But, as I said before, looking back from a little way along the road I can see all the hazards and pitfalls and I do so very much want you – both of you – to be happy. I feel that in your case it could be so easy to accept everything that's offered, perhaps get a bit lazy about seeing the other person's point of view. I'm not saying you will, but I'm sure I would have if I'd married someone so much older, and more experienced—'

'And richer.'

'And richer, though that's not so important. If you marry someone your own age, you grow together, for better or worse, you *have* to work on it to survive. In your case it would be easy to sit back and just let it all come to you.' There was silence, Elvi looked down at her clasped hands, her coppery hair falling down like curtains to shield her face on either side. When she looked up there were tears in her eyes but she was smiling.

'I will try, Jean. I *will.*'

'I know you will.' Jean put out a hand and laid it for a moment on her cheek. 'I've said my older-and-wiser piece now, and if I don't put this in the oven we'll all go hungry.'

And that, as far as it went, was that. The exchange resulted in Elvi feeling chastened, and if anything more confused, and in Jean feeling guilty. She told Ian as much, but he was unsympathetic.

'You're a public nuisance,' he told her jovially. 'The poor lass comes all the way up here for a little sabbatical and all you can do is probe her innermost soul.'

'It wasn't meant to be like that at all. I was acting on my instincts as a friend.'

'You've got an overdeveloped sense of responsibility, that's your trouble. Whatever you may think to the contrary, that girl is grown up and capable of reaching her own conclusions. I really think you should let it be.'

'Oh God, I'm sorry.' Jean rubbed her fingers through her hair, overcome with remorse. 'What have I done?'

'Nothing at all so far, I should imagine. Don't upset yourself. But I should leave it at that.'

'You're right, I will. By the way, I see there's a dance on in the village hall on Saturday. It'll be almost the end of her stay, she might like to go.'

'Yes, I'm sure she would, but not by herself. She doesn't know anyone.'

'That's what I'm afraid of. You go with her, Ian. She's so fond of you. Then she can enjoy herself, and I needn't worry.'

'Let's get a babysitter, and all go.'

'No, there are things I can do when you're all out from under my feet, and you and I can go any time we like. You take her, it'll do her good to have fun and dance, and mix with some other young people before she goes back and faces up to marriage.'

'Yes, you're right. Okay. I'll be a nice safe escort and let's hope the lass won't mind being seen with a clodhopper like me.'

'She'll be proud. Or she ought to be.' Jean gave him a kiss on the cheek. 'Thank you.'

That night at supper Ian mentioned the dance.

'There's a village hop on the Saturday night before you

leave us. Would you like to come along?'

'Oh, lovely!' Elvi's face lit up. 'It's ages since I've been dancing.'

'It's nothing grand, you understand. Just Jimmy Shand music, and the locals having a good time.'

'What could be nicer? But can you get a babysitter easily?'

Jean glanced at Ian. 'We shan't need one – I'm not coming.'

'Why ever not? You *must* come – you've been working so hard for all of us, you need an evening off.'

'Don't worry, I shall have one.' Jean smiled. 'I shall get all sorts of things done and enjoy my own company. Besides, I can go to a village hop any time, they're no novelty for me. You go with Ian and enjoy yourself, and we'll all have a celebration lunch on Sunday.'

Elvi could see that Jean's mind was made up. 'Very well. I can't pretend I wouldn't love to go. Poor Ian – am I a duty and a burden?'

'Of course not.' Ian was gallant. 'I'll be the envy of every man in the room.'

'Flatterer.'

And so it was agreed. Elvi found she was looking forward to this small social event with quite disproportionate excitement. It was indeed a long time since she had been to a dance, and mixed with people of her own age. She supposed that the one 'in case' dress would have to do. She wasn't fussy, if no one else was. She tried it on on Thursday night and stood inspecting herself before the long mirror on the wardrobe door. The dress was a soft knobbly cream wool, with a simple shirt-shape and voluminous sleeves caught into tight cuffs. She had had it for years, but continued to wear it because it was so comfortable. She couldn't bear to feel restricted in clothes and this particular dress was so soft and loose that she hardly knew she was wearing it. She pulled her hair back and considered the effect, twisting from side to side speculatively. Then she released it again and shook her head to spread it over her shoulder. This was how Alan preferred it – lots of hair. She had to admit it did suit her best, and yet she nursed an uneasy suspicion that it also made her look younger, something she definitely did not need.

She rummaged in a drawer among woolly socks and scarves and found the string of beads she'd brought with her – chunky, softly-glowing amber, translucent as barley sugar, bought for her by Alan. This last fact caused her that familiar pang of unease, made sharper by her recent conversation with Jean. She decided to ring him that evening.

His voice, when it eventually came crackling over the rather bad line, sounded so strange and unreal that she could think of nothing to say.

'Hallo? Hallo?' He obviously thought he had been cut off.

'Hallo, Alan.'

'Darling, how lovely to hear from you. Are you having a wonderful holiday?'

'Jean and Ian have been fantastic as usual, I'm really one of the family up here—' She smiled at Jean who was passing through the hall with a pile of washing off the line. 'And how about you – I suppose you've been slaving away all the hours that God gives.'

'That's right. But it's been worth it. Things will be much easier when you get back, we'll be able to do things together – I am looking forward to seeing you again, you know.' He had lowered his voice in that earnest, tender way he had that made something inside her draw back and curl up.

She said brightly, 'I'm having a fling on Saturday night.'

'A Highland fling?'

'Something like that!' She laughed, relieved to have lightened the tone of the conversation. 'Ian's taking me to a dance in the village hall.'

'It sounds marvellous. I can't say I don't envy Ian, but from what I hear I can trust him to take care of you.'

'Oh, I shan't need much taking care of, I intend to dance every dance and be so energetic there'll be no time left for anything else.'

'Well, enjoy yourself. Don't think of me.' He said it not

pathetically but as a sort of amiable warning. She responded in kind.

'I won't. I'll see you very soon.'

'That's right. I love you. Hurry back.'

'Bye, darling.' She pressed the receiver down abruptly, hoping he would assume the line had been cut off. Jean came back into the hall, this time with mugs of coffee on a tray.

'That was quick. Coffee?'

'Please. No, I don't like the telephone: we never talk for long.'

'I know what you mean.' Jean could sympathize with this. She remembered all too vividly the unsatisfactory nature of phone calls when she and Ian had been apart. The silences, the misunderstandings, the inability to express those feelings which crowded the line but which needed physical closeness for their expression. She glanced at Elvi – she looked tense and slightly flushed. Jean decided that perhaps she had been too hard on her.

Saturday night was wild and wet. The wind cut across the side of the hill like a knife, rattling the window frames and hurling the rain like handfuls of gravel against the glass. Ian, sitting over a pint and sausages and mash at the kitchen table, glanced at Elvi who was spreading herself a sandwich.

'Still want to go?'

'Of course – we're not dancing out of doors I take it?'

'Take no notice,' said Jean, 'he's trying to wriggle out of it.'

Elvi was at once remorseful. 'That's different. I don't want to drag you out if—'

'See what you've done, clumsy?' Jean gave her husband's head a playful push. 'The poor girl feels a nuisance now.' She turned to Elvi. 'He'll enjoy it when he gets there, he always does.'

'I'm sure I will.' Ian, looking more and more sheepish, drained his beer and stood up. 'I meant nothing by it. I'm misunderstood, that's the trouble.'

'Poor old thing. Go and get changed the pair of you. Elvi,

I wish you'd have something more to eat before you go – let me cook you a bacon and egg while you're changing.'

'No, thanks, I'll take this up with me.' Elvi brandished the cheese sandwich. 'I'll be fine.'

When she came down twenty minutes later, Ian was ready and waiting, standing in the hall looking self-conscious in his tweed suit. He was struck as never before by her beauty – she seemed all copper and amber and pale gold – brilliant, but not hard, rather glowing as if lit by some gentle fire. He took her coat and held it for her to put on.

'You look lovely,' he said simply. Jean appeared in the doorway of the sitting room, smiling benignly.

'She does, too. You look after her.'

Elvi flicked her hair over the collar of her coat with the backs of her hands and beamed.

'You're a love to stay at home while we go gadding off.'

'No, I'm not, I shall have a lovely quiet time. Go on or the evening will be half over.' She stepped forward on an impulse and kissed her goddaughter. 'Run along.'

She watched them leave, the wind pouring through the door when they opened it, lashing their coats round their legs and lifting the well-worn mat in the hall. The wild darkness swallowed them, the door closed and the house settled back into an unusual quietness.

The village hall was already humming when they arrived. Elvi went to leave her coat in the tiny, cold cloakroom. The moments of quick preparation, the electricity in her hair making it fly and crackle when she brushed it, the goosepimples – not only of cold – beneath her loose sleeves – everything added to her feeling of excitement. When she re-emerged into the tiny outer hall Ian was standing at the table by the door, buying tickets from a plump, elderly woman with skin as weathered as a windfall apple. As Elvi approached she beamed at her with such warmth that Elvi at once felt welcome and approved. The woman's hands, moving slowly over the old biscuit tin full of change and the dog-eared books of tickets, were large and red, cracked by the wind. As Elvi and Ian turned to go into the hall she said softly, 'Have a dance for me, lassie.' She spoke so quietly that Elvi only half-turned in acknowledgement, uncertain whether she had heard a voice or not, but the words were still with her as the warmth and light and music of the dance washed over them.

'Let me get you a drink,' Ian said. 'What will you have, whisky?'

There was a twinkle in his eye. Elvi made a face. 'You know I can't take the stuff – I'd probably disgrace you. I'll have a glass of wine if I can get it.'

'I don't know about that – if they do have it, it'll be pretty rough. What do you want otherwise?'

'Lemonade.'

'Mad fool. Come on.' They went over to the small bar – no more than a couple of sheet-covered trestles, manned by two perspiring local worthies, coats off and shirtsleeves rolled up in the heat of the hall. Ian, towering a head and shoulders above the crush, hailed them by name and placed his order. He was well-known and well-liked and there were various teasing greetings, which he parried with easy good humour. Elvi felt the glances, even, in some cases, the frank stares, which fell on her, and found herself beaming broadly as Ian introduced her generally as 'my popsy' to roars of disbelieving delight. She had barely got the cool, brimming glass of pop – there was no wine – when someone caught her by the elbow and turned her firmly towards the dance floor. Ian bellowed affectionately: 'Don't be frightened, lassie, it's only Bill MacIntyre, the wild man of Kirkmuir!'

It was obvious that the wild man intended to dance with her whether she wanted to or not, and she thrust her glass into Ian's outstretched hands and allowed herself to be propelled on to the floor, where couples were already forming up for Strip the Willow. Once there, the bright, strident pulse of the music melted her nervousness, and she prepared to dance with all her might. All the faces lined up opposite her were smiling benignly, and she was relieved to discover that the one directly opposite was far from wild and not unpleasing. Bill MacIntytre was a dapper, silver-haired man in his sixties who turned out to be as light on his feet as a fifteen-year-old. The exhilaration of whirling down the line, feeling the firm swing of arm after arm, was like flying. This is how dancing was supposed to be – fast and furious and fun, too quick for conversation, too energetic for all but the most glancing flirtation. When the music finished she felt quite light-headed, laughing breathlessly, and, almost without knowing it, she found herself swept into another dance by another partner. She caught a glimpse of Ian's face, beaming broadly over the bobbing crowd of heads at the bar. She was blissfully elated and happy. She was a good dancer and tonight a tireless one and it was another hour before she managed to extricate herself from her partner and rejoin Ian.

As she approached he held out a half-pint mug of lemonade.

'It's a fresh one – the other one went flat.'

'I'm *sorry*.' She was laughing. 'I couldn't get away!'

'And not trying very hard, either, by the look of it – talk about not sticking to the man you came in with!' Ian turned for support to his companion at the bar. 'By the way, Elvi, this is a young friend of ours, Callum Sheil.'

'Hallo, Callum Sheil.' Elvi stretched across Ian to offer a hand, and felt it grasped very firmly – even rather hard, by a thin, bony hand.

'Callum's a newshound.'

'A reporter, really?' Elvi was intrigued. 'On which paper?'

'Only the local one, I fear.' His voice was very soft, but clear – it reached her quite distinctly despite the congenial hubbub all round. 'And I'm certainly not a newshound yet, I've a long way to go. But I intend to go the distance, I promise you.' He presented her with a sudden brilliant smile, of such sweetness and intensity that she felt herself blushing. It was like a beautiful compliment, intimate and unexpected.

'Will you dance?' She nodded and he walked ahead of her on to the floor. It was a lilting, tuneful waltz. His arm round

59

her was firm but light. She was struck again by his thinness, it was like dancing with a boy, except that his lead was sure and his movements poised. He was exactly her height, no taller, and she was very conscious of his eyes directly before hers. They were dark and animated, set in a narrow, mobile face with a long nose, and a mouth which was both severe and sensuous. He's a Celt, thought Elvi, he's got a timeless face. His hair was black and springy, with a disarrayed appearance which she guessed was probably natural and permanent but which still looked as though he ran his fingers through it continually.

Now as they danced, he was quiet, but Elvi could feel him watching her, his thin frame exuding a current of energy and animation. She realized that she herself felt a tension and excitement which was quite different to the carefree exhilaration of the previous hour's dancing. She was expectant, waiting for something, though she didn't know what. When the music stopped he dropped his arms but remained standing very close to her. She found she was quite unable to step back and so they stood there together, as if held by some invisible thread, until the music began again and he put his arm round her. Feeling that she must speak, to break the mysterious spell which seemed to be creeping over them, she said: 'Have you lived around here all your life?'

'No. Just the last three years since my father died. I was in Edinburgh before that.'

'And what made you come? I mean, why didn't you join a local paper there? I should have thought there would have been more opportunities.'

'I didn't join a paper there for the simple reason that I wasn't interested in journalism at the time. I came here to be a hermit.'

'And were you a successful hermit?'

'Very successful. I lived in a croft, and grew a few vegetables, and made things, and coughed and sneezed a lot.'

His lack of pretension was appealing. Elvi looked into his face and laughed aloud. He rewarded her with another of those dazzling, generous smiles.

'So you decided the fleshpots of the press were preferable to the rigors of self-sufficiency?'

'More or less. I wrote an article for the *Chronicle* about the problems of the hermit's life and when they said they'd buy it I told them, Right! I've had enough of hermitry, how about giving me a job?'

'And they did? Just like that?'

'Just like that.' A mischievous look flitted across his face. Elvi could imagine how easily the job had become his. She had seldom met anyone with this special ability to please – he conveyed the impression of wishing to delight only her. If he switched on that high voltage smile she could think of no one who could fail to be ensnared.

The music stopped once again, and amid the clapping and laughter and hoots of exuberant Scots enjoyment they stood still, and close and together.

'Would you like a drink?' he enquired.

'I wouldn't mind something – a shandy or something. It's hot in here and I'm thirsty.'

'So am I. Come on.' They went back to the bar and he left her on the fringes of the crush while he fought his way through. Small and thin as he was, he was soon swallowed up by the crowd. Elvi found herself staring hard at the phalanx of broad backs and fast-reddening faces, concentrating on his reappearance. Ridiculously, she missed him, she wanted him back by her side. Her exuberance had gone, she now no longer wished to dance with anyone else, she dreaded an approach or an invitation, she felt solitary and vulnerable because he was not standing close to her. It was not a sensation she was used to. The face she usually presented to the world, a face of which she had never before been aware, had slipped. She felt very much herself, and yet a stranger.

When he came back, carrying a can of light ale for himself and a shandy for her, she felt pleasure and relief flood through her. He gave her her drink and then concentrated on pouring and drinking his own. He did this with a quiet, careful deliberation, like a boy savouring an illicit ginger beer. After the first long swig he looked at her and licked the moustache of foam off his top lip with relish: 'That's good.' He kept his eyes on her, as if waiting for some reaction, when he added: 'I must go in a few minutes.'

'Oh?' To her embarrassment she could hear the naked surprise and disappointment in her own voice. In an attempt to lighten the impression she said, 'What a pity – just as we were getting to know each other!'

'Yes.' He was serious. 'It is a pity. But I've got an early start tomorrow, I'm afraid.'

'That's sensible of you.' Elvi was trying not to let her annoyance show. Suddenly it seemed arrogant of him to announce his departure so abruptly when he must know that she cared so much for his company. And the excuse about an early start seemed nothing short of insultingly weak. Her face reddened, she felt foolish and awkward, until suddenly she felt his thin hand lightly touch hers where it clutched her glass.

'I am sorry,' he said softly.

She looked up and met his eyes and knew that he meant it.

'That's all right. I feel so foolish.'

'Why?'

'Because you must have seen how disappointed I am that you're going.'

'I'm flattered for one thing. And for another it's nice to see some good straightforward feeling displayed now and again. Don't you think?'

'I suppose so . . .' She was unconvinced.

'I know I like it. You're staying with Jean and Ian?'

'That's right.'

'I'll come tomorrow. I know them well and I often drop in. We could go for a walk or something.'

'Yes – yes, that would be nice, I'd like that.'

'Good, it's settled. Now I'll escort you back to the man you came in with, like a gentleman should.' He grinned and took her arm. She felt again the peculiar thrill of vitality which emanated from him. He looked so young and insubstantial and yet he seemed to have a double helping of life force, spilling over from his slight frame, charging everything with which he came into contact. Ian was still in the same place at the bar.

'Hallo, you young things!' he greeted them, amid the kind of undue hilarity which a weak joke enjoys among drinkers. Callum's composure remained unruffled.

'Have you been propping up the bar all this time, Doctor?'

'Indeed I have! I came in with a girl but she hasn't been near me since!' More hilarity. Elvi blushed furiously.

Callum said: 'I merely rescued this lady from her inattentive escort.'

'That's your story and you're sticking to it, I suppose. Going home now are you? Casting her off like a worn-out glove?'

'That's right.' Both men were obviously enjoying the exchange. There was no rancour in it, but Elvi felt humiliated and embarrassed. She thought briefly, and for the first time, of Alan. Alan, whose world centred around her, whose courtesy and consideration were things to be relied upon at all times.

'Please stop it,' she snapped. 'I am *here*, you know!' To her chagrin this outburst was met with a hoot of laughter from Ian, but Callum put his arm lightly round her.

'You mustn't mind, Elvi. It's only a joke. I'll see you tomorrow.'

By the time she had turned to say goodbye he had already been swallowed up by the crowd. She turned back to Ian, who was wagging an admonishing finger at her.

'Coming tomorrow, is he? Poor old Alan! I've never met the chap but I feel sorry for him already.'

'Don't be ridiculous. It's just a friendly call. I didn't realize you got so facetious when you drank.' As soon as she had spoken she was terrified lest she'd overstepped the mark. She had never before been so rude to anyone in her life, especially Ian, whom she liked and admired so much. But to her amazement the people around her laughed and patted her on the back and Ian gave a rueful smile and placed his glass on the bar with an air of finality.

'You're too sharp for me tonight, lassie. Come on and I'll dance with you before my reputation's ruined.' They went on to the floor and joined a group for the Dashing White Sergeant. She was glad it was a quick, vigorous dance, so that she could twirl and stamp and laugh and hide her new vulnerability behind a façade of gaiety. There seemed to be a dark, quiet place deep inside her now, a secret place where something was growing like a tiny frail new plant in the early spring. In her mind's eye she could see Callum, walking home in the dark, as thin as a sapling in the buffeting wind.

The next morning at breakfast, Ian was morose, and Jean reproving.

'Fancy taking Elvi to a dance and spending half the night propping up the bar!'

'I've said I'm sorry. The lass enjoyed herself anyway, didn't you, Elvi?'

'Oh, I did, tremendously. Jean, don't be cross with him, he was lovely and I had the time of my life.'

'I daresay you did, but it certainly wasn't because of him. He's got the head of a lifetime this morning.'

'Then he's paying for his social shortcomings, isn't he?' Elvi smiled encouragingly at Ian, who was stirring his spoon in a cup of soupy black coffee.

'All I can say is,' he announced mournfully, 'that if I behaved badly, I'm sorry. I must get to the surgery.'

'God help the patients.' Jean was acid, tilting her cheek to be kissed without looking at her husband.

As he pulled his coat on in the hall he said: 'Give my regards to Callum when he calls.' As he left, he slammed the door behind him, and Jean winced exaggeratedly. Elvi got up to pour herself more coffee.

'Don't be hard on him,' she said. 'He's the nicest man I know.'

'He's the nicest man *I* know, that's why it gets my goat when he doesn't come up to scratch.'

'Well . . . it was a lovely evening, anyway.'

'You met Callum Sheil then, did you?'

'That's right, Ian bumped into him and he said he might pop round today.' Elvi could feel Jean's steady, perceptive gaze resting on her and turned back to the table to escape it.

'We're very fond of Callum,' said Jean. 'He's got no one in the world, perhaps that's why he's so canny at making other people like him.'

'I didn't know that. But you're right, he's very pleasant.'

'Hm.' Jean began clearing the table fast and furiously.

To change the subject, Elvi enquired: 'Where are the children? I haven't seen them this morning.'

'They've gone to friends for the day. I've got to go into Oban. It looks as though you'll be entertaining Callum by yourself.'

'That's alright.'

'The children will be sorry to have missed him. They adore that boy.'

'Yes, I should imagine he'd be very good with children.'

'That's right.'

Elvi was sharply conscious of Jean's suspicions. Again she tried to deflect the subject of Callum.

'I must check with the station about train times for Monday.'

'Don't worry, I might as well do that as I'm in town anyway today.'

'Thanks Jean. Are you sure you'll have time?'

'Quite sure. If you're here for lunch there's some cold pie in the larder and plenty of cheese and stuff, just help yourself.'

'That's marvellous. Can I do anything about the evening meal, to help you out?'

'I shouldn't worry, we'll take pot luck or I can bring something back with me. I must dash now or the morning will be gone.'

'What about the kids, do I collect them?'

Jean's voice floated down the stairs: 'No, I'll do that on my way back this afternoon.'

After Jean had gone, still as irritable as an east wind and driving the Land Rover with such ferocity that a sheet of mud spurted from beneath its wheels as she pulled away, Elvi gave herself up to the feeling of joyful excitement which she had been warding off all morning. She had been frightened of letting her defences waver even for a minute in case her whole face spread into a great stupid grin and she started to jump up and down like a child on Christmas morning.

Now, to find some echo of her own delight she switched the kitchen radio on to continuous music and began to busy herself with meaningless preparation. She made a pot of fresh coffee, picked some new daffodils from the muddy garden and stuck them in a jug on the table. Jean had left things in a most uncharacteristic mess, but Elvi took delight in cleaning and tidying, putting homemade shortbread on a plate and then dashing upstairs to check on her appearance. When she looked in her mirror she found that her own face surprised her. The eyes looked back, fiercely bright, the lips were full and red, the cheeks flushed. She looked as though someone had taken the original painting of herself and touched it up in every department, so that it had a heightened, colourful intensity. Even her hair, always springy and rich, had an extra vibrancy this morning, like a mass of glowing wires. She put her hands to this strange, brilliant face. No wonder Jean had been suspicious. But nothing could make her guilty or sad today. Today she was happy, and that was all that mattered. She thought of Alan, but he seemed unreal beside the excitement of the here and now. She dragged a brush over her hair, toyed with and rejected the idea of changing out of her trousers and sweater. She knew instinctively that there was no need to dress up or to pretend. When she heard a knock on the back door she got there so fast she could not even remember running down the stairs.

'Hallo.'

'Hallo. Come in.'

He entered. He was wearing a dark navy fisherman's sweater, which accentuated the paleness of his face and the almost febrile brightness of his eyes. He has a burnt-out look, thought Elvi, as though his extra energy eats at him.

Now he looked around, head tilted. 'It's quiet. All alone?'

'Yes, I'm afraid—'

'I'm glad.' She smiled, he was so honest. 'Is that coffee I smell?'

'It is, and freshly made. Sit down and we'll have some. There's some of Jean's homemade shortbread, too.'

'Ah, Jean's famous shortbread.' He took a piece and ate with obvious enjoyment. He smiled as he watched her pour the coffee. As she set his cup in front of him she asked, 'Why are you smiling like that? Have I got a smut on my nose?'

'No, I just like watching women go all domestic.'

'Why? It's boring, surely.'

'No, not at all. You move so nicely when you're busy. Your hands are so quick.'

'We have plenty of practice.'

'Do I detect a hint of resentment?'

'No, I like it. I've looked after my father for years, and I enjoy it.'

'He's lucky to have you.'

'I'm lucky to have him.'

Elvi told him about her life at home, carefully skirting round the subject of Alan, but he was too direct for her.

'You have a boyfriend in England?'

'There is – somebody about.'

'How enigmatic. Does he lurk in the grounds awaiting his chance to carry you off?'

'I only meant – it's nothing serious.'

The cock had crowed. Elvi rose abruptly, put the cups in the sink and said: 'Shall we go out?'

'By all means.'

Elvi pulled on an extra sweater and boots and they set off up the mountainside. After they had walked a few hundred yards in silence, he held out his hand.

'Hold my hand,' he said. Elvi placed her hand in his and it felt as though their two persons were fused together by that small link. She felt that he knew her and understood her more than any other person she had known, although they had only met a few hours ago. And she felt also that she wanted to give something back, to show in some measure the gloriousness of her sensations, to demonstrate how precious was his mere presence. Some deep-rooted reserve held her back, but he, as usual, was over the boundary before her.

'I can only dare to hope,' he said, facing straight ahead, 'that you feel the way I feel.'

'Yes . . . yes, I do.' It seemed so absolutely right that he should have said that. There was no need for more. He stopped and gently pulled her round to face him.

'We're fools,' he said. 'But because you're off home the day after tomorrow, and because I want to anyway—' He kissed her. And Elvi realized then with a shock of excitement and remorse, that this was how it ought to be. She was transcended and overcome, she felt at once tender, feeling his acute thinness, and passionate at the insistence of his kiss. She wanted him fiercely and he was all she wanted. Then as they drew apart there were tears of pleading in her eyes. As they spilled over he put out his hand and brushed them away with thin fingers which he then put to his lips and licked with the sensuality of a cat.

'We are fools, you know,' he repeated softly. 'Let's say no more.'

'I can't!' Elvi's words came in a harsh sob. 'Please, don't leave me. Please, don't.'

'You're leaving me. Remember? And that's as it should be, you must go back where you belong, and I must get on with my life here.'

'But I feel now as if *this* is where I belong.'

'It isn't.' He was emphatic. But then he suddenly drew her to him again, pressing her cheek against his shoulder, and when he spoke again there was a tightness in his voice, keeping something back, and his hand on the back of her head was hard as though he forcibly prevented her from looking at him. 'You just have to believe me when I say you *must* go back.'

Frantically, shamelessly, Elvi clung to him, the tears pouring down her face. She had no pride left, and no rational
argument that seemed strong enough to deprive her of this
new-found love.

'Please, *please* . . . there is no one else, there's nothing to
prevent us – we have to see each other. Why should I have to do
without you when you're everything I want? Why should I?'

Quietly, over her sobs, he said: 'You sound like a child.' But
the words were a caress, not an accusation. When she looked into
his face he was smiling. A tiny spark of hope kindled in her.

'You will come? Oh please come to me.'

'I'll come. I'll contact you. I'm a thousand kinds of idiot
for saying so, but I'll come.'

And that was how it was. They had walked back to the house
clinging to each other in the buffeting spring wind, learning
each other by sound and touch as a blind person imprints an
image on his inner darkness. Just as they got back, the rain
had started and they had felt themselves cut off and imprisoned
within their love. It had seemed simply right and logical to lie
together in the little whitewashed bedroom, with the fury of
the spring storm outside and the warm, close secret of their
joined bodies within. Callum showed her, with infinite care,
and humour and consideration, a land that she had never
even dreamed existed. A land of discovery and adventure
and incredible sweetness. She truly recognized, for the first
time, her own beauty, and delighted in it, and was overjoyed
that she could in turn show her pleasure in his.

Afterwards he had become very quiet, still and serious, and
she did not try to change that. He left with the renewed promise
of a visit, and she had felt no sadness at his departure, only
intense joy at what had happened to her.

How glad she had been of the last-minute activity which
had carried her through Sunday! Packing and checking trains
and making telephone calls. She was certain that if she had
not been so busy her exhilaration would have been plain for

all to see, and she would have been obliged to shout out loud that which she most wanted to keep secret. She found it frighteningly easy to lie about Callum's visit, to say how sorry he was not to have seen the children, to make it sound casual and inconsequential. Jean appeared thoughtful and was full of little gestures of kindness – magazines and homemade sweets for the train, a bottle of whisky for the Major, kind messages to Alan: the latter delivered with a little too much weight, but Elvi was flying too high to be brought down.

As she settled into the train she thought to herself: we cannot fail, we are right. Everything will happen for the best. All we need is time.

Six

As her long journey reached its end, the reality of her home situation impinged on Elvi's consciousness as it had not been able to do while she was in Scotland. Small details began to drift back to her haphazardly. She remembered that her father, when she had spoken to him on the phone, had said that Alan would be meeting her train. At the time, in her euphoric happiness, she had barely taken it in, let alone given it any consideration, but now as the grey outskirts of London began to process past the windows, and people began to lift down cases and put on coats, she felt the full weight of its implication. She was going to have to face him now, at once, when the memory of Callum's voice, and face, and touch, were still fresh and tender on her like new burns. She again had the sensation of extreme vulnerability that she had experienced when Callum had first left her side. She was only half a person, and now the shell which had kept her safe for so many years had been removed, she was open to pain in a way she had never been before.

As the train glided to a halt at Euston she made a forcible effort to recall Alan, as a person, to whom she could react as she always had done. But it was impossible. The events of the last few days had turned him into a name, a shadow that fell between her and Callum, but no longer a real flesh-and-blood man. Whereas Callum . . . She closed her eyes for a second and his face swam before her, with those burning dark eyes generating their extraordinary current of vitality.

Dully and mechanically, she collected together her things and joined the crowd of people walking up the ramp to the ticket barrier. She felt no panic, only a terrible numbness. Almost

71

as soon as she was through the barrier she felt a hand on her arm.

'Hallo, darling. Let me take that.' She felt her case taken from her and the hand guided her through the crush out into the great brightly-lit echoing vault of the main hall. She turned, with hopeless resignation, to face him.

'Hallo, Alan. Thank you for meeting me.'

'Don't be silly, how could I not? Did you have a marvellous time?'

She nodded.

'How were they all? I had an awfully nice letter from Jean – they were so delighted you went.'

'Yes . . . yes, they're lovely people.' She thought, he must be able to tell, my smile feels like a grotesque mask, my voice sounds flat and dead, how can he not tell? But it appeared that he did not, for he was talking and smiling, and his arm was across her shoulders like a yoke. A pressing need to apologize for something, anything, urged her to interrupt him with: 'You shouldn't have bothered to come. I know how busy you are. I could easily have got a taxi over to Victoria.'

'We're going to do that anyway, I wasn't about to drive the Merc across town at this time of day. But will you please stop telling me I shouldn't have come? What on earth do you think I've been doing with myself for the past few days, but waiting to see you again? I went down to the house myself on Saturday, just to see how McReady's were getting on, but it was like a museum without you. You'll be glad to hear that your instructions are being carried out to the letter, and they've made a lot of progress since we went down last.'

He squeezed her and inclined his head to look into her face – he liked to watch her pleasure when the house was being discussed. But she made a pretence of rummaging in her pocket for something in order to avoid his eyes. The house. Her pride and joy, her hope for the future, the anchor which had kept her wayward emotions from casting adrift and being wrecked on doubt. Now it inspired not a flicker of interest. Indeed, the thought of it frightened her, it was no longer an anchor but a weight tied round her neck to hamper her escape.

They only had to wait a couple of minutes at the taxi rank, and then they were off, the moment she dreaded, in the strange seclusion which the back of a cab affords, so welcome to lovers, but to her, a terrible ordeal.

Alan put his hand on her cheek and turned her face towards him.

'Glad to see me?' She nodded, but kept her lips pressed firmly together. She could not trust herself to speak. He leaned forward and kissed her lightly and she remained still and passive. As he drew back she detected for the first time something quizzical in his look.

'I wish I could come down with you now,' he said, in a brighter, conversational tone. 'But I'll be down on Friday night, ready and willing to perform whatever complex administrative tasks you want done. Your wish will be my command.'

'Thank you. That will be marvellous, really.'

'What about that curtain stuff we chose in Liberty's?' He was making a big effort now. 'Do you want me to go in and see if it's arrived?'

'No, that's going to be delivered. In fact it may be at home already.'

'Fine. I really liked that. You have such good taste and I have none at all in those matters.'

Elvi smiled briefly and then, feeling that that was not enough, added, 'Yes, you have,' and caught again that quizzical look in his eyes. He felt in his breast pocket for his cigarette case and lighter. He had a careful, precise way of putting the cigarette between his lips – she had always liked to watch him, but now she could not look and averted her eyes to the window. Every tiny thing which was rooted in her past feeling for him was now just a sad, hollow echo that she preferred not to acknowledge.

The smell of cigarette smoke drifted round the cab. Alan rested his forearm on her shoulder and played idly with her hair.

'I love you, you know,' he said in the same conversational tone. She knew, oh, how well she knew, that he was trying not to pressure her, striving in his usual considerate way not to press on the nerve that was sensitive although he had no idea what the pain was. How hard he made it for her. She looked at him directly for the first time.

'I know you do,' she said.

'Just so long as you remember it. It's something you can rely on.'

'I know.'

'That's all right then.'

But it was very far from all right. He saw her into her homebound train at Victoria very quietly and unfussily, smoothing her path in his expert, unruffled way. And through-out this and his leave-taking she could feel the knot inside her drawn tighter and tighter until she was stiff and aching with the tension of it. He saw her drawn expression and found a reason for it which he himself only half-believed.

'You look exhausted. Try and sleep on the way down.'

'Yes, I will.' She was relieved to have a ready-made excuse. 'Thanks again for everything.'

'Don't mention it. I mean that.' He smiled to take the firmness out of the words. 'I'll be down on Friday and we'll be the archetypal engaged couple. Isn't it time we went to see the vicar again or something?'

'Probably . . . I don't know actually, I haven't really thought—'

'Of course you haven't. Give my love to your father. I'll ring tomorrow evening when you've had a good rest. Good-bye, my love.' He kissed her forehead, pressed her hand and was gone. Elvi could feel the indulgent looks of the other passengers resting on her, and sank down in her seat to escape them. If they only knew.

For the next two hours she sat stock still, staring at her reflection in the darkening window. Her head ached but she could not sleep and when she attempted to look at the magazine the words swam before her eyes like so many meaningless dots. It was as though the conflict raged in her head so that there was no room left.

Her father had arranged a taxi for her at the village station. It was one of the two local taxis, driven by Reg and Derek Adams, father and son. Reg, who was there to meet her on the platform, had known her since she was a child.

'Evening, miss. Had a good holiday?'

'Yes, thanks, Reg.'

'Not long now to the big day, eh?' He put her case in the boot and held open the door of the battered black saloon.

'No, not long.' There was no denying that inescapable fact. Elvi wished she did not know Reg, that she could sit quietly and anonymously and be driven quickly home. Fortunately he was garrulous and did not require much from her in the way of conversation except the occasional affirmation. When they got home his last words were: 'See you on the way to church, then!' Delivered with a roguish grin.

'Whatever did he mean by that?' she asked her father as they walked up the steps to the front door.

'He's driving us to the church, remember?'

'Yes, of course . . .' But she didn't. Things she had said, little matters she had arranged, were like another world. This house, with all its happy memories and associations, held no magic now, all that it stood for was so far away. It was as though in the space of a few days she made a great leap forward into womanhood and quite suddenly 'put away childish things'.

In the hall her father said: 'There are a few messages and whatnot but they'll wait till you've had some supper and made yourself comfortable. It's wonderful to have you home, my dear.'

'It's wonderful to see you,' said Elvi, and thought, that's about the only honest thing I've said all day. She went into her room and was touched to see that the Major had been in himself and got it ready for her – the bed was turned back invitingly, the curtains drawn and the bedside light on, and there was a little lustre jug filled with primroses on her dressing table. In the corner was a pile of recently arrived wedding presents, and beside them the bulging carton containing the nursery school's multiple offering. The sight of this last was too much for Elvi. For the first time the tears came and she sank down on the bed and gave herself up to the blessed relief and luxury of weeping, not bothering to wipe her cheeks, or hold back the sobs that came thick and fast.

When the storm had subsided she went to the basin and splashed her face with cold water. She ran a comb though her hair and took a cursory look at the cards on the parcels. So many people wishing her well, so many people eager to push her forward into a new life.

She left the parcels unopened and went downstairs to her father.

It turned out that both the florist and Miss Markham were eager to see her, and the Major also suggested she pay a call on the vicar and confirm the music she wanted for the service. To her distress he seemed to have become more positive about the wedding in her absence, to have made up his mind that he was looking forward to it. His enthusiasm carried the evening and she simply agreed to do this and that and went early and gratefully to bed soon after supper.

The days that followed were a kind of limbo for Elvi. Because she had no pretext for not doing so, she had to visit people and make arrangements which now seemed totally pointless. And it was not only that they concerned herself and Alan, but they seemed in themselves so trivial and foolish. Why had she cared so much about this wedding, the dress, the flowers, the hymns? She now knew for sure that they were so much empty ceremony, that she had used them to camouflage the essential emptiness of her feelings. The dress was finished but she could not bring herself to take it home. Instead she made some feeble excuse about it being safer with Miss Markham, and hurried away. She discovered to her horror that her father had written and sent off most of the invitations in her absence, leaving only a few whose names and addresses he was unsure of. They lay on the hall table like a reproach, but she put off writing on them out of sheer cowardice. Jean rang up, and she longed to ask after Callum, but did not dare. Remembering his words to her she suddenly grew terrified that he would not contact her, that whatever had worried him in the first place would loom large again now that she was gone, and that he would simply let things drift. But then she remembered the afternoon, with the rain battering on the windows and their fantastic journey of discovery, and she knew he would come.

On Thursday night he rang. She had only just put down the receiver from talking to Alan, who had confirmed his arrival the following evening at about eight. She stopped, halfway across the hall, and turned back to look at the phone as though it were some importunate stranger tapping on her shoulder.

'Hallo,' he said, 'it's me.'

'Thank God. I've been so frightened, so worried.'

'Why? I told you I'd be in touch.'

'Yes, I know, but—'

'But me no buts. Listen, I'm in London.'

'Callum!'

'It's not so crazy as it sounds. I have to come down for a meeting every couple of months so I brought my next one forward a bit. I'll be free from about eleven onwards tomorrow, just tell me where you are and I'll catch the train straight down.'

'No! No, you can't do that.'

'Why not? I can and I will.'

'No – you see my father – I told you about him – he's really not too well at the moment.' She lowered her voice, but her father was watching television in the sitting room and was unlikely to overhear. 'Let me come up to town, I'd like to anyway. We can have all day, but I mustn't be too late back. I think there's a train that gets me into Victoria about twenty past eleven, where shall we meet?'

'I'll be at the station. I have to have every minute there is with you, do you understand?'

'Yes.'

'Are you quite sure you should leave your father?'

'He'll be fine, I'll leave everything for him. He's not in bed or anything, he's just having a lot of pain from his leg.'

'Okay then, tomorrow it is. Be there, Elvi.'

'And you. Goodbye.'

'*Au revoir.*'

When she had replaced the receiver she sat for a full minute savouring the warm wave of excitement. As before, it swept anxiety and guilt before it so that she could think of nothing except that she was to see him very soon, feel his kiss and hear his voice and bask in his presence.

'Who was that?' the Major asked as she re-entered the sitting room.

'No one. I mean, Alan. He'll be down tomorrow at eight.'

'Good. But wasn't there another call after?'

'Yes. That was no one – wrong number.'

As the train pulled into the station at eleven eighteen on Friday morning, Elvi thought how different were her feelings now to the last time she had prepared to step down from a train. Then she had been so dispirited, so wretched and so full of foreboding, now she was buoyantly happy, waiting with her hand on the door handle for the gentle bump that meant they had truly arrived and she could run, run up the platform to greet him.

He was standing a little behind the others waiting at the barrier, his hands pushed deep into the pockets of a corduroy jacket. As she made her way towards him he remained very still but his smile went out to greet her. When she was close he enfolded her in his arms, and she could feel him still smiling against her hair. After a moment she drew back a little and ran her fingers lightly over his face, reminding herself of every plane and hollow. There seemed to be everything and nothing to say. She was whole again.

As they left the station, hand in hand, he asked: 'Where shall we go?'

'I don't mind. Nowhere smart.'

'Certainly not. Look at me.'

'I have been.'

He kissed her. 'Let's get a bus up to Hampstead. We could walk over Parliament Hill and have lunch at the Spaniards.'

'That sounds marvellous. I didn't expect you to know London so well.'

'Everyone knows London a bit, don't they? I mean most people have misspent at least part of their youth here, and you never forget places where you were young and foolish.'

'You're talking as if you're middle-aged already and I bet you're not much older than me!'

'Maybe, but I started young.' He flashed her a wicked look. 'Quick, a bus!'

A number 24 was pulling away from the stop but with a frantic dash they made it and scrambled, laughing and breathless, up to the front of the top deck. Callum sat back and propped up his feet on the metal partition in front.

'This is the life!' he said, with immense satisfaction. 'I consider this to be one of the great pleasures of London, a nice long ride on top of a double-decker bus.'

'Yes, you get a marvellous view. I've never done it before.'

'Never done it before?' He turned on her a look of exaggerated astonishment. 'Elvi, where have you been all your life?'

'Being sheltered, I suppose. Unlike most of the population, my youth was spent, not misspent, out of London.'

'Well, well, we have got ground to cover, I can see that. I shall have to force myself to do this more often.' He put his arm round her shoulders and drew her close, snuggling her up to him protectively. It was odd that for all his slight build he seemed to stand between her and the world like the mightiest of defences. 'This, then, is a guided tour,' he said. 'Pay attention. If you don't, I'll rip all your clothes off and make love to you in front of all these good people.' He jerked his head to indicate the two elderly women who sat a few seats back.

Through the half-hour journey he talked, and pointed out landmarks and little things he thought would interest her –

79

cafés he knew, second-hand bookshops, streets where famous people had lived, little grubby parks he had walked in.

'The thing about London,' he said, 'is that people are robust about it. They don't wilt under their urban surroundings, they make the most of them, and grow cabbages in their window-boxes, and enjoy every small postage-stamp of grass they've got. I like that, it's realistic.'

'I don't think I could bear it,' she said, looking out at the ranks of blackened buildings, the litter-strewn pavements and endlessly surging traffic. 'I like the country – it's peaceful.'

'Of course you could bear it.' He was firm. 'Most people can bear almost anything. You'd have to adjust your response to it, though. The thing is not to compare it with the country. It's a different animal, with different characteristics. Comparisons are odious, remember.'

'I can't help it. I suppose I'm a bumpkin.'

'You may be that, but you're not grown up till you can enjoy the city as well, and love it for what it is. At least –' he suddenly smiled to dispel pomposity – 'that's the way I see it.'

'You certainly put it forcefully.'

'No sense in mentioning it otherwise.' They sat quietly for a while and Elvi considered this last remark. It was true, he never said anything unless he meant it, it was as though he had carefully and deliberately honed down his conversation so that it was not only strictly truthful in the factual sense but also true to himself. That he set such store by this absolute truthfulness implied something like an animal's conservation of energy for the essentials of life. And now, like a cat curled on a favourite cushion he sat completely still, relaxed but watchful, his eyes on the moving picture outside the window.

They reached the terminus at South End Green and began the walk up Parliament Hill to the great domed sweep of the heath beyond. Up here there was a stiff wind, as always, and the kite-flyers were out in force, but the weather was getting milder every day now and it was not cold. As they walked, they talked, and Callum told her about his work. It was something Alan never discussed, since both he and she assumed that the topic would be tedious to her, but Callum had no such inhibitions.

'I like journalism,' he said, 'just because it's so ephemeral. I don't have the urge to write an epic novel or a great play, although I admire those who can. I want to write about the here and now, as it happens, and to convey my impressions as quickly as possible to other people, for what they're worth. It's immediacy that counts for me. That and directness, the ability to communicate quickly and clearly and vividly.' His enthusiasm seemed to release some extra force in him, for as he talked he began to walk more quickly, so that Elvi had to half-run to keep pace with him, and he released her hand in order to use his own for emphasis.

'And where do you want to get to?'

'The top. Or at worst some way up the ladder.'

'What is the top then? I don't know much about it.'

'The top is Fleet Street, the scribblers' Broadway! I used to love those corny films full of men in belted raincoats, and fedoras with press cards tucked in the band.'

'But it's not really like that, surely?'

'S-s-s-h, them's my dreams you're trampling on!'

Elvi laughed. He made her laugh a lot. It was so marvellous to laugh out loud because something struck her as funny and not, as was so often the case with Alan, to deflect some difficult situation which she could not otherwise have handled.

They began to come down off the wind-combed grassy hill into the sheltered dip by the ponds, and then to climb again through the wooded outskirts of Kenwood, where the cheeky grey squirrels pattered along the path as bold as brass, begging for titbits.

'Tree rats,' observed Callum, 'but they're rather nice, aren't they?'

'Not as pretty as the red ones.'

'There you go again, making comparisons.' He was reproving. 'That's a habit you have to get out of. Whatever the ecological pros and cons of the argument, the tree rat is not merely the yobbish poor relation of the cute red squirrel. He's a character

81

in his own right. Look at him –' he crouched down and held out his hand, which was immediately approached and investigated by the nearest of the squirrels, '– he's really adapted to life in the city. Good for him.' He looked up at her, the squirrel still nibbling at his fingers. 'What?'

'I didn't say anything.'

'I know. But surely you were going to.'

'No.' She began to laugh. 'You win.'

'I doubt it.' He jumped to his feet, took her hand and began to walk briskly along the path. 'All of a sudden I'm peckish. And thirsty.'

They reached the Spaniards at twelve thirty and were just early enough to get themselves a cosy corner table before the crowd of regular lunch-time drinkers arrived. They both had stout, but Elvi, who hadn't had it before, didn't care for it, so Callum went back for a glass of white wine and appropriated hers for himself. The ploughman's lunch seemed a feast after their walk, and they tucked in in silence.

When he had finished, Callum sat back, with his hands clasped behind his head, and said: 'Now I shall come over horribly sleepy. Do you know what I should like?'

She shook her head. 'What?'

'I should like to have some nice snug, sleazy little room to go back to with a meter for the gas and an iron bedstead. And then we could turn on the fire and make coffee and love.'

'But there's nowhere to go.'

'No. I can't afford to pay for somewhere and I don't know anyone well enough down here any more to ring up and borrow.'

'I don't either.'

'So there we are. And I can hardly bear it.' Characteristically he did not touch her at all, but simply sat back surveying her with such a hungry look of love and longing that she put out her hand to him.

'We are together anyway.' She knew it sounded feeble.

'That's not enough. Not now, at the moment. I want to make love to you to convince myself of you properly.'

'Why? Don't you believe in me?'

'I believe in you, but not in you and me.'

'That's too complicated.'

'Not at all, quite simple. I told you before. I'm not objectively in favour of the two of us. I don't think I'm the man for the job.'

'You're mad!' She was laughing.

'That's right. And selfish, and ambitious and niggardly with my favours. Ask anyone.'

'Why?' She was teasing him. 'Are there so many who know?'

'You know what I mean. I cannot bring myself to believe that this other chap wouldn't be much better for you than me.' This glancing reminder of Alan, and her casual betrayal of him, sent a chill through Elvi. She did not want to be made to feel that load of guilt and unhappiness, just now, when she was so happy. And because she had not told the truth Callum was casually, conversationally, turning the knife in the wound.

'I picture him,' he went on, 'very honest and upright and dependable, all qualities I much admire. He wouldn't be doing so much of this hanging about if he wasn't. A fellow of great moral fibre, I should think.' He did not sound mocking or facetious, he seemed quite genuinely to be describing a picture in his mind's eye. When he'd finished he glanced at her face. 'Am I right?'

'I suppose so – partly, anyway. He really isn't that important.'

'Not that important to *you*, poor chap. There is a difference.'

'Stop trapping me. I meant nothing by it.'

'I'm sorry, I wasn't trying to trap you and I'm sorry if I sounded pompous. I'll sound worse in a moment when I tell you not to expect too much of me.'

'What should I expect?'

'I don't know, and I wasn't saying that you *should*, just that you mustn't look for anything in the way of – permanence, if you like.'

'I don't look for anything but you.' It was the honest truth.

'What would happen if one day, it might even be quite soon, you looked and I wasn't there?'

'I can't think about it.'

'Try, for me.'

'I suppose life would go on. The trouble is I'm so happy right now I just can't imagine you not being there. I've felt only half-alive this past week without you, and now I'm alive-and-a-half because I'm with you. And anyway, why do you ask? Are you likely to stop feeling as you do now quite so abruptly?'

'Oh no, not that. But I might physically have moved on. I'm very pushy, you see, there are lots of things I want to do in a short time.'

'Your time's no shorter than anyone else's.'

'Perhaps not, but because I've mapped it out so thoroughly it seems so. I can't say in all conscience that I wouldn't take every opportunity that came my way even if it meant leaving you for a while.'

'I'm not such a delicate plant that I couldn't survive a separation,' she protested. 'I told you, I'd be like a hibernating animal, waiting for the spring.'

Her hand still lay on his knee and now she looked hard into his face, hoping to see exactly how he received this, what he made of it. But the dark eyes were secretive. There was a little pause during which she sensed something inconclusive in the air. She did not know what she had to say to resolve the uncertainty, and Callum seemed unwilling to.

Suddenly he appeared to come back to reality with a bump. He stood up, took her hand and said, 'Let's go.'

They walked back mostly in silence, and slowly, their strides matched. When they got back to South End Green he said: 'I'd like to buy you something, a present.'

'You mustn't do that, I don't want a present.'

'But I want to give you one. Does that make any difference?'

'Well . . . if you put it that way, but don't go spending too much.'

'That all depends,' he said mischievously, 'on whether you want a sable coat or a string of beads.'

'That's unfair.'

'Okay, I've got an idea.'

He had, it transpired, got several ideas. He took her into a little craft and antique shop and together they selected a beaten copper choker and earrings. It was a delight to shop with him because his enthusiasm was infectious and his taste sure. When Elvi baulked at the earrings – 'I never wear them!' – he told her: 'Then try.' She at once pulled her hair back but he restrained her.

'Don't do that.'

'But they won't show otherwise.'

'Yes, they will, a naughty gleam when your hair swings. Like a slave girl. You look terrific, believe me.' She peered into the small speckled mirror which was all the shop provided and saw that he was right. The warm glow of the copper complimented her colouring perfectly and the earrings, just glimpsed beneath her hair, gave her a dashing look she'd never thought herself capable of.

'I think you're right.' She looked round at him in delight.

'Yes, I am.' He turned to the girl at the counter. 'We'll have those, thanks.' Elvi began to remove them.

'Keep them on, why don't you?'

'Won't they look a bit odd with—?' She glanced doubtfully at her shaggy jacket and dungarees.

'Not a bit of it. I like it, anyway.'

'All right, I will!'

'You see?' Callum addressed the smiling assistant. 'She looks great, doesn't she?'

'Yes, she does.'

By the time they had taken the bus back into town it was well after four and Elvi remembered with horror that Alan was expected that evening. She became more and more uneasy.

'I think I should catch the first train I can,' she said as they alighted from the bus outside Victoria.

'Why? You said not too late, but it's still afternoon.'

'I told Father I'd be back by eight.'

'You can stay another hour and a half and still do that with time to spare.'

'I know, but I do worry a little, and he doesn't know about you . . .'

'I'm a dark secret, am I?'

'Not dark or a secret, really. He just doesn't know I've been with you, that's all. He's very conservative.'

'He must be! Do you always conduct your affairs in such a clandestine manner? It's like the Barretts of Wimpole Street.'

'No, it's *not*!' Elvi felt suddenly close to tears. Deception did not suit her, at least not the deliberate deception of others. The awfulness of having to face Alan again, the indecision, the pain of leaving Callum, the whole sad, sorry, confusing *mess* was all at once too much for her. At once he saw, and his arms went round her as the early-rush-hour crowds scurried past them into the station.

'It's all right, it's all right . . .' he soothed, stroking her hair. 'I'm sorry. Of course you must get back to him.'

'What about you? What are you going to do?'

'I was going back on the sleeper tonight anyway, I'm due in the office tomorrow morning. I'll probably go and see a film, have some supper and get on the train. They'll let me on at about ten thirty with a bit of luck.'

'I'm sorry. I'm sorry I'm so feeble . . .'

'You're not feeble. Your father's got a far stronger claim to your time and attention just now than I have.'

She shook her head miserably, helplessly. There was nothing she could say.

'Come on,' he said, 'let's go and find you a train.'

It turned out that there was one waiting, due to leave in about fifteen minutes. He bought a platform ticket and boarded it with her. They sat huddled close on the seat, the station noises ringing like a parrot-house outside the grimy glass. Some wit had defaced the 'No Smoking' sticker, turning each of the Os into little faces, each puffing on a fat cigar. Callum pointed to this and smiled.

'I like that,' he said. And then: 'Don't go away unhappy, Elvi. How can I bear it?'

'But what do you expect? It's been so short and you said – you said . . .'

She could not bring herself to repeat the words that turned over again and again in her mind.

'I said you might look and I'd be gone. What conceit!' For the first time she heard his voice full of self-hate, of violence, and it brought her up short.

'I can't say I didn't mean it,' he went on more gently, 'but that won't be yet. We've a long way to go together yet, Elvi, and I don't want to miss a step. I'll be back, as soon as I can. You can rely on that.' The last words were like an echo of Alan's. She turned and clung to him.

When the guard's whistle blew Callum had to unfasten her hands and place them on her lap, otherwise she would not have let him go. She wasn't crying now, but was white-faced and stiff with unhappiness.

'*Au revoir*,' he said, and when he was on the platform he put his hand flat on the glass by her pale face. But the cold glass came in between and she could only look out at him like a trapped animal.

For as far as he could, until he was breathless, Callum ran by the window and when he gave up, he stood and watched as the train snaked out from under the station canopy and gathered momentum round the long bend. When they were out of the station Elvi removed the earrings and choker and put them in her bag. She did so slowly and reverently as though she were undressing a corpse for burial.

She caught the bus back to the end of the lane and walked the rest of the way home. She had had to wait for the bus, and she felt tired and cold. It was seven o'clock.

She let herself in and called to her father. 'I'm back!' As she removed her coat she was conscious of the sitting-room door opening. A warm shaft of light spread into the hall, broken by the shadow of a figure in the doorway. She turned to greet her father, and saw Alan.

'Hallo, my darling,' he said. 'I got here early.'

'Where's Father?' She could only think of how things should have been. What had gone wrong? She walked past him into the sitting room. There was no one else there. 'Where's Father?' she repeated.

'Don't worry, he's all right but he was very tired. So when I arrived I suggested he spend the evening in bed. He's up there if you want to go and see him.'

'But what's the matter?' Panic about the whole situation boiled up inside her. 'Why does he suddenly have to spend an evening in bed?'

'It was obvious his leg was very bad—'

'My God, I should never have gone!'

'Of course you should, I simply thought—' But she was already flying up the stairs. She burst into her father's bedroom.

'Father – are you all right?'

'Right as rain.' She bent over the bed and he kissed her. He did, indeed, look comfortable enough, sitting there in his dressing gown with a glass of whisky on the bedside table and his book open on his lap. 'I'm a fraud really, but the leg began playing up a bit his afternoon, and when Alan arrived early and suggested I come up, I didn't need much persuading. It's sheer indulgence.'

'I should never have gone!' She plumped down on the bed, her fingers twined tightly, in an agony of guilt. Alan appeared at the doorway.

'Don't get yourself into a state. Come on down and have a drink yourself and leave your poor father to his well-earned rest.'

'He's right.' The Major leaned forward and patted her shoulder. 'Go and tell Alan what you've been up to in town today and leave me to my book.'

She rose stiffly and went past Alan and down the stairs. The sitting room was bright and cosy, the fire lit and the curtains drawn. On the table by the sofa stood Alan's half-full tumbler of whisky and an ashtray with a smoking cigarette resting on its lip. The familiar neat pink oblong of the *Financial Times* lay on the sofa. Alan came in behind her and went over to the corner cupboard.

'Martini?'

'Thank you.' He brought her the drink and sat down on the sofa, by his own. Moving the newspaper, he indicated that she should do the same.

'You look all-in,' he commented.

'London is tiring.'

'That's right. Especially if you're not used to it. Sometimes I think I've learned to shut most of it out just from sheer habit – you do if you spend most of your life there. But to go up for the day,' he grimaced, '– horrible!'

'What brought you here early, then?'

'The meeting was off and there was nothing else I could usefully do at that time on a Friday afternoon, so I thought, Why not?'

Elvi thought: This is terrible. Here they were, sat at either end of the sofa, he too kind and courteous to press his attentions, she too miserable and fearful to say what had to be said. She sat rigidly, staring down into her glass and as she sat she heard him ask, as though over a great distance: 'Who were you lunching with?'

She did not answer at first. She did not believe that he had said it, his voice sounded so quiet and concerned. But then he asked again: 'I wondered who it was you were lunching with.'

'What?'

'At the Spaniards.'

'Nobody.'

'On the contrary. Definitely not a nobody.' There was no sarcasm in his voice, he sounded sad and serious. 'I noticed him particularly. He was the sort of person one notices.'

'You were there.' It was not a question.

'Only briefly. Dick Porter and I stopped there for a beer and a sandwich on the way back from a meeting in Muswell Hill. I saw you just before we left.'

'Why didn't you come over?' The cold hostility in her own voice frightened her. She felt no pity for Alan now, she felt nothing at all except a terrible, fierce desire to defend herself.

'I didn't come over,' said Alan, 'because it would have been inappropriate. I could see that it would have been totally – out of place.'

'What do you mean?'

'You know what I mean, my darling.'

'I don't! You're being so damned civilized and smug and accusing—'

'Elvi – I have never felt less smug in my life, believe me, and I have not spoken a single word of accusation. I only mention this because I don't want you to tell me lies out of kindness.'

'Why should I tell you lies?'

'You tell me.' He stubbed out his cigarette and lit another. Elvi, not looking at him, heard the small sounds that went with the ritual she knew so well: the faint click of the cigarette case, the slither of it being returned to his pocket, the second smaller click of the lighter, and then the faint whiff of smoke as he exhaled. Then nothing. He sat very still and absolutely silent. Obviously, it was her turn to speak.

'Why did you think it would have been "out of place" as you put it, to come over and speak to me?'

'Because you were in love, the two of you. That's why.' His tone was matter of fact.

'What an extraordinary thing to say!'

'I don't know that it is.'

'You can't possible look at two people in a pub and say they're in love. Nobody could!'

'You're *not* just anybody, Elvi. Remember I know you very well. I'm in love with you myself. And the look you were giving him is the one you can't bring yourself to give me. I'd recognize it anywhere.'

'Oh, Alan.' For the first time Elvi turned to look at him. His face was impassive. She could not pretend any longer. 'You're right. What can I say?'

'Whatever you like. For the moment, I've run out of conversation.'

'I can't think of anything that will do.'

'*Anything* will do. Tide me over for a moment, Elvi . . .'

She saw with horror, all at once, what she was doing to him. She began to talk, very fast.

'He's called Callum, I met him when I was in Scotland. It was very quick and sudden for both of us, we hardly knew what was happening until it had already happened. I've never experienced anything like it before, you have to believe me, Alan. It was a shock, I wasn't ready for it. He doesn't know about you, I was too afraid to tell him, so you mustn't blame him. He's a very gentle person, the last thing he'd want to do is hurt anyone and the last, the last thing I want to do is hurt you. I never knew it could be so easy to cause so much unhappiness. What else can I tell you? He's a journalist, he's very ambitious, he's very young – And you're right, I'm in love with him.' She shrugged her shoulders hopelessly.

'I see. So what happens now?'

'We must call the wedding off.' That was the one thing she knew was right, the nettle she was sure had to be grasped. 'Whatever else happens let's do that, Alan, let's give ourselves time! And the house, we must sell the house.'

'You really want to do that?'

'Yes, I do, we have to. Can't you see, we're trapped by all the paraphernalia, we don't stand a chance!'

'But aren't you forgetting something?' he asked.

'What?'

'I love you. I want to marry you.'

'But you *can't*!'

'I can try, Elvi. And I will.'

Seven

For a moment Elvi was stunned. Everything she had felt and said and understood from the last dreadful minutes had pointed towards one inevitable outcome: Alan's departure, however painful, was what she had expected. And now he sat there calmly telling her that when all was said and done he still loved her. That he would not go.

'You can't,' she said again.

'Why? Do you intend to marry this other man?'

'His name's Callum.'

'Are you going to marry him?'

'I've no idea – no – that is, we've only known each other such a short while.'

'Where do you see it all leading?'

'Is it so important that it leads anywhere?'

'I think so.'

'It may be for you, Alan!' She made a gesture of impatience.

'You're no rebel yourself.'

'Maybe not, but he's made me see things differently. I don't care what comes of it, as long as I can be with him *now*.'

'Does he feel the same?'

'I think so.' She was defiant. 'And he's been honest with me. He told me he's ambitious, that there are a lot of things he wants to do with his life. He may not always be around.'

'And what sort of future is that, Elvi?'

'Stop talking about the future as though every step of it had to be marked out and planned like a timetable!' She rose and walked round behind the sofa to avoid his gaze. 'I told you my expectations have changed.'

'Let me put it this way.' Alan was reasonable, persuasive, but she would not turn to look at him. 'Compare the two deals. Don't think I don't understand how it is.' He gave a wry smile. 'I know only too well. Let me just say that I think we could have a good marriage, we could *make* a good marriage between us. I won't ask for more than you can give, I'd be content to make you as happy as I could. Elvi, I could lavish love on you. I'd always be there, I could earn your love in the end. I believe in marriage, you see. I believe that it's something two people of goodwill create for themselves. We've been happy till now, haven't we?'

She was silent. Abruptly Alan rose and came to her, taking her by the shoulders and turned her round to face him. 'Haven't we?'

'Not really.' She amazed herself by her frankness. A few weeks ago she would have died rather than admit her fears, now she was about to explain them without a qualm.

'I know now,' she went on quietly, 'that I've never loved you – not properly, Alan. What I was in love with was the idea of marrying you, of being your wife, of arranging the house, of everything that went with being Mrs Neilson. I half-realized it was no good but I was too timid and naïve and deluded to admit it, even to myself. But now I can't deny it any more, I know what I feel for Callum is real, and complete. I don't need any of those other things. Do you see?'

'Yes, I see.' He released her and went over to the fireplace, standing with his back to her, gazing into the flames. 'I think I knew that, too.'

'You knew? Then why, why, did you let us blunder on with it? Why couldn't we have stopped the whole sham and talked to each other?'

'We're doing that now.'

'But too late, Alan, much too late.'

'I can't accept that. I say I knew, but the reason I didn't mention it was because I was sure we could come through just the same. And I still feel that, Elvi!' The fierce determination in his voice frightened her. Would he never accept defeat?

'I'm going to tell you something, Elvi,' he said firmly. 'Something changed your feelings for me, but now I think it can only help you to see things my way. I've been married before.'

Of all the things Elvi might have expected him to say this was the least likely. She felt momentarily thrown off balance by the series of rapid adjustments taking place in her head. It was like being told that a picture you had always taken for granted was in fact a picture of something totally different, and should be hung the other way up or in a different light. She sank down on the window seat.

'Tell me, then,' she said.

'It was a disaster.' He sounded hard, as if speaking of it roused all the old bitterness and frustration. 'Both Pru and I were far too young. We rushed into it, we thought all we needed was each other.'

'You mean you didn't have security?' She was scornful.

'We had no security, but that's not what I meant. We weren't prepared to *try*, Elvi, we were hopelessly entangled in our own feelings and it made us selfish.'

'You can't have loved each other enough,' she said simply.

'Our marriage *died* of *love*!' It was the first time she had seen Alan angry. 'Don't you understand? The sort of love you mean is the kind which is like paper burning in a grate, a quick, brilliant flame, and then gone. Then there's only the smoke – the jealousy, the recrimination, and guilt. The love which two people can share for a lifetime is the kind you build with care and effort and kindness, it's the kind of fire that's warm and glowing even when the flames have subsided. Pru and I thought we could give up the world for love, but in the end the world got us, and destroyed us. She went, and we divorced and it was hell, the having to admit defeat, the knowledge that all we thought we had wasn't enough to see us through. I tell you, Elvi, I never thought I'd let myself in for that again. Until I met you.'

'Please don't say any more.'

'Let me finish. I resisted the way I felt for you for a long time. But like you with your Callum I knew it was real and in the end I couldn't deny it. And this time I knew what had to be done. I understood the bricks and mortar of the thing. I asked you to marry me because I felt I had the strength to go through with it again and this time to make it work. I knew I might never have another chance, I'd never have got into this if I hadn't had faith in our ability to last. Remember I can be strong for both of us.'

'But that's not enough!' Elvi was almost crying with frustration. 'What about me? Am I to be some kind of helpless passenger? Aren't *I* supposed to feel anything, or is that the preserve of men of experience like you?'

'How can you say that? You know all I want is your happiness.'

'Don't be so patronizing!' She was shouting now, she didn't notice her father appear in the doorway. 'I want something for myself, can't you see that? I don't want to be happy and protected and looked after and *suffered* just because you think you're big enough to carry the load. I want to do a little living on my own account—'

'What on earth is going on?' The Major entered, white-faced, leaning heavily on his stick. Elvi covered her face with her hands but Alan spoke quietly and reasonably.

'I'm so sorry, sir. It looks as though a lot of things have needed to be said for a long time.'

'What do you mean?' Elvi's father sank down in to a chair. He looked very old.

'I mean we have to put off the wedding.'

'Dear God. What have you two been doing to each other? I don't understand. You can't put off the wedding at this late stage.'

'We shall have to. I think it would be best.' Although he was addressing her father, Alan's eyes remained fixed on Elvi. She realized helplessly that his strength lay in his understanding of the older man, that he could hold his ground while the Major was with them. He went on: 'Nothing is final, and I don't want it to be, but Elvi needs more time to make up her mind.'

'For goodness sake, child—' Dick Beecham's voice was harsh.

'Don't call me a child!'

'You are my child and I shall call you what I like! What have you been saying, have you gone mad?'

'Alan's right. I felt trapped, Father.'

'You're being immature, you've simply got last-minute nerves. I've no intention of going back on everything now.'

'With all due respect, sir –' it was Alan at his most authoritative – 'it is we who are going back, it has to be our decision. I support Elvi in it. I shall make all the necessary arrangements, you need have nothing to do with it. I must insist.'

'You say this, but what am I to think? What am I to say?'

'It won't be so hard. Nobody judges, these days. And as I say, it is only a postponement.'

'Is there another date?'

'An indefinite postponement,' put in Elvi.

'I see . . .' Dick Beecham drooped his head in his hand for a moment. When he looked up again his eyes were moist. 'You'll have to excuse me . . . I don't see at all . . .' He rose slowly and left the room. Alan and Elvi watched him. In the doorway he turned, as if he wanted to say something or perhaps to ask one final question that would clarify everything, but he decided against it and left, closing the door behind him.

'So,' said Elvi, 'we postpone it. That's not what I *want*, Alan, can't you see? I want my freedom. Completely. Now.'

'I know that. But I suppose I do have some interest in the matter as well? This is a reasonable compromise. Don't let's burn all our boats yet.'

'But how can I think, how can I work things out – with this on my finger?' She held up her left hand on which Alan's ring glittered. He stepped forward and clasped her hand, bringing it quickly to his lips and then folding it in both his own.

'Don't wear it then. But keep it, and keep it safe. I'll ask nothing of you, Elvi, you can be as free as a bird. I promise that. I won't try and contact you, I won't write, or enquire – I'll disappear. But I'll be there if you need me. Then, if you are quite sure in a few months' or even a year's time, we'll call it a day.'

'And what about all the wedding arrangements?'

'I said I'd see to that, and I will. You tell the locals, they're your friends and they'll appreciate hearing from you direct. But I'll write to the other people, don't worry.'

'And the house?'

'I'll go ahead with that for the moment, the work might as well be finished even if it has to be put on the market again after that. It's an investment and I prefer to guard it for the moment. It's a nice house, anyway.'

'Yes, it is . . .' She caught his eye and felt a wave of sadness for him, for herself, for the house and what might have been. 'Oh Alan, what can I say? Sorry isn't enough. The last thing I ever wanted to do was to hurt you, of all people.' She leaned against him and his arm stole around her, like a shield, but touching her only lightly as though he did not trust himself to hold her close.

'Don't say anything. Words keep people apart.'

She felt his hand on her hair before he stepped swiftly back and his tone changed to one of businesslike preparation.

'I'm going now.'

'But it's late, and you've only just arrived . . .'

'Nevertheless. Best to go.' He picked up his paper and glanced round. 'My other things are in the hall. Tell your father I'll be writing to him.'

'But shall I see you – we have things to discuss?' His abruptness unnerved her, surely there should be some kind of ritual, to end it all. But he was already out in the hall, putting on his coat, collecting his case and briefcase. He seemed to be moving further away every second.

'Please, Alan, don't go like this.'

'Like what? There is nothing else to say. I shall contact as many people as possible tomorrow and I suggest you do the same. The sooner that's done, the more time you will have to make up your mind.'

'You sound hard. It's not like you.'

'It is me, my darling, it's my way of grasping the nettle.' He crossed to her and kissed her on the forehead, a cool, light kiss like the touch of an autumn leaf. 'Goodbye.'

He was gone, closing the front door behind him, and when Elvi reached the porch the lights of the Merc were already swinging out of the drive, to be swallowed up between the tall dark banks of the lane.

With a heavy tread, Elvi went up to her father.

The decision to go back to Scotland was much assisted by the fact that Major Beecham encouraged it. He was low, both mentally and physically, but insisted that she should go.

'I don't want to know what all this is about, but you should go to be with someone who can apply good sense. Jean's the one. Go to her.'

'But what about you?'

'I daresay I can persuade Mrs Thing to live in for a couple of weeks, she's done it before.'

'All right, I would like to.' She could hardly contain her relief. And her excitement.

'If you're sure you'll be all right.'

'Yes, yes.' He sounded weary and defeated. Elvi put her arms round his neck.

'I can't help it, Father, it has to be like this.'

'I understand.' He patted her shoulders gently. 'Or I try to. But whatever it is you've discovered in life, remember other people have feelings, too, and those feelings have value. Everything doesn't change because you do, and you must make allowances.'

'You mean Alan?'

'Alan. And myself.'

'Father, I'm so *sorry* . . .' She cried now, child-like tears of remorse that she was no longer perfect in his eyes, but even as he rocked her and soothed her she thought of Callum.

*   *   *

And it was that thought which gave her the courage to visit people and tell them about the postponement. The vicar, the nursery school, the taxi service, the florist, numerous friends and acquaintances, and Miss Markham. All were sympathetic, subdued and embarrassed, she sensed their need to get away from her and discuss the matter uninhibitedly with somebody else. Up until now, she had only been the subject of kindly, affectionate gossip – now there would be speculation and suspicion, to some extent justified. But Miss Markham was the worst. She came straight to the point.

'Why?'

They were sitting in the small, cluttered, cosy room where Elvi had come so often. The dress, finished now, hung like a limp white ghost in its polythene bag from the picture rail. Miss Markham was outraged and upset. Elvi felt wretched.

'I'm sorry, Miss Markham, your beautiful dress . . .'

'I'm not bothered about the *dress*! It's you I'm thinking about, girl, what are you playing at?'

'I'm certainly not playing at anything,' Elvi bridled. 'Believe me, I'm trying to do the sensible thing.'

'Sensible!' Miss Markham spat out the word in scorn. 'You're throwing up everything so that you can have some kind of last fling.'

'No, it's not like that. I just need more time. I'm not sure I want to marry at all.'

'Now she tells us! I don't understand it, I really don't. And the Major's heartbroken, I suppose.' It was not a question, but Elvi chose to take it as such.

'No, he understands. Of course it was hard on him but he can see the sense of it. I'd hoped other people would, too.'

'I don't know, I really don't. It's a wicked shame.'

That was it, thought Elvi, as she trudged home. People don't like a mess. They like things to fit in with their preconceptions and come up to their expectations, and if you rock the boat, watch out. And yet this particular mess was the only way she could find some kind of pattern or order, it was the only way she could extract a kernel of truth for herself. She felt invigorated by the morning's encounter as though she'd sloughed off an old skin and emerged bright and clean and new. It was a new beginning.

On Sunday evening she rang Jean and told her. Practice had made it easier, and she came straight to the point.

'I'm sorry,' said Jean. 'But I suppose I knew, really.'

'You knew? How could you possibly?'

'I sensed something wasn't right. It's sad, Elvi, but you're doing the right thing.'

'Jean, I'm so glad you said that. But Father won't be. He thinks you're going to make me "see sense".'

'He's wrong, then, isn't he? Much as I love and admire your father, I think he can't see the wood for the trees in this case. I'm certain you're doing the right thing. By all means come.'

'Thank you, Jean. Really, thank you.'

'There's just one thing. We're due to be away for the second week, we're going over to Edinburgh to visit Ian's folks. I can't put it off, they're getting on now and we haven't seen them for ages. Shall you mind being on your tod?'

Elvi's heart leapt. 'No, of course not. I can look after the place for you.'

'Yes, I suppose so.' There was a little pause. 'Okay then, that's settled. Be in touch and let us know which train, we'll talk it over when you get here.'

For a second Elvi wondered whether Jean knew about Callum. But she dismissed the idea as being unlikely. She did not want anyone to know, not yet, it would make things doubly hard. Now she must get in touch with him, but how? She realized that she did not have his address and he had not given her his number. What was she doing, throwing over marriage for someone whose telephone number she didn't even know?

The idea delighted her. She scribbled a hasty note care of his newspaper, being careful to keep it strictly formal in case of someone else opening it, and asking him to ring as soon as possible. It was four days before he did so, by which time she had reached an unbearable pitch of anxiety.

'What's kept you, for goodness sake? Didn't you get my note?'

'Yes, this morning.'

'This morning? But I posted it four days ago!'

'If something comes to the office it tends to get snowed under. I'm sorry, you should have sent it to my digs.'

'I don't know the address. In fact, I don't know anything.'

'Nor you do. How ridiculous.' He laughed. 'But you're coming up.'

'Yes, I'm coming to the Andersons'. But to see you.'

'What day? I'll be there.'

'No, I'd rather you waited. They're going to be away the second week, we can spend all the time together we want. I've got so much to tell you, so much has happened. I'm sure we'll meet anyway, but don't come there specially to see me until they've gone. Will you?'

'Very well, if it's important.' He sounded puzzled. 'It seems a little clandestine, though.'

'There is a reason. I'm afraid I wasn't entirely honest with you.'

'Oh?' His voice gave nothing away.

'No. There was somebody else. I was engaged.'

'Sweet Jesus.' She was not prepared for the shock and horror in his voice. There was a silence so long she felt compelled to break it.

'Callum? What's the matter?'

'I had no idea. Elvi. What have you done?'

'Finished it.'

'My God.'

'I did what I thought best.'

'Yes, yes, of course . . .'

'So you see I *do* have a dark secret. Jean and Ian know about that, but they don't know about you. And I don't intend that they should for a while longer.'

'You're right, we have a lot to talk about. Be in touch. I'll see you soon.'

He rang off, and Elvi knew that it was to marshall his thoughts. He had been genuinely appalled, but why? What would he have expected of her? It was true she had not told him about Alan, but if he had known, what difference would it have made? She could not have gone on with Alan with things as they were.

She went up to her room and sat on her bed. It was May now, and the evenings were becoming longer and softer. She could hear her father out in the garden, the occasional snip of the secateurs, and the sound of his measured, quiet movements as he examined his beloved roses. Every day now he seemed older. While she had still been his treasure, his gift to Alan, she had looked up to him and deferred to him in everything. Her care of him was in return for his enveloping protection. Now that she had voluntarily thrown off her old self she realized, not without sadness, that while she loved him more, she respected him less. The balance was tipped. It was as though he had now washed his hands of any influence over her, and was handing over the initiative to her, sinking quietly into old age. She looked round at her room. The only present that remained was the box from the nursery school, she had wrapped the others and sent them back the previous day. Each dreaded task turned out to be easier than she expected. She had discovered a new toughness in herself, a resolution which surprised her. The photo of Alan still stood on the little white-painted dressing table and now she removed it and put it face down in the bottom drawer. The act was purely practical, she imbued it with no significance. His ring she had placed in the bottom shelf of her jewel case. She had done this at once, and without regret. The room looked neat, childish, pretty. It was just as it had been since she was about ten. There were the primrose-patterned curtains, faded in vertical bars from the bright sun of many summers; the little mantelshelf over the gas fire, where all her much-loved china animals stood; the big colourful alarm clock with a grinning face that Jean had given her when she was thirteen; and the bookcase which reflected her tastes from Arthur Ransome to Margaret Drabble.

It was a room, she now felt, that belonged to someone else. She would clear it out before she left.

Eight

When Alan had got back to his flat he was full of a kind of jittery energy. He threw his case down on the bed but did not unpack. Instead, he went to his desk in the living room. He sat down and began to go through the drawers and compartments systematically. All the papers pertaining to his own life alone – bills for the flat, car documents, business papers – he heaped together. He had always been scrupulously tidy and methodical in his business affairs, everything was in order. Elvi's letters he put all together into a large buff envelope together with an assortment of other letters and papers to do with the wedding, the house and various major domestic purchases. The air tickets for Corfu he studied for a moment and then placed on the small telephone table inside the front door. He was not quite sure yet what he would do with those. He put his writing paper, envelopes and pen on top of the desk, with a list of the proposed wedding guests. The thought of writing dozens of letters of postponement and apology did not appal him. He would derive some satisfaction out of formulating the right phrases, striking the right note – and besides, each letter might prove to be a kind of catharsis, so that by the end of the exercise he would feel tired, but purged.

Finally he unlocked one of the small drawers directly beneath the lid of the desk and took out a dog-eared assortment of photographs, envelopes and scraps of paper. He picked up the top photograph, a postcard-sized black and white snapshot, and studied it.

Pru. Unaccountably he felt a great surge of closeness and

affection for her, a desire to salute her. There she sat, in all her slightly dated glory, a diminutive girl with a huge grin, her hands thrust deep into the pockets of a baggy duffle coat, her curly mop of hair whipped across her face by the stiff sea breeze: he remembered now that he had taken that one on the seafront at Brighton, one stormy bank holiday Monday before they were married. She had laughed at him.

'Whatever did you want to come to *Brighton* for?'

'I like Brighton.'

'Yes, but not in a force eight gale. Even the pier's swaying.'

'I think it's nice.' They'd both been laughing and he could see now that it was rather ridiculous. They'd had to shout above the wind, and the sea was choppy and irritable, building up as it drew nearer into great rearing waves that crashed and sucked at the pebbly beach. Pru had kissed him.

'I know why you wanted to come here!' she yelled. 'Because it's where people bring their mistresses!'

'That's right. That's *it*! I knew there was a reason.'

'Well, I'll tell you why people bring their mistresses here.'

'What's that?'

'It's too damn windy to go out, that's why!'

They had staggered along the prom as far as the shelter of the cliff, and the lacy white ironwork of the Aquarium, kissed and cuddled for a bit there and then fought their way back again against the ever-strengthening gale to their prim, drab little hotel just off the front. They'd made love in the small twin-bedded room and the delicious guilt they felt at their small deception added to their enjoyment. In his mind's eye he could see with extraordinary clarity Pru's face, flushed with the cold wind and excitement, her grey eyes bright with a frosty, electric sparkle, her lips smiling and asking to be kissed again. She had been the most loving and giving of partners, he reflected; she seemed to present herself, beaming and radiant, as a kind of constant open invitation to bed, her own enjoyment making up a major part of his own. They had, he remembered, drifted along in a cosy cocoon, intent on their own pleasure, impossibly pleased with themselves for being so happy. So when they had been forced to mature, to emerge from the chrysalis all brittle and vulnerable into the cold hard light of day – they had simply withered and given up. The disappointment had been too great, they had not been able to cope.

He found a wedding photograph. Neither of them had any close family so they'd had a very informal wedding at a little church in World's End. Pru had worn a pretty, short dress and a floppy hat. The dress looked too short now, of course, like fancy dress. They had had lots of friends at the wedding, there had been a riotous reception at a bistro where they'd eaten many Saturday-night canellonis. The staff knew them and did them proud, and one of Pru's old schoolfriends had disgraced herself and dismayed her staid upper-crust escort by doing an abandoned and amorous tango with one of the waiters.

It seemed aeons ago. Alan did not even know where most of those friends were now. Marriage had swallowed up Pru and him, and divorce had spat them out as different people, to start all over again.

He riffled through the rest of the photos, noticing sadly that they chronicled not only the short downward path of their marriage, but also the change in Pru. In the space of a year or two she changed from a laughing, pretty, sexy girl into a woman with a closed face. It was not that she lost her looks, but that the light went out.

There was the house in Paddington where they'd had the first-floor flat, much to be desired on account of its small railed balcony. In the picture (he remembered taking it) you could just see the top rung of the clothes-horse on the balcony, with a row of Pru's smalls, like pennants on a yacht, drying in the dusty sunshine.

There was the holiday in Wales, their first (and only) car, destined to fail its test ignominiously after only a few months; their cat, Terence, taken from inside their tiny living room as he sat curled on the veranda, majestically scruffy. To think what Terence had witnessed, sitting there or, in the winter, on the bumpy chaise longue. He had sharpened his claws, and washed himself, and occasionally chased the ubiquitous balls of fluff that go with cheap rugs on parquet flooring. And all the time their marriage had been cracking, shifting, sinking until the terrible cataclysmic evening when Pru had screamed: 'I hate you!' with her face all white and twisted with fury, and they both knew that they couldn't drag each other down any longer.

It seemed that neither of them had the morsel of extra strength that was needed to start them on the long and arduous climb back to self-esteem and mutual respect. For that was what they had lost, thought Alan. They had allowed disillusionment to strip them naked of all pride. By the end they valued themselves and each other at nothing, so that even the wounds they inflicted on each other were like old scabs nicked to see if they would bleed. But here there had been no gradual healing. Instead the scars became infected, they could hardly bear to be together because each was a warning and a reproach to the other.

So they had divorced. And there had been the dreadful formalities masking all those dark, changeable fears and pains; the demoralizing realization that the best form of defence was attack, the guilt of knowing that everything was not black and white, but sickly swirling grey, like city fog.

He had not thought that either of them would ever recover. It was as though the acquisition of that little bit of paper that freed you of each other left you so drained and disgusted that you were fit for nothing. They, who had been so much in love, so full of life, so buoyantly confident in their ability to survive – they had been decreed 'incompatible'. As if there were no more to it than not being able to get along.

Alan dropped his head into his hand. That had been that: and now there was Elvi. He was overcome with a wracking sense of failure. What was the matter with him? The essential selfishness of their love had destroyed Pru and him and now, when he was prepared to give everything he had, to sacrifice every vestige of self-interest, he had failed again, apparently for that very reason. He must be maimed, stunted, an emotional cripple not to handle things better. For the first time since he had met Elvi he felt his self-confidence collapse. He had been able to cope with her vague fears, her capricious changes of mood, even her diffidence to his physical advances; but this new, fiercely determined young woman, all candour and clarity and aggression – this metamorphosis had taken him by surprise. Even worse had been her sudden, last-minute pang of pity, that had been the final twist of the knife. He had offered her everything and all she had been able to give in return was her sympathy.

How ironic, he reflected, that when the flame was finally kindled it should be by somebody else, and he was quite powerless to understand why or how. He loved her so much, he wanted her, he cared for her, but that was not enough. Perhaps even his refusal to let her go completely would militate against him, but he would not alter that, it was his last-ditch stand. If he could maintain some kind of continued background presence, no matter how distant, in the next few months, she might still feel able to turn to him if need be. Whereas if he capitulated and withdrew completely, pride would prevent her from ever approaching him again. Making a quick decision, he put the piles of papers away, all the personal ones in the bottom drawer, which he locked. He stared at the pen, notepaper and list of names which were all that remained on top of the desk, and got up to pour himself a drink.

Everything in this flat had been carefully chosen, and yet the whole was no more an expression of his personal taste than the office where he worked. After the divorce he had lived with married friends for a while, and when he had bought this place he had determined to make it comfortable and elegant, but impersonal. Nothing of his life with Pru remained. They had both agreed to give up the tenancy of the flat in Paddington, and though Pru had kept a few items of furniture (and Terence) he had wanted nothing. The initial purchase of the flat had left him broke and he had managed at the outset with a few saucepans, a sleeping bag and some cushions. But the acute loneliness and the need to pay Pru's alimony had made him ambitious. His career advanced apace and he was able to buy, bit by bit, the furniture, pictures and so forth that he needed. He went for modernity – clean lines, not too much colour, a feeling of space and light. That was all. Detail did not interest him and nor did ambience. Far from wanting to fill the place with expressions of his own personality, he wanted it to be like someone else's apartment – restful, removed, undemanding. In this he had succeeded. As he went back to the desk with a tumbler of whisky he thought of Elvi and her flair for decoration. There was no doubt that wherever she lived there would be flowers and colour and rich, varied textures, and the hundred well-thought-out, apparently random touches, that make a house a home. Now it seemed likely that he would never share such a home with her.

He picked up the pen and began to write.

Callum had been more shocked than he could say at Elvi's revelation on the telephone. It sent a cold blast of misgiving right through him so that he became anxious and fidgety. It was hard to keep his mind on his work and this fact did not pass unnoticed in the offices of the *Chronicle*. Eddie, the chief sub, waxed voluble on the subject, it was his speciality.

'Would it be remiss of me to ask what ails our star reporter?' Eddie was a hard-bitten Mancunian, educated chiefly in the school of experience, but he had perfected a quasi-professorial mode of speech which served him well in the berating of junior colleagues. Now several heads were raised, anticipated verbal pyrotechnics.

'I have been waiting,' he went on, 'for the promised copy concerning the bypass planning enquiry. I have been awaiting it, expecting it, looking forward to its arrival on my desk with baited breath. I have never for a moment doubted that it would be concise, informative and even perspicacious where perspicacity was proper, but I am distressed to find it *late!*'

This was the worst accusation in Eddie's large arsenal of invective. His entire professional life had been devoted to the prevention of, or punishment for, lateness. He saw himself in the role of the anchorman who never failed to keep faith with the printing presses in spite of the burden of lax staff. Callum received the outburst quietly, he knew very well that it was intended as a demonstration rather than a personal attack.

'Sorry, Eddie. It'll be on your desk in about an hour.'

'"It'll be on your desk in about an hour"!' Eddie mimicked. 'Promises, promises. It should have been on my desk an hour ago.'

'As long as it's finished by the end of today, it's not going to hold anything up.' The chief sub lowered his hornrims and glowered over the top of them, his gaze raking round the office balefully.

'I suppose,' he said menacingly, 'that it is of no consequence that *I* am being held up? That I am obliged to sit here and twiddle my thumbs while Mr Sheil completes his penetrating analysis of the planning enquiry?' Callum ostentatiously began to type again. Eddie glared at him. 'I can only hope and pray that the copy will be completed in good time so that not only Mr Sheil, but the sub-editors as well can get back in time for their supper tonight!' With this he returned to his work – of which there seemed to be plenty, despite his remarks about twiddling thumbs – and the rest of the office settled back to its various tasks.

Callum finished the article in forty minutes. He remained a further half-hour while Eddie and his minions went through it exhaustively for errors and literals, but their efforts went unrewarded and at six thirty Callum left the office.

After the stifling atmosphere at the *Chronicle*, the cool, damp Scottish evening was bliss. The paper was produced in the upper storey of a block in the high street, the ground floor being occupied by the office of the local Labour party. For all its limitations and shortcomings Callum believed in the *Chronicle*. Until ten years ago the outlying villages had no sounding board for their news and views, no vehicle for information or advertising. They had been dependant on the Oban paper and this had not always been available in the local shops.

The *Chronicle* had been the brainchild of a local man,

Max Myers, not himself a journalist, but a firm believer in village autonomy. He had been right, the *Chronicle* proved both popular and functional and, though it did not make money, it paid for itself.

Callum usually felt satisfied at the end of the day. At least a couple of evenings a week he'd go into the Star and Garter hotel and have a drink with Max and one or two of the others. But this evening he set off up the high street towards the mountain. He needed to walk, and to think. He passed his digs and went in to tell Mrs Mackintosh not to wait for supper. She received this instruction with her usual disapproving gloom, but Callum knew that something would be waiting in the oven for him when he got back just the same. Mrs Mackintosh came from a tradition of landladies who treated their PGs like dogs, but looked after them like kings.

Callum turned his collar up and headed out of the village. He glanced up at the Andersons' house: it looked snug and inviting but he resisted the temptation to go there. It was his own company he needed tonight, and besides he would feel a Judas among those people who liked and cared for him and, more importantly, for Elvi. He took a sheep track off to the right, following the valley that encircled the base of the mountain. The fantastic scale of his surroundings comforted him, made his anxieties seem less because of his sheer physical smallness. The path was narrow, and his trousers were soon heavy and sodden from the continual brushing of the wet heather on either side. To his right the ground rolled away to a false crest, dotted with rocks. These rocks seemed to possess life of their own. Despite their random positioning, as though some gigantic hand had cast dice on the hillside, theirs was a watchful presence which no amount of geological information could dispel. He remembered feeling the same once about some radar scanners, strung out in a row in the Suffolk countryside. There they were, mere artefacts, and yet they exuded a sense of their own identity, their great concave faces turned to the wide sky, a group of silent giants, gazing into space.

He turned off the track and made for a large pile of

stones near the top of the crest. From here he could see the further rise of the ground beyond, the soaring grandeur of the mountain and, straggling down the valley to his left, the huddled, tenacious houses of Kirkmuir, like tickbirds on the shoulders of buffalo.

From here he could also see the narrow white ribbon of the path where he had walked with Elvi. The soft mist on his face recalled her tears. She loved him. And because he loved her too he had done nothing – or not enough – to stop her. And now she had given up someone else for him – little undernourished Callum Sheil, all ambition and no prospects. He had created for himself a life of independence, self-contained and organized, with only a few close friends. His parents had died some years before, and his elder brother lived in Canada with his family. There was no one to whom he owed a thing. But now . . . now all that had gone out of the window, all the planning and rationalizing counted for nothing, because he had allowed himself to fall in love and, most foolish of all, had admitted to it. He had really torn it this time. And the crux of the matter was that he felt totally disinclined to stop the ball that was now rolling so fatefully, and ever faster, downhill.

It was getting cold. He rose and looked about him. The rocks stood impassively about him, their shoulders hunched up against the weather. The mist was beginning to drift down the valley now, he would have to start back before it became too dense to see. As he began walking down the slope to the path he said aloud: 'Hell and damnation!' But the only reply was his own footsteps crashing through the heather.

Dick Beecham discovered Elvi clearing out her room. She was doing it thoroughly, and with tremendous speed and energy as though she could no longer stand it in its previous state.

When he appeared in the doorway she looked up and said: 'High time, really.'

'I suppose so. Are you throwing all those things out?' He

indicated a large carton full of china ornaments and books, and another bulging with clothes.

'I am.'

'Whatever am I going to do with them?'

She laughed. '*You* haven't got to do anything with them, Father. I'll put them in the loft for the meantime. At least, I'll take the clothes to the next available jumble sale and keep the rest till I've made up my mind.'

'The Morgans have asked me to lunch, do you mind?'

'Go ahead. Actually it's a blessing because there isn't a lot for lunch here today. I've ordered a pile of stuff for delivery tomorrow, then Mrs Dix won't have to bother too much with shopping while I'm away.'

'Good, good. I'll be off then.'

'Bye.' She went back to her sorting and rummaging with obvious enjoyment.

The Major set off to walk to the village. It was a walk he particularly liked and its familiarity enhanced rather than detracted from it. He liked to see it in all the different seasons. In summer when the fields were packed with yellow hosts of corn, sparked with poppies like an army brilliant on parade; and autumn when the colours grew soft and the hedges were studded with fruit and berries; even winter, whose coldness and damp he dreaded more each year, brought an especial beauty to the country – he liked to see everything so bare and hard and exposed: everything was so very much *itself* in the winter. And now as he walked along the side of the field – no longer all brown, but covered with fresh green spikes – he liked it best of all. Its optimistic newness, its unfailing reliability, its combination of beauty, delicacy and stamina. Here was something you could rely on.

Of people, he was no longer so sure. For the first time in many long years he felt very much alone. After his wife's death he had invested so much of himself in his daughter – not too much, he had thought, as he watched her grow straight, and sweet and beautiful. And the prospect of her marriage, while he was reluctant to lose her, was something he had accepted and come to terms with because Alan had been so absolutely right. Now all that security and rightness had gone, all his notions of what the future was to be had been shattered and cast to the winds. He was no fool, he did not blame or accuse his daughter, for he could recognize something in her that had grown and matured and could see also that it has a natural process. If anything, he blamed himself. He had been too careful. If he had allowed that process of growth to happen earlier, as perhaps it should have done, all this pain and disappointment might have been avoided. But then, it was not Elvi who felt the pain and disappointment: on the contrary, she was full of hope and happiness and spirit; it was he and Alan who were retiring to lick their wounds. He supposed there was another man, and then smiled to himself for thinking in such old-fashioned terms. Of course, there were many other men – the world was full of them and any one of them could have caused his daughter to change, to see things differently. Dick Beecham knew that his regret and his sense of loss were selfish, but knowing that did not made them easier to bear.

When he arrived at the Morgans, Bob Morgan was out in the garden. He hailed the Major, and opened the wicket gate to let him in.

'Don't tell me you've walked all the way!'

'Yes, indeed. It's very pleasant.'

'How about the leg?'

'Does it good.'

They walked together over the lawn and Joan Morgan waved from the kitchen window. We are three old people, thought Dick. I must get used to being old and standing back. I always thought that getting old was something that happened gradually and naturally, but it's not so. It's the decision to act the part, a decision you take quickly and voluntarily, that's what it is. And when people speak of 'growing old gracefully', they mean that a person has taken that decision in good time, so as not to cause anyone else embarrassment.

As he sat down in the Morgans' comfortable drawing room

while his friend poured the drinks, he realized also that his leg was stiffening up. Tonight it would hurt, and all because he had taken a walk in the spring sun. He looked out of the window at the burgeoning May garden and felt cold and tired and sad.

Nine

'Of course,' said Jean, 'all the trappings of a big wedding make it twice as hard for you. If you had been planning an unpretentious register office affair you could have un-planned it with no hassle at all. As it is, you've gone out on a limb to publicize the whole thing.'

'I know.' They were sitting out in the garden. Between them on the bumpy hillside grass lay the tea tray with mugs and a plate of biscuits. Alasdair and Fiona were busy digging over by the grey stone wall. It was a beautiful evening with a high, clear sky and the odd cloud casting its melting, moving shadow over the mountainside as it passed. Elvi was absently pulling at a tussock of heather which had forced its way through the thin covering of man-imposed garden. The heather stalks were incredibly strong and wiry, almost cutting her fingers, and yet the flowers were tiny and delicate, their misty pink that was a haze in the distance, was brittle and detailed close to. She strained off a handful of them and sifted them from hand to hand.

'It all seems so foolish now,' she said, half to herself, half in reply to Jean. 'It was me, not Alan. I suppose I wanted to hide behind it, like a great big smokescreen.'

'It must have been ghastly telling everyone.'

'Not really. In a funny sort of way it was therapeutic, good for me. I was coming out in my true colours. Of course it was sad when people were genuinely disappointed and didn't understand, but I can't help that.

'You've changed.' Jean gazed at her appraisingly.

'Oh yes, I've changed all right.' There was something wry

115

and self-mocking in Elvi's voice. 'I hardly know what to make of myself these days.'

'Why?'

'I suppose because if you change too quickly you surprise yourself.'

'No. I mean why *did* you change?'

'Oh, I see.' Elvi went back to her lump of heather. 'That's the thousand-dollar question.'

'Tell me.'

'I suppose –' Elvi watched the heather flowers tumble from hand to hand like the tick of a metronome conducting her thoughts – 'I saw the light. I realized I was kidding myself about Alan. That I mistook being gratified by his love for actually loving him. I'm afraid I've hurt him terribly.'

'That's for sure. But there's no point in castigating yourself on that score. If what you say is true you'd have done infinitely worse and more far-reaching damage by marrying him.'

'Yes. Yes, I think so. But it's ironic really – now that I've told him, and he's gone and I'm not tied to him any more I can appreciate what a special kind of person he is. Was.'

'He's still alive, my love.'

'Yes, it's silly the way one thinks of someone in the past tense just because they no longer have anything to do with you personally.'

'And he no longer has anything to do with you?'

'No. The postponement was a spoonful of sugar as far as I was concerned, and I don't mean to be hard. I think he realizes that too, but it's a good luck charm to help him through the next few months, if you like.'

'Let him down gently?'

'I know it sounds corny and heartless put like that, but yes, that's exactly it. I probably like him more than I ever have done and for that reason it seemed the least I could do.'

'Oh Elvi, Elvi . . .' Jean lay back with her hands clasped

behind her head, her eyes closed. 'I wish you all the luck in the world. You're going to need it.'

'Why?' Elvi looked up and laughed. 'You sound very gloomy and foreboding.

'I didn't mean to. But you've embarked on a pretty rough trail. The truth game.'

'I don't see why. It should be much easier.'

Jean shook her head, eyes still closed and smiled up at the sky.

'Don't you believe it. It's going to work both ways, you see.'

'Of course.'

'All right, all right, I won't pursue that one. In any event I'm proud of you.' She rolled her head to face Elvi and opened her eyes, screwed up against the westering sun. 'Is there anyone else?'

Elvi was totally unprepared for the question, and her surprise made her truthful.

'Do you mind if I don't tell at present, Jean?'

'Of course I don't mind. Keep me posted, though.'

'I will. I promise I'll tell you soon. It's just that there's so much that isn't clear, to me even, so many things I have to sort out and think through. If I tell you it will somehow – crystallize everything before it's properly grown.'

'I understand.' Jean sat up and sighed. 'And what's more I must cast aside these idle natterings and get the children in the bath. Hair-washing night.'

'I'll help.' Elvi jumped up and picked up the tray. 'I'd like to.'

'I know you would, you're a sucker for punishment. Tell you what, you deal with them, I'll do supper. Then we can both sit down and have a drink like ladies of leisure after they've gone to bed.'

'It's a deal. Here.' Elvi handed Jean the tray and ran over to where the children had dug, with their small plastic seaside spades, a trench of impressive proportions.

'Good heavens, what's this for?' she asked. Alasdair looked

up at her like a man disturbed from cosmic reflections by the buzzing of a fly. 'It's a moat,' he said scathingly, 'to keep the enemy out.'

'Of course it is, sorry. Who's the enemy?'

'The weasels.'

'And Cut-Throat Jake,' added Fiona.

'Good heavens, how bloodthirsty: anyway, it looks enough to keep anyone out.'

'No, it's not. Not yet.' Alasdair was firm. 'There's a lot needs doing to it yet.'

'I tell you one thing, though. It's a fact that people work better in the morning. So come and have your bath now and leave the final touches until tomorrow.'

'All right.' Fiona was gullible, and anyway tired of being a labourer under such a hard task-master. 'Are you bathing us?'

'Yes, if you'll let me.'

Alasdair sighed at such out-and-out corniness, and stuck his spade in the pile of earth as though finishing off an opponent. He led the way back to the house and Fiona followed, slipping her small cold hand confidingly into Elvi's.

'I'm glad you're going to bath us.'

'I like doing it. We'll wash your hair tonight, too.'

'I don't like shampoo in my eyes.'

'Don't worry, we'll be very careful. You'll have to tell me how Mummy does it.'

'She does it very, very quickly because it's a job that just has to be done.'

Elvi smiled at this obviously accurate quotation and the small treachery it illustrated.

'Mummies have a lot to do,' she said lamely.

After the somewhat riotous bath that followed she sat in the children's room for a while as they sat in bed. The effect of the hairdrier was to make them look soft and fluffy as ducklings. Fiona's hair, normally dead straight, stuck out in two small wings over her ears. She pulled the blankets up under her chin and stared penetratingly at Elvi.

'Will you be a mummy soon?' she enquired.

'No. Why do you ask?'

'She's asking because she knows you're getting married soon and when we asked about it last time Mum said—'

'Asked about what?'

'About babies,' Alasdair explained patiently. 'When we asked her about babies she told us all about the seed and the egg and said the man gave it to the woman when they were married.'

'Oh, I *see* . . .' Elvi had to laugh at this last-minute evasion of Jean's. But Fiona pressed home the question.

'So we wondered if Alan was going to give you a seed?'

'Well . . .' Elvi realized there was no escape. 'Actually I'm not going to marry Alan any more.'

'Why not?' asked Alasdair conversationally. She was grateful for the practicality of children. But still, she had to tell them the truth, not muddle them with platitudes.

'I realized I didn't love him enough,' she said. Fiona leaned up on her elbow, her curiosity roused even further by this simple remark.

'Was he horrible and ugly?'

'Heavens, no!' What could she say? 'There was nothing the matter with *Alan*, he looked nice – he *was* nice, and kind, and everything. But I changed my mind.'

This more selfish angle went down better. Alasdair nodded. 'I do that sometimes,' he averred, 'and it drives Mummy *round the bend.*'

'Did it drive Alan round the bend?' Fiona, little Sir Echo.

'Yes – yes, it did. It's annoying when people do it, but sometimes they have to. I had to. After all, it wouldn't have been right to marry someone I didn't love enough, would it? We might both have been very unhappy later on.'

'And get divorced!' said Alasdair triumphantly. Elvi was surprised.

'Who told you about divorce?'

'Ted Simpson, in my class at school. He's divorced.'

'You mean his parents are,' corrected Elvi, thinking how painfully appropriate was the original.

'Yes. Well they are. He sees his real daddy only sometimes and they do fantastic things *always*.' Alasdair's voice displayed naked envy which Elvi did not feel she could allow to pass.

'Yes, but what's the point of doing fantastic things and only seeing your daddy once a month? You wouldn't like it if Daddy wasn't here, would you?'

'But Ted's got another daddy now, one who lives there.' There seemed no answer to this and Elvi was saved from slipping further into the slough of misunderstanding by the appearance of Jean.

'Come on, you lot. Lights out time.'

'Oh *Mum*!'

'Come on, no messing. Have you cleaned your teeth?'

'Yes,' Elvi nodded affirmation.

'Right, snuggle down then.'

Jean gave each of them a kiss and turned out the light. As they went downstairs she asked: 'You were deep in conversation, what were they on about?'

'They were asking whether I was going to have a baby.'

'Good Lord, the cheeky monkeys! Whatever put that idea into their heads? I mean it's hardly casual conversation, is it?'

'I think you'd told them something about a man and a woman getting married and—'

'Okay, okay, I admit it! I got rather bogged down with all that. So they, I suppose, thought that Alan and you . . . Poor old Elvi, they did put you through it.'

'I don't mind. They're so guileless, it wasn't in the least painful. Quite the opposite, in fact.'

'Hm. Still, they'll have to learn to be a bit more restrained.'

They went into the sitting room and Jean poured two glasses of white wine.

'I hope you don't mind the home brew.'

'It's delicious. You are clever, Jean.'

'No, this isn't one of my specials, this is Ian's kit that

he buys at the chemist, but it's not bad. Ah . . .' Jean sat down on the sofa and kicked her shoes off. 'This is the best bit of the day.'

'What time will Ian be back tonight?'

'Lord knows. He's got an evening surgery up in the next village, and when he does get back he'll be on call anyway.'

'He works so hard. Doesn't it ever upset you that he's out so much?'

'It's no more than I expected when I married him. He's always been energetic, and kind, and conscientious – they're three of his nicest qualities and his job demands that he employ them to the full. Of course it drives me round the bend if we've got people coming and I've cooked a special dinner and made a huge effort, and then he's out half the evening, but it's only annoyance, not real hair tearing. That's not something I go in for much. Too lazy.' She took a long swig of wine, and reached for the bottle. Elvi smiled to herself. She liked and admired Jean. Her life here was hard, Elvi knew, and the material benefits minimal and yet she brought to it so much vigour and energy that you couldn't help but envy her.

'You really love Ian, don't you,' she said. It was not a question. Jean's eyebrows shot up.

'Of course. Most of the time.'

'I mean it, it's so encouraging somehow, to be with you, because you show that it can work.'

'Yes, we're perfect paragons of marital virtue!' Jean mocked, curling her legs up beside her on the sofa.

'Don't run yourself down. It's true. I can't help it if it sounds sentimental, that's just the way it is.'

'All right, I'll accept the compliment graciously. But don't run away with the idea that we always see eye to eye, that we're always in perfect harmony, sweetness and light, all that twaddle.'

'I know *that* – can I have another drop? – it wouldn't be nearly so impressive if you didn't quarrel occasionally. Like saying people are brave when they're never afraid.'

'Very prettily put – hey, who can that be?' There were a

couple of staccato blasts on the front-door bell. Jean put down her glass and went into the hall. Elvi suddenly knew who it would be.

'Callum!' Jean's voice drifted through from the hall. 'Long time no see. Come in and have a glass of something. Elvi and I were just hitting the plonk.'

'I really won't stay . . .' he protested half-heartedly as Jean led him into the room. It was odd to hear him talk like that, he who was usually so incisive, so decided and to the point. He smiled at Elvi – she could feel its warmth like the breath of a closely whispered endearment.

'Hallo.' She was amazed at her own composure. The acute pleasure she felt in his just being there did not cause her to blush. She felt calm and content – he was back.

'Oh, I'd forgotten you two had met,' said Jean, bustling in with another glass. 'Come on, Callum, you'll have a drop. We'll feel embarrassed boozing away in front of you.'

'All right, I'd like that.' He shrugged off his donkey jacket and sat down. As Jean poured the wine, his eyes remained on Elvi, but as he took the glass he said casually: 'As a matter of fact it was the good doctor I called to see.'

'Oh, I'm sorry, love, he's up at Muirhaven this evening, and then on call. It's anybody's guess when he'll be around.'

'I should have known I ought to have rung first. Still, it was a nice evening, I might as well drop in here as anywhere else.'

'What did you want him for? Maybe I can help?'

'I wanted him to let me interview him about this proposed new health centre.'

'Struth!' Jean threw her head back and laughed. 'Are you *sure* it's my dear husband you want to interview?'

'That's right.'

'But he's *dead* against the location.'

'I know. I might as well stir things up a bit while I'm about it. I'll get an interview with one of the people behind the scheme as well.'

'You'd better. He whips himself into the most towering rage every time the wretched thing's mentioned. I'll tell you what.

Come the day after tomorrow at about eleven thirty. He always has an hour or two midday on a Wednesday after the local surgery, and then you can stay to lunch afterwards. The kids would like that, too.'

'But are you sure that's going to be okay with Ian?'

'Of course I'm sure. It'll do him good to get it all off his chest to someone who actually wants to listen.'

Callum turned to Elvi. 'How long are you here for?'

'About a fortnight.'

'You ought to come and live here.'

'Do you think so?'

'Since you like it so much. Save on train fares, you know.'

'Don't tease the poor girl.' It was Jean. 'She's had a bit of a rough ride recently, and she's getting away from it all.'

'I see.' He sounded quite serious again. 'I'm sorry, I didn't mean to be flippant.'

'That's all right.'

'Well look, I'll be getting along. I've got work to do.' He got up. 'I'll see you on Wednesday. Tell Ian to call me at the *Chronicle* if the arrangement doesn't suit.'

'I will,' said Jean, 'but I'm sure it will be fine.'

He looked at Elvi. 'I'll see you again soon, then.'

'Yes.' The urge to touch him was so strong that she took a step towards him and then, flustered for the first time, held out her hand. He shook it, managing to make the gesture seem perfectly natural, and the brief contact was electric.

The front door closed, and Jean re-entered the room. In order to establish her position as a casual acquaintance of Callum's, Elvi remarked: 'He's nice.'

'Yes, isn't he? He's almost one of the family. Like you.'

'So I gather.'

The following morning she received a letter from her father.

> Dear Elvi, I hope that Scotland's doing you good. I think
> we all needed a space in our lives to think over the new
> state of affairs.

That bit made her smile. So military.

> I can't pretend to understand why things have changed,
> but it's very important that you should be happy and I
> won't stand in the way of that. Alan must have done his
> job very quickly and thoroughly because I've had a few
> letters from people – they've all been most considerate
> and tactful, you need have no fears on that score.

It was he who had the fears, thought Elvi. She read on:

> I don't want to push or influence you in any way, but I
> feel I'd have failed in my duty if I didn't suggest that
> you reconsider. Alan is a good man whose only concern
> is for your happiness. I believe him to be extremely
> unhappy about the postponement although he appears
> so businesslike. All I ask is that you do not dismiss the
> idea altogether before you've had time to think.
> The garden's looking nice, now, and Mrs Dix is doing
> me proud, though sometimes I feel she fusses round me
> a little too much – it's not good for me at my age. I shall
> ossify completely unless I'm allowed to do for myself
> a bit. I'm looking forward to having you back. By the
> way, I met your friend from the kindergarten the other
> day and she said you'd be welcome to go back there for
> a while until you decide what you want to do. Everyone
> is very kind . . .

Elvi suddenly grew impatient with the tone of the letter
and screwed it up. Why did he have to be so apologetic, so
anxious? She knew Alan far better than he did, she knew
exactly how things stood. For the first time in her life she
dreaded going back. Home, where she had always been happy,
now seemed a sort of trap where she could flounder about
helplessly in an enveloping net of affection and advice until
she eventually suffocated like a landed fish. Perhaps she could

stay here . . . ? But she dismissed the idea. It wouldn't work, not yet. She had to talk to Callum again, they had to decide together what was best to do, and she would have to go home this time, however briefly, to tie up the loose ends of her old life.

There was another letter, from Alan. It was short and to the point, his immaculate small black handwriting covering only about a third of the sheet of cream paper.

> . . . so all that has been dealt with. Please get in touch if there's anything you need to know. I'll sign off and get on with my life, Alan.

She tore that up, too, and dropped it in the fire. There was simply no point in keeping it. The pieces of paper, curling and flaring in the grate seemed to underline her sense of her own change. She would never have done that a few months ago. She felt sorrow for the departed old self, and then a fierce delight in her new independence.

On Wednesday she left the house at eleven thirty to collect Fiona from her playgroup in the village, and met Callum trudging up the lane. It was what she had intended. She walked into his arms as if she could have dissolved completely and become part of him.

'Hey, steady,' he said softly, 'it's a bit exposed here, you know.'

'Jean's in the kitchen at the back. She can't see.' She kissed his face again and again, teasing.

'Anyone could come along. Have you no shame?'

'Nope. I love you. I love you.'

'What a woman!'

'How on earth am I going to get through lunch and every-thing with you sitting there? I'd rather eat *you*.'

'I daresay, but this is business.'

'You could have done it before I came. You're deliberately teasing.'

'That isn't so. The story only presented itself a couple of days ago. This was the logical time to do it. Incidentally, climb down,

125

because the good doctor's expected back at any moment.'

Elvi released him and sank back on the low stone wall that bordered the lane. Callum sat down beside her.

'I don't really know why we're making such a secret of it,' she said, not entirely truthfully. 'I've made a clean breast of it with Alan. What are we waiting for?'

'People need to time to adjust to one change before they're presented with another. At any rate, as far as I'm aware we're not too sure of the next step ourselves.'

'We want to be together,' she said simply.

'That's true, but not necessarily feasible, not right away. There's no cause for any cloak and dagger stuff, we can be seen to like each other, for God's sake. Just try for everyone's sake to keep your hands off my person in public.' He grinned. He looked like some mischievous Celtic sprite, perched on the wall, his hair sticking up in black spikes, his eyes too big and bright for his narrow, mobile face. He's an oddity, thought Elvi, and took one of his hands in both hers.

'Nobody can see,' she whispered theatrically, and then: 'Why are you so horribly thin?'

'I just am. Always have been.'

'It can't be right. It's because you live in digs and don't look after yourself and burn the midnight oil.'

'It may suit you to think that,' he said, 'but as a matter of fact my landlady's a first-rate cook, the house is warm and, as you should remember, I go to bed early. I have a life of considerable comfort.'

'Then you ought to look better on it.'

'Thanks! I may be a ten-stone weakling with eyes permanently reddened from having sand kicked in my face, but I'm a healthy ten-stone weakling.'

'Good.' She rubbed her hand up his arm. He felt anything but weak: there was about him that coiled-spring quality which excited her so much.

The Land Rover screeched to a halt beside them and Ian leaned across from the driver's seat.

'Come on, man, I'll run you the rest of the way. We might

as well get this ghastly business over, eh?'

'Indeed.' Callum rose and climbed into the passenger seat, winking at Elvi. Ian peered round at her.

'Where are you off to? Nothing better to do than sit on stone walls gossiping with the local hack writer?'

'I'm going to fetch your daughter from playgroup and then collect Alasdair from school.'

'I thought he had school dinners?'

'He does, but Jean asked if he could come home today as Callum was lunching.'

'Hell's bells, so much for my dream of a civilized meal enhanced by witty adult conversation. See you later.' The Land Rover lurched away and Elvi began to walk, and then to run, down the hill towards the village.

At lunch Callum became the children's personal property. They seemed to enjoy watching and listening to him as though he were some kind of rare and novel sideshow. The answers to particular questions seemed unimportant, it was the manner of their answering that counted. Elvi noticed that his success with them depended largely on making no concessions whatever to their tender years. He was amusing and described everything graphically, but he made no effort to use simple words or to simplify the subject matter. He had brought with him a small dictaphone.

'Can we record our voices – *please*, Callum.'

'Yes, after lunch. But you'll have to do it properly. I'll show you how it works and then you can made the recording. But now you must think of what you're going to say. I don't want just any old rubbish cluttering up my tape.'

'So there,' said Jean, dishing up apple crumble, 'you'd better put your minds to that. Custard?'

This project provided a diversion for a while, and Callum said to Elvi: 'Aren't you a nursery teacher? I seem to remember . . .'

'I'd like to be. At the moment – until recently – I'm just an assistant and bottle-washer at the local nursery school at home. I love doing it, but I'm not in the least trained.'

'Perhaps you should be.'

'Yes, it is a possibility, you're not the first person who's suggested it. I must be the only twenty-year-old in Britain with no qualifications and no ambitions.' She laughed, slightly embarrassed. Without the justification of imminent marriage she had in fact begun to feel this lack more acutely. Ian said: 'Twenty's nothing, girl. Go and do the training now if you want to, you're not superannuated.'

'Well – I might, I suppose. It's certainly something I enjoy.'

'And I bet you're good at it.' This was Callum looking across at her with such pride that she felt everyone must notice. She dropped her eyes to the plate and made a business of starting to eat. Nobody said anything so she looked up and observed: 'You seem to be pretty popular with these two yourself!'

'He is,' averred Ian. 'But his line is to treat children like small adults.'

'Hey, come on, that sounds terrible. I don't expect them to be "little ladies and gentlemen", do I?'

'No, not in that way, but you don't regard them as a race apart, as some people do.'

'Well, they're not, are you?' Callum tapped Alasdair, who was sitting next to him, on the shoulder. Alasdair fought with bulging cheeks to swallow a gigantic mouthful of crumble.

'What?' he managed.

'I beg your pardon,' corrected Jean automatically.

'Children aren't a race apart, are they?' asked Callum. Ian caught Elvi's eye and raised his shoulder theatrically as though to ask, 'See what I mean?' Alasdair pondered the question, interpreted it, considered his reply, and delivered it.

'No. We're the same.'

'There's your answer!' Callum was triumphant.

'What's a racer-part?' asked Fiona.

'It means different, a different kind of thing to everything else,' explained Callum seriously.

'Oh. Can I have more pudding?'

'You can wait till everyone else has finished,' said Jean.

When they had got down, Callum produced the dictaphone.

'What's it to be then?' he asked Alasdair.

'We're going to sing "Away in a Manger".'

'How unseasonal! We ought to have "Summer is a-Comin' in".'

'Nobody's going to know it's not Christmas,' said Alasdair with blinding logic. 'And Fiona knows it.'

'I'll leave the recording artists to it,' said Jean. 'Coffee everyone?'

'Yes, but make it quick, woman, I've got calls to make.'

'I'll wash up,' offered Elvi.

'Don't let's bother now. Later, perhaps. Ian, will you be able to take Alasdair back to school on your way?'

'Yes, yes. Away with you for the coffee.'

Callum demonstrated the use of the machine and the children did their piece. He gets totally involved in whatever he's doing, thought Elvi, as she watched him. He kept his eyes on the children's faces as they sang, and when they'd finished, he said, 'Right, let's hear what that sounds like, shall we?' and sat down on the floor with them to listen to the recording. His face in repose was thoughtful and closed. He listened intently to the playback and when it had finished he asked: 'What did you think of that?'

'We sounded funny,' said Fiona.

'You did a bit. But there you are, you see, that's what you sound like to other people.'

'We could do it better.' This was Alasdair. 'We could do it over again and make it better.'

'Now you're talking!' Callum beamed. 'That's what it's all about, eh, Alasdair? You're right, we could improve on it.'

'But not indefinitely. Coffee time.' Jean re-entered with the tray and Callum got up from the floor to take it from her and put it on the table. Then he sat down on the high-backed sofa by Elvi. It was only a two-seater and she could feel his warmth. She thought how nice it would be if they could tell Jean and Ian and the children right now, and they could celebrate, and be happy together, and she and Callum could bask in their approval. But she checked herself. Ultimately it did not matter what anyone thought of them; even the approval of dear friends like these was irrelevant. She would not get caught in that trap again. Patience: all she needed now was his love, and that she had. And his company, which she was to have in full in only a short while.

When Ian got up to go Callum rose also. 'Can I hitch down to the bottom of the hill?'

'Do. How did you think the – er – thing was?'

'The interview? It was good. You were good.'

'Please,' said Jean, 'he'll be seeing himself as the great media doctor next, pontificating on telly five nights a week.'

'*Oh* no.' Callum laughed. 'That he'll never be.'

'Thank you, friends, for boosting my morale.'

'I meant you're far too honest—'

'—and opinionated,' put in Jean.

'And too involved, I was going to say.'

'Well, that's my future sewn up then.' Ian went into the hall. 'Are you lot coming with me or not?'

Elvi went to the front door. Ian went on ahead and loaded Alasdair into the back of the Land Rover. Callum stopped by Elvi and touched her hand lightly.

'Not long,' he said, 'we'll be together.'

'I know. Goodbye.'

'*Au revoir*, my love.'

She turned to see Jean standing in the hall. She could read nothing in her face, it was impossible to tell whether she had seen or heard anything.

'So much for farewells,' she said, and went back to the kitchen.

Ten

The first time he came, when the family had gone, there seemed no need of words. He arrived after leaving work at six. It was raining and he looked cold and bedraggled. Elvi had lit a fire in the sitting room and she helped him pull his wet sweater over his head and rubbed his hair with a towel as though he were a child. He sat on the hearthrug in his shirtsleeves, shoulders hunched, fingers spread to the blaze. She pulled off his shoes and rubbed his damp feet with her hands – he got cold because there was no flesh on him, she could feel every bone. She put her arms round him from behind, leaning herself along his bumpy spine as though to transmit some heat by sheer physical pressure. They remained like this for a moment, simply savouring this long-awaited moment when they were together, and alone. Then quickly he slipped round to face her and they kissed, kneeling in front of the fire. As they made love the fluttering of the flames and their dancing light and warmth was like a blessing.

Afterwards, as they lay back, the fire was the only light in the room, a soft, changeable glow that moved over them like water. The rain outside had subsided and was now falling as a soft Scotch mist, a hazy curtain outside the window.

'The fire's nice,' he said quietly.

'Yes, cheerful . . . It was so wet and miserable.'

'And firelight's so sexy.' He ran his hand down her flank. 'You're beautiful. I've never known anyone beautiful before.'

'You must have done.'

'No – lots of people are very attractive, they have their own particular brand of beauty. But I've never know anyone of whom I could quite objectively say, "She is beautiful," and know that it was a fact, that everyone would agree.'

'You make me sound grand.' For some reason Elvi felt tears pricking her eyes. 'I'm not grand. You shouldn't say things like that.'

'Nonsense – hey, Elvi darling, what is it?' Suddenly concerned he leaned up on his elbow and drew the hair back from her face. 'I'm sorry – the last thing I meant was to upset you.' He put his arms round her and laid his cheek against hers. 'I love you, that's all, and it gives me pleasure to talk about you.'

'I know . . .' She was crying softly. 'But please don't – set me up as something I'm not. I can't cope with it, I can't.'

'Believe me. I don't set you up as anything. There's no pedestal under your feet, Elvi Beecham, certainly not one put there by me.' She could hear him smiling now, it was completely comforting. He went on, rocking her slightly to soothe her: 'I think I know at least some of the weak points, and very consoling they are too. I love you warts and all. And I very much hope that you've noticed a few on me – or the ones that I care to show, that is. There are plenty more, take my word for it.'

She laughed now, and asked: 'Have you got a hanky?'

'In my jeans.' He stretched up and pulled his clothes down off the chair where they lay in a heap. 'There.' As she blew her nose and mopped her eyes he watched her and suddenly burst out laughing.

'What's the matter?' She gave him back the hanky.

'I was just thinking – it's one of the ludicrous aspects of sex that as soon as you produce one item of ordinary, everyday clothing the whole thing looks comical. There you are, naked as the day you were born, bathed in the firelight's glow and so forth and trumpeting into my hanky for all your worth. You looked so damn funny!'

She began to laugh. 'Like people on the beach in socks . . . ?'

'Something like that.' They laughed themselves silly and then, because Callum was goosepimples all over, they dressed and curled up together on the sofa. Callum stroked her hair gently.

'And now for the bad news,' he said.

'I know. I'm sorry I didn't tell you before, and I hope you won't think too badly of me.'

'It's not that. You did what you thought was the best and most honest thing – well, didn't you?'

'Yes.'

'So that's all right, I suppose, though God knows I feel sorry for him. But what troubles me most of all is that you've done it all for me.'

'For *me*. It was entirely selfish. I wanted to be free to enjoy you.'

'Okay, put it like that. It still worries me. I told you this can be nothing permanent.'

'If you mean marriage—'

'No, I'm not talking about marriage, even.' He was conscious of the maze of half-truths into which he had led them, and yet he could not at this moment summon the courage to come clean.

He said lamely: 'I'm sorry. I'm scared shitless of the responsibility. I never imagined that anyone would see fit to alter the entire course of their lives because of me. How can I deserve that?'

'Look –' she wanted more than anything to reassure him of his own worth, of his value to her – '*you* altered the course of my life, the moment I met you. I didn't. Breaking with Alan was just a natural result of that – something that had to be done.'

'But I can't make any promises. Even now you're free I can't promise anything.'

'I understand.' She kissed his forehead, smoothing the lines of worry with her fingers.

'I wish you did,' he said, and had never meant anything more fervently in his life. He would tell her, he resolved. He would think of a way – a way that would not arouse her pity, which he dreaded, or her guilt, which would be as bad. Either

133

of those could corrode their love in an instant. He had to present facts, not emotions, so that she was neither driven away or tied to him. He had to deliver the thunderbolt in such a way that nothing was changed. God, it was impossible.

He asked, with sudden irritation: 'Why me, anyway? Tell me. Why me and not – Alan, isn't it? What is he like? I deserve to know.'

She looked at him, uncertain of his mood, wanting to say the right thing. 'I didn't love him.'

'Then why the hell were you going to marry him?'

'Because I didn't know then what love was.'

'You mean sex.' He sounded fiercely bitter. He seemed to want her to denigrate both of them. She wouldn't let him, she decided. She'd ride the storm, he wouldn't trap her.

'Sex was part of it,' she said evenly. 'Or rather it wasn't. I was very, very fond of Alan, but I didn't want him.'

'Poor sod.' He laughed in a coldly sarcastic way that she had never heard from him before. 'Poor bloody sod.'

'I think he knew. I think he always knew, but he thought he could make it right.'

'And you? You were so carried away by your quick success with me, your first-date tumble, that you rammed his good intentions right down his throat?'

'No.' Elvi could feel the tears rising, but she knew she had to be strong. Whatever battle it was that Callum was fighting with himself she would not help him win it by asking for pity. 'No, that's not true. I'd never have made love with you if I hadn't known from the first that I wanted to.'

'Thanks.' He was no longer angry, but bleak.

'Look,' she said, taking her courage in both hands, 'I was a virgin. I was *scared* of sex. As I said before, I'd led a very sheltered life. Alan couldn't make me want it although he was patient, kind, considerate – everything he should have been. You never had to do a thing. I wanted you, it was as simple as that. I was taken by storm. Making love was the obvious, natural thing to do. And,' she added, 'if you don't believe me, you can go to hell.'

'Why, Elvi Beecham!' She had at last shocked him out of his one-man war. 'You're attacking me.'

'I'm not. I couldn't.' She turned in his arms and buried her face on his shoulder. 'But you were saying such dreadful things, and you *know* they aren't true. I mean – it was the same for you, wasn't it? I haven't made a complete fool of myself?'

'We both have. God knows. I apologize.'

'Don't.'

'Okay, let it stand and put it down to experience.'

He thought: I will tell her, I owe it to her. I will tell her soon that I'm not worth it. And that I may be leaving.

But the days slipped by, and he did not. By putting it off he made it assume an enormous importance, a portentousness almost which made it harder. By rehearsing the words in his mind over and over again they began to take on a hollow and melodramatic ring. The right moment had passed and now the business of selecting another one was an unbearable strain. He considered writing it down, but that seemed coy – and then, if he put it in letter form she would keep that letter and brood over it and read things into it that were never intended. He realized that the longer he left it the more impact it would have, and despised his own vacillation. He became cranky and preoccupied at the *Chronicle*, and was under the lash of Eddie's tongue almost continually.

And then, two nights before the Andersons were due to return, something happened that effectively made up his mind for him.

He got back to his digs at about midnight, and opened the door of his room to find that Mrs Mackintosh had pushed a letter beneath it. Not, he noticed, the usual spikily-written note from the landlady herself reminding him about laundry, or rent, but a long white oblong envelope, the address typewritten, and with a London postmark. He hadn't the least idea who it could be from. He propped it on the mantelpiece while he lit the gas fire and made himself a cup of coffee and then sat down on the

135

bed and opened it. It was from the office of one of the quality London Sunday papers.

> Dear Mr Sheil, I have had your letter on my desk for some while, and I must say I am interested in the idea you put forward. I think it's right for us, but I would need to know a little more about how you propose to present it. I'm sure you understand that we need to be fairly sure of a project these days before we send someone off to Italy, all expenses paid. Could you give my secretary a ring and make an appointment to come and talk it over? Your fares will be paid, of course. I look forward to meeting you soon. Yours faithfully, Alec Dalmyer, Editor.

Callum put the letter down. That was rich. After four long months, they had finally responded. And by God they liked it! He picked the letter up again and read it through once more, trying to absorb the implications. '. . . send someone off to Italy, all expenses paid.' Send who? Him? He went back a couple of lines: '. . . how you propose to present it.' They did intend to send him. But first there was the trip to London – the onus was on him to convince them. He was sure he could do it. For a moment he felt wildly elated, a tremendous childish delight in his own success. And then he remembered Elvi. If the job came off it would involve spending several months in Florence. As he recalled he had proposed chronicling the writing of Paul Donati's next novel. It would mean being with the Booker-winning writer almost all the time, sharing his life, giving up everything for that space of time. He had once met Donati and they had got on well. He had received a promise of co-operation if ever such a series proved feasible. It could be done, he would do it, it would be fascinating, exclusive – and entirely his. But again, there was Elvi. There would be no point in her coming, even if she could afford to. The truth was, he didn't want her, or anyone, there to distract him.

And yet . . . maybe it was the test they needed. Perhaps both of them would find out something about themselves and their feelings during that time. His own elation over the project made this seem a perfectly acceptable scheme: time would fly, they would write to each other, it would be healthier for both of them. Elvi might even meet someone else. This idea brought him up short. She might indeed.

He broached the subject with her the following evening. They had walked up the hill path after supper and were sitting on the stone bluff overlooking the valley. It was a beautiful evening, the scenery ravishing the eye on every side, the air soft and mellow, full of the promise of the long summer. High above them in the failing blue hovered a kestrel as still as a watching eye. Elvi leaned back on the rough stone, her eyes closed.

'I could die now,' she said cheerfully.

'Great.'

'I mean I could die happy. Just melt away into the rocks and the sunset.'

'And what about me?'

'You could always come too.' She put out her hand, eyes still closed, and felt for his.

He said, truthfully: 'I don't like death talk. I've got something else to talk about.'

'Oh?' She opened one eye. 'That sounds ominous.'

'Not really. Here.' He passed her the letter. She sat up and read it, then gave it back to him with a shrug.

'So? You'll have to fill me in on the details. That's a bit cryptic.'

'I wrote to this bloke about four months ago with an idea for an article, or series of articles.'

'What about?'

'A writer called Paul Donati.'

'I have heard of him, but I can't say I've read anything of his.'

'No, well, neither had I until I met him a couple of years back. He's an astounding man, I've never been so impressed by anyone's sheer intellectual drive . . . anyway, after that I read most of his stuff and I wrote him an extremely callow and effusive letter saying how much I'd got out

137

of the books, and would he one day let me write about him.'

'You want to sit at the feet of the master.'

'Something like that. He wrote back and said yes.'

'I don't suppose for a moment he imagined you'd ever take him up on it.'

'Yes, I think he knew I might. He wasn't being patronizing, he never is. He takes people for what they are.'

'You do think a lot of him.'

'Yes, I do. Anyway, I read somewhere that he was going to be in Tuscany for the summer writing a new novel. What I suggested to them – ' he tapped the letter – 'was that they allow me to go out there and do a fly-on-the-wall account of the writing of the last few chapters, all the problems and bad patches, the writer's life in Italy, everything. Imagine.'

'I can.' Elvi lifted his hand to her cheek. 'You are clever.'

'I haven't done it yet. It's extremely ambitious – I've got to go down to London and convince them it's worth doing. It's going to cost them.'

'I suppose so.' Her eyes took on a thoughtful look and she began to rub his hand against her face. 'You'd go to Italy soon.'

'That's right.'

'How long for?'

'For however long it takes. The essence of the thing is to be there—'

'—at the finish.'

'Something like that.'

'And if it's something you really want to do, then of course you must.'

There was a resignation in her voice that plucked at his heart, but he shouldered it away. 'You're right, Elvi, I must. I'd be mad not to take this opportunity.' He threw in a dirty trick for good measure. 'I knew you'd understand.'

'I *know* that I understand,' she said. 'But I don't *feel* that I do.'

'A distinction without a difference.'

She hadn't heard him, her voice brightened. 'Callum – what's to stop me coming to Italy with you? Surely I could. I've got savings, I could find a job—'

'You speak Italian?' She shook her head. 'Where would you live?' She shrugged one shoulder, crestfallen. 'Think about it. I shall be living with Donati, and my work will be cut out for me. The object of the exercise is to be with him most of the time, observing. I shan't have any free time. I need to concentrate on that.'

'Yes. Yes, of course. You'll get on better without me.'

'Now that's—'

'You will. I can see that. And you're right, I couldn't live over there. But I can visit, and you can come back for the odd weekend, surely—'

'No, Elvi. I told you, it's total immersion.'

'Fine.'

He took her hand, but she didn't respond to his grasp. 'Don't make me seem callous. I'm not, just realistic. I shall miss you, too. Like hell.'

She gave a little laugh, her face turned away. 'You mustn't let that affect your work.'

'I'll have not to.' He released her hand. There followed a silence in which he sensed her regrouping, gathering her forces. When she spoke again she was composed.

'What about the *Chronicle*?'

'I'd have to hand in my notice. It's sad in a way, it would be the end of an era for me and God knows I'd still be a failed hermit if it wasn't for them – but there it is. Time to move on.'

'It would mean good money, I suppose.'

'Pretty good. No one these days can afford to chuck it about, even prestigious outfits like that, but obviously if I could get more commissions – it would make a difference.'

'And you'd move to London?'

'Only if they offered me a staff job. As a freelance I could be based where I chose, but I imagine it would be more convenient to be down south.'

'That's good news.' She smiled at him, a brief, cold little smile, stiff with anxiety. 'At least we could be closer.'

'Yes.' He didn't know what to say or do to help her. Heaven knows, he had prepared her for separation, but now it was so difficult, more painful on both sides than he could have expected. He rose, and pulled her up beside him.

'Anyway,' he said, 'we're counting our chickens. I've got to go to town and sell them the idea first. Who knows? They may take one look at me and decide I'm a bad investment. After all, a ten-stone weakling from the Highlands . . .' Suddenly she put her arms round his neck and clung to him. He could feel her tears on his shoulder. When she lifted her face she had regained her composure but only just.

'The trouble is,' she said ruefully, 'I love you.'

'I know. It's a problem. You'll have to learn to live with it.' She smiled in spite of herself, and they began to walk down the hill.

When the Andersons returned, the house which had been so private became noisy and bustling again. The children swarmed over Elvi's room as she tried to pack, chattering non-stop, anxious to show her presents from their grandparents. Elvi had never before found them a nuisance, but she did so now. The noise grated on her, their loud, boisterous presence seemed an intolerable intrusion.

At one point, when Alasdair bounced on the open lid of her case, almost wrenching it off its hinges, she shouted: 'Will you *stop* that? Go away, both of you, I'm busy and I've had enough!'

The effect was staggering. The children had never heard her raise her voice before and this, combined with the fact that she was flushed and obviously near tears, drove them into hasty silent retreat. As they scurried out, Jean came in.

'I'm sorry, love, have they been a pest?'

'I'm sorry, too . . . Damn.' Elvi sat down on the edge of the bed and dropped her face in her hands with a sob. 'I'm sorry, please take no notice . . .'

'I never saw a thing.' Jean came and sat down by her and offered her a tissue. 'Dry up and tell me all about it.'

'There's nothing to tell.' Elvi mopped her face and blew her nose. 'I was overcome with the prospect of going back home and facing up to everything again.' She lied easily – at least it was partly the truth. Jean nodded.

'I know. I daresay it will be tough for a while. But you don't regret what you did?'

'It's not that. But everything had been building up to the wedding for so long – it had filled the horizon. Now there's a lot of empty future and I've got to get down to filling it with something else.'

'Yes. Perhaps you should think seriously about the nursery teaching course.'

'I will. I'm sure I'll be more rational when I'm back home. It's partly leaving all you lovely people.' She smiled and put out her hand to take Jean's. 'You've been so good to me, I don't know how to thank you.'

'Sure, we've been the perfect hosts, going off and leaving you to fend for yourself for a week. No wonder you're feeling down, I blame myself – whatever have you been doing with yourself?'

'It's been lovely, really,' said Elvi hastily, anxious to dispel any impression of self-pity. 'I've walked and read, and Callum's been round.' She thought it best to admit to a little to preclude being suspected of a lot. Jean nodded.

'I'm glad you've seen something of each other. He's one of the good guys.'

'And the rest of the time I've been quite content with my own company. I assure you I haven't been moping for the past week.'

'Good. Well the main thing is you must keep us posted, ring up whenever you feel like it, even if it's only to have a good moan. Very necessary the occasional good moan.'

'Yes . . . yes, I will.' She began to pick things up from the bed and toss them into the suitcase in a desultory way. 'I hate packing.'

'You hate change. You always have.'

'I suppose you're right . . .' Elvi was in the mood to allow her godmother to dictate to her. It prevented her from wallowing in her own feelings.

Jean said: 'I'm sure I'm right. That's why I admire you so much for what you're doing now.'

'I suddenly got selfish that's all.'

'Well, we won't go over all that again.' Jean rose and patted her shoulder. 'Supper will be on in about half an hour, we'll have a bottle of plonk. I'm afraid I've said the children could stay up as it's your last night.'

'Don't say it like that.' Elvi was overcome with remorse. 'I feel so awful for shouting at them, especially as they're only just back – honestly, it wasn't so much them as the whole situation, I was feeling scratchy—'

'My love, I know the feeling well.' Jean smiled. 'They've forgotten about it already, and anyway it'll do them no harm to realize that you're human too.'

All through the meal Elvi felt close to tears. The fact of its being a farewell meal, combined with the emotional strain she was under anyway, produced a sort of heightened sensitivity: faces took on a special meaning, as though she were trying to print them on her memory. The wine went to her head and people's voices seemed strangely removed – she was quite cut off from her surroundings. When the phone rang towards the end of the meal she barely noticed it.

When Ian re-entered the room he said: 'That's Callum for you, Elvi. He must be sweet on you or something, he wants to run you to the station tomorrow.'

'Does he?'

'Cut along, and talk to him then.'

She rose unsteadily and went out into the hall. 'Hallo?'

'Elvi – look, I've borrowed a friend's car for tomorrow, why don't I run you to the station? The Andersons will

The Divided Heart

accept gladly, they'll be busy having only just got back. What time?'

'Hideously early – the train's eight forty. It means leaving here at quarter to.'

'No sweat, I'll be there. See you.'

'Bye.' She walked slowly back into the dining room. The children were being sent up to bed and the ensuing kisses and hugs served to cover her awkwardness. When Jean had gone upstairs with them, Ian said to her: 'All fixed up?'

'Yes, I must say it's very kind of him.'

'I'm sure he's only too pleased. To be honest it will be a help, I've got an early start tomorrow.'

'I know. You always ferry me about, you're much too soft with me.'

'We don't see you that often. Eat up.'

Elvi managed a few more mouthfuls and then put down her spoon, defeated.

'I'm sorry, this isn't like me. I couldn't manage another bite.'

'Another glass?'

'Heavens no, I'm sloshed already, it's making me maudlin . . .' She felt the lump in her throat rising to choke her, the tears welling up. Jean came back into the room.

'Elvi, they want you to go up and say good-night. I said you'd already – what's the matter?' She looked from Ian to Elvi and back. 'What have you been doing to the girl?'

Ian shrugged. 'She's having a weep, it's a free country.' Elvi was grateful for his matter-of-fact manner.

'I'm okay,' she said, 'I'll go up to them.'

'Are you sure—?'

'Perfectly. Do me good.' She hurried from the room.

The children's bedroom was in twilight, the curtains drawn against the last rays of evening sunshine. It reminded her of the set for a production of *Coppelia* that friends had taken her to when she was about nine, the toys sitting and standing

143

about in a kind of anticipatory stillness. She could almost believe that some of them would really come alive the moment she had closed the door again.

'I've come to say good-night,' she whispered, 'and then you must go to sleep.'

'Come and sit on my bed.' It was Alasdair, patting the edge of his duvet invitingly. She glanced at Fiona – already spark out, so there was no fear of being accused of favouritism. She went and sat by the little boy.

'We must whisper, because Fiona's asleep,' she said, putting her finger to her lips.

'There's no need, she sleeps like the dead once she's gone,' came the obviously plagiarized reply. 'Two seconds ago she was wide awake, calling for you,' he added rather scornfully.

'She's only little.'

'When are you going?'

'Early in the morning.'

'Callum's taking you.'

'How did you know that?'

'I've been listening to your conversation, you can hear everything up here, you know. Will you marry Callum?'

'Good gracious, no!' Elvi tried to sound properly taken aback.

'It would be very convenient.'

She had to laugh. 'For what?'

'For all of us. You'd be living here then.'

'Not necessarily, and anyway I'm not marrying anyone at the moment. I've got to go back home and do all sorts of boring things – find myself a job, for one.'

'What job?'

'Teaching small children, probably.'

'Gosh, I wish you were our teacher.'

'Do you indeed? Even if I shouted at you like I did before supper?'

'That was *nothing*, you should hear Mrs Parkes!'

'All the same, I'm sorry. I was tired, that's all.'

He was not interested in her apology. 'On the way back we saw a tank.'

'Did you? Was it a big one?'

'Huge! It had a gun in front, and there were soldiers in lorries on either side.'

Elvi sensed a conversational digging-in and rose to her feet. 'Come on, you must get to sleep. You've had a long day and I must go down and give Mummy a hand – she hasn't had time to unpack her things yet!'

'I'll see you in the morning.' It was a statement.

'Of course. Night-night.'

''Night.' She went out and pulled the door to behind her. She felt calmer. Downstairs the table had been cleared and Jean and Ian were at the sink.

'Here, let me do that.' She moved Jean gently aside. 'You'll be glad to hear I am no longer weepy. You two go and unpack and I'll make you some coffee.'

'It's a deal.'

The rest of the evening was quiet and cosy and Elvi found herself looking forward to the next morning, when she would see Callum. He had said that he would try and make it to the station, but this would be even better. She did not allow herself to think of the moment of departure, nor of the Italian trip. It would turn out right, she would manage, and there was no point in agonizing over it.

The farewells were mercifully brief, as Ian was hurrying down to surgery and Jean was in the throes of getting the children breakfasted. Callum was unusually quiet.

They drove for about twenty minutes in silence before he said abruptly: 'I'll be down to London at the end of the week. My appointment's at ten, I'm arriving on the sleeper. Will you come and meet me?'

'What do you think?' Her hand was resting lightly on the back of his neck, stroking the springy black hair. 'Of course. I shall want to hear all about it.'

'Hm.' He glanced at her. 'You may not. It may be Florence

the week after that.' There was something of the harshness in his manner that she remembered from their dreadful discussion of Alan. She was wary, uncertain of his mood or of her ground.

'We've talked about that,' she said.

'Ah yes, I forgot, it's all been safely discussed, and filed under OK.'

'Don't be like this.' She folded her hands in her lap and turned to look out of the window. A purple, grey and green hillside; rocks; sheep; a solitary man with two darting collies – gone. And now there was a stretch of silky water with a reflection printed on it. It was all so beautiful and it had nothing to do with her. The satisfaction she had once gleaned from the countryside had been taken from her. She was now hopelessly dependent for her happiness on him.

'I don't know what you want me to say,' she said with some resentment.

'Neither do I.'

'Then don't bully me. I do my best.'

'Please.' The sarcasm in his voice appalled her. 'Don't be plaintive, it doesn't suit you.'

'I simply want us to work it out.'

His only response to this was to put his foot down on the accelerator so that the car shot forward.

'Be careful!' Elvi shouted, genuinely frightened.

'Why?'

'I don't want to get killed even if you do!'

'Suicide pact! Just the job!' He yelled crazily and screeched round a long bend so that Elvi's stomach heaved.

'Stop! Please stop!'

'All right,' he agreed, with sudden sweet reasonableness. They drove the rest of the way in fraught silence.

At the station his mood seemed to abate but he appeared morose and introspective. As they waited on the draughty platform he put his arm round her and pulled her roughly against him.

'I suppose I have to say sorry.'

146

'You don't.'

'Yes, I do. I'm not apologizing for my mood or my feelings, you understand. I'm apologizing for my rudeness.'

'Accepted. But why?'

'I feel confused. And guilty. And I'm not used to it.'

'You know –' she kissed him lightly on the cheek – 'it's crazy. When I first met you that was how I felt. Now it's different – I'm free and happy and I love you; I'm even quite brave. But now *you're* tearing yourself to bits. What's the matter with us?'

He smiled the old brilliant smile for the first time that morning and Elvi felt warmed by it. 'Perhaps we've been reading too many novels,' he remarked. 'We've forgotten how to be content.'

'Perhaps. Please don't let's worry too much about this job. It's great news really, and I've been thinking, maybe I could come out too for at least part of the time—'

'No.'

'But why not?'

'It would be hopeless, I'll be virtually living with Donati. And anyway I can't afford to pay for you, and where would you get the cash from? Forget it.'

The train appeared, snaking into the station, at first no more than a distant rattling rhythm, then a rush of noise as it drew alongside them. The deafening sound enveloped them, Callum folded Elvi in his arms, then hurried her aboard and put her cases in the rack.

As the train drew away she saw him mouth the words 'Take care.' But he did not wait to wave and the last she saw of him was his receding back view, hands in pockets and head bowed, leaving the station.

147

Eleven

Alan decided on the spur of the moment to contact Alec Dalmyer. He could not have said himself what his motives were – some obscure desire to re-establish himself as separate from Elvi, to go back to where he had left off after the separation with Pru. Or perhaps sheer vulgar curiosity – he knew that Dalmyer had done well for himself, was now the editor of a prestigious Sunday paper, and still unmarried. Alan found himself wondering about this – whether Alec had tried and failed, or whether he had simply managed to remain independent through choice. Alan recalled that at one stage he and Alec had been thick as thieves, he had always been an amusing and stimulating companion, with a Peter Pan quality, a glittering boyishness.

Alan thought of him as born out of his time – he should have been one of the Coward generation, a bright young thing with a knife-edge wit and a fanatical desire to amuse and be amused. Now what would he be like? Alan craved some company that bore no relation whatever to recent events, or to the way he felt. Alec, he was sure, would be gloriously un-curious, far too bound up in self-admiration and the propagation of his own image to be concerned about Alan.

He rang on Monday morning. A crisp, upper-class secretary answered the phone.

'Hallo, Editor's office?'

'Good morning. Might I speak to Mr Dalmyer?'

'A-ah,' (a practised pause, here) '– I *think* he's rather tied up at the moment . . .'

'Then can I leave a message – he could ring me back.'

'Perhaps that would be best. Could I have your name, please?'

'It's Neilson, Alan Neilson.'

'Mr Neilson. Right—'

There was some kind of quick exchange in the background, rather muffled. Alan guessed she had her hand over the receiver, and then he heard Alec's unmistakeable boyish tones.

'Alan! My dear fellow, a voice from the past!'

'I thought you were rather tied up,' observed Alan wryly.

'We-ell . . . a good secretary, Annette.'

'She protects you from the world.'

Alec laughed, that light, fluting laugh that Alan could remember ringing out at so many sweaty youthful parties. 'The world is always too much with us, I'm sure you find the same.'

'Yes, I do. I rang to find out if we could have lunch some time.'

'Of course we *must*. Now let's see, we must go somewhere gentlemanly and full-blooded where we can size each other up and review the ravages of time in the greatest possible luxury.'

'You just say where.'

After some studied consideration Alec decided on Rules, but not until the end of the week. 'Endless lunches in this job – but I can put off that terrible woman on Friday, can't I, Annette?' There was a murmur of assent in the background. 'Shall we say one?'

'That's fine. I'll look forward to it.'

In the event Alan found himself out of a meeting in the Strand at twelve fifteen, and decided to walk up the Embankment to Fleet Street and meet Alec in his office. In any case he was curious to see him in context.

When he reached the appropriate floor he was obliged to wait, corralled in a reception area under the beady, well made-up stare of the girl there who announced his presence over the phone.

'A Mr Neilson is here for the Editor,' she said in a stereotypical nasal sing-song, her eyes watching him sightlessly as she listened to the response. Then she put down the receiver and resumed studying a sheet of paper on her desk, while filing her nails beneath it. Alan wondered whether it was as bad as this for people who came to see him, and decided that it was not. His office was more businesslike, surely, less exclusive, less image-concious. He was obliged to admit to himself that he was unused to being an outsider. In his own field he was reasonably well-known, a force to be reckoned with, if not always deferred to. He was rarely kept waiting, and the terms of any meeting were usually his. It was chastening to be regarded merely as just another someone, with whom the Editor was having lunch: that girl, he reflected, probably assumed he was a sponger, a practised butterer-up, trying to get a story commissioned.

Another girl, a tall, pale, lanky beauty, appeared in the reception area.

'Mr Neilson?'

'That's me.'

'You didn't have an appointment?' It was the gentlest accusation.

'No – I was going to meet Mr Dalmyer at Rules, but I was early, so I came along here.'

'I see.' She smiled coolly, her point made. 'He has someone with him at present. Are you quite happy to wait for a few more minutes?'

'I'm here now.'

'Right.' She beamed triumphantly. 'He won't be long.' She moved over to the desk and began to talk in a hushed, intense way, to the receptionist. Both girls had the soignée, expressionless beauty that he associated with magazine covers. It was odd, he thought, how so many good-looking women strove to make themselves look identical. Beauty editors seemed dedicated to the principle of uniformity. A big nose? Make it look smaller. Thin face? It had to look rounder. Deep-set eyes? Surround them in white so that they stand out. He sighed and the tall girl cast him a withering look.

150

'See you,' she said to the receptionist, and drifted away.

About a quarter of an hour later, Alec appeared, bidding an effulgent farewell to his previous meeting.

Alan rose as his friend bounded over to him.

'My dear chap, I do apologize. I didn't expect you to turn up here, you know—'

'I was early, so I thought I would. I hope that was all right.'

'Please! Let's go and have lunch, we've got ten years to catch up on.'

Alan enjoyed the lunch. Alec was a good talker. Listening was not his strong suit, but Alan was glad of that, had been counting on it, even. He found it soothing simply to sit there, in the plushy, dated snugness of Rules, to eat, and drink champagne, and let Alec wax expansive. He had changed, thought Alan, but only in precisely the ways one would have expected. Fashions had played into his hands, he looked slim, and fit and elegant, his hair worn longish, but well-cut, his eternal air of boyish insouciance now heightened to one of urbane camp. He was unmarried through choice and there was little doubt now where his proclivities lay. He had 'come out'. But with it all Alan noticed a slight underlying nerviness – a brittle layer of self-defence that underscored all the breezy gaiety. He felt sorry for Alec. He was not one of the new generation, raised in an atmosphere of tolerance, in the certainty that gay was good. Alec had years of anxiety and caution to overcome, and those years had left their legacy.

'You could say life has treated me well,' he announced, with a complacent, but not wholly unlikeable smile. 'But I'm not long for this job.'

'Why ever not? I should have thought it was what you'd been aiming for – you've got where you wanted to be. The top.'

'Ah, but the trouble with always wanting to be somewhere is that when you get there it's almost bound to be an anticlimax. Besides, they don't like me.'

'I find that very hard to believe,' said Alan truthfully.

'How kind of you to say so. But no, it's true. Fleet Street is very *virile*, you know Alan, they equate ability with a particular brand of scruffy, hard-drinking, heterosexual prowess. I'm amazed to have got this far, really. But then, I can do the job, I'm rather good at it, and they don't care for that. It doesn't sit well with their prejudices.'

'I think you're being paranoid.'

'In my old age? Perhaps. In any event I shall move on soon.'

'Where to?' Alan was genuinely interested.

'I shall sit in my flat overlooking Parliament Hill and write a dirty book. I've made a lot of money, I've been disciplined, I've proved something about and to myself. Now it's self-indulgence time.'

'I'm sure you'll write an excellent book.'

'Thank you, friend. You won't read it, that's for sure.'

'What makes you think that?'

'I don't suppose you read novels. You never did then, and you haven't changed much.'

'No, I don't read. I prefer the truth.'

'Ah yes, the good old plain, unvarnished truth – so often far more titillating and fanciful than anything the average imagination could make up . . . another brandy?'

'No, I must get back to the office.'

'So must I, but I'm a quick drinker. Keep me company.' Alan refused again, but two brandies were brought. Alec paid the bill with a casual handful of notes, waving aside Alan's offer.

'For God's sake, I asked you,' Alan insisted.

'But I suggested Rules. And anyway, I'm a far better host than I am a guest. You ought to come round for dinner at my place some evening, I'm a first-rate cook.'

'I'd like that.'

Alec watched him, cat-like, over the edge of his glass for a second and then remarked: 'I heard about you and Pru. What a crying shame.'

'But a long time ago, too.'

'Still, Pru was a lovely girl, a free spirit. I'm sorry you lost her.'

'But you blame me.'

'Who, me? Blame? My dear Alan, blaming is something I simply do not do. I don't blame a living soul for anything. But I did feel a sense of waste about you and Pru: it was something I thought was absolutely *right*. I am chastened to be proved wrong.'

'Yes. It was a waste.'

'And has there been no other lovely lady to brighten your life since Pru's departure? It's most remiss of me not to have enquired before.'

'Not at all.' Alan knew perfectly well that this was a well stage-managed ploy. Alec was leaving the important questions about him till last, so that no matter what bombshell he cared to drop about his private life there would only be time for Alec to dispense a quick, witty and articulate response before escaping. He was a sympathetic man in the general sense – as the French say, *'sympathique'* – but he had had too many problems of his own to want to share anyone else's. He would adorn your life, make it easier to bear by making it more fun, but it was no good expecting him to share the load. He had borne his own, alone and privately for too long, and had wept on no one's shoulder. He had been there and he wasn't going back. Alan understood this.

'I am engaged actually.'

'*Engaged*? Alan, how terribly fifties of you.'

'It was what Elvi wanted.'

'Elvi. And when will the knot be tied?'

'I don't know. There are things that need sorting out.'

'Ah me. You have your troubles still.'

'That's right.' There was a moment's silence. The two men looked at each other across the table. Alan thought, how strange, it's years since we saw each other, so much has happened, but in the last analysis we're simply using each other to reinforce our own defences.

As they walked back to the Strand to pick up a cab, Alan felt curiously disappointed. Alec waved down a taxi.

'Where to?' he asked Alan.

'Moorgate. We'll drop you off and I'll pay the other end. Least I can do.'

'As you wish.' Alec gave the driver instructions and they settled into the seat. 'So. When shall we two meet again?'

'I don't know.'

'Such wild enthusiasm! Would you like to come round to dinner some time?'

'Yes, I would.'

'With the lovely Elvi?'

'No.'

'Right then. I shall adjust the company accordingly.' He must have read something in Alan's face, for he added: 'Don't worry, I am not going to impose anything too outré on you. I was very well brought up.'

'I know that. Please don't think—'

'I'll telephone you at your place of work.'

'Yes.'

'You're very sotto all of a sudden, what ails?'

'I'm tired.'

'Ah, the great escape. It's a form of laziness, you know. I doubt that you're physically tired, you're just backing away from some nasty thing that's reared its ugly head in your mind. I have not the slightest desire to know what it is but I'm perfectly certain you'd do better to go and examine its teeth than to retire and take aspirins.'

Alan laughed. 'Probably.'

'Certainly. Here we are.' The cab drew into the curb and Alec got out. Through the open door he remarked: 'It was very – reassuring to see you again. Thank you for being in touch.'

'Thank *you* for a superb lunch.'

'*De nada.* I'll ring about dinner.' He slammed the door and tapped the roof of the taxi as if geeing up a horse. As it drew away down Fleet Street towards Ludgate Circus Alan saw Alec turn, encounter someone on the steps of the building and enter with them, obviously deep in animated conversation. The sight saddened him a little – it seemed to emphasize Alec's resilience, his independence, his sociability. What I lack, thought Alan, is the ability to diffuse my affections. I put all my eggs in one basket and then wonder why it's so bad when the basket gets dropped. He looked out of the window as they stopped at traffic lights. A red-headed girl crossed the road in front of them and for a moment she reminded him of Elvi. But when she turned towards them and he saw her face, he saw that she was not a bit like her and he felt irritated and disappointed as though she had deliberately tried to trick him.

When he got back to the office there was a flap on. Cavendish had been on the phone from Birmingham with a tale of sales contracts not honoured, eager to pass the buck. His secretary was on the verge of tears, there were a couple of terse and 'urgent' memos on his desk from the sales manager (also a victim of Cavendish's panic measures) and the phone was ringing yet again as he entered. Mentally calling down a plague on all their houses, he snapped at Sandra to pull herself together and refused to answer the phone for a full minute although its persistent ring was grating on the nerves of all present. He should, he thought bitterly, never have allowed himself the luxury of lunch with an old friend. His life wasn't like Alec's, and nor was his job. Two hours at Rules had left him with chaos for the afternoon. He demanded coffee from the already flustered Sandra and prepared to do battle with Cavendish.

Elvi and Callum met at the bar of the National Film Theatre. She had been surprised that he was a member.

'It's one aspect of my deprived urban youth that I decided to continue,' he told her. 'Before I had you to waste my time for me I used to come to a film here every time I was in town – it's useful for catching up on things you haven't seen. And it's much more comfortable than going to the pictures in the West End.'

The bar at lunchtime was quiet, and had the desolate air of

a night-club first thing in the morning. They collected cheese rolls and light ale and sat at a table by the wall.

'Well?' she asked. 'What happened?'

'He's for it. I'm going.'

'When?'

'Well, I've got to finalize things with Donati, and hand in my notice at the *Chronicle* – I shall aim to be out there at the end of next month.'

'For how long?'

'I can't say. As long as it takes. The whole thing depends on seeing it through. Living it – it would be hopeless to set a time limit.'

'Yes, yes, you said before. So –' she smiled brightly, knowing it mattered to him – 'that's terrific news. You must feel very proud of yourself.'

'I'm pleased. I don't want to leave you. I feel very mixed.'

'You mustn't. Go ahead and do it for all you're worth.'

He smiled and put his hand over hers. 'Thanks.'

'By the way, what was he like?'

'The editor? Chap called Alec Dalmyer – very charming, very able, very gay.'

'How can you tell?'

'Darling Elvi – he didn't stand with his hand on his hip, or make a pass at me, if that's what you're thinking. It was just obvious, that's all. At any rate, he's extremely astute and hard-headed and very good to work for, I should think.'

'What will they do – keep you in bed and board for three months?'

'No, just my fares, and necessary extras. I intend asking Paul if I can stay with him.'

'That's very bold of you.'

'Not at all, he's that sort of a man. He'll appreciate that if the piece is to work, I need to be on the field of battle, so to speak.'

'And you will find time to write to me?'

'Of course.'

Callum thought she was more beautiful than ever today. There was something poignant and bittersweet about her determined effort to be responsible, to be sensible and unselfish at all costs. She was wearing a plain black shirt, with the necklace and earrings he had given her. Her face was pale, her red hair pulled back and caught with a narrow black ribbon. Knowing her, he was sure she had calculated no special effect and yet she had a waif-like, tragic appearance, like some lovely Spanish infanta.

'You're looking very –' he searched for the right word – 'heart-rending.'

'Do I say thank you?'

'It was intended as a compliment.'

'I suppose all this black is rather funereal. It doesn't really suit me.'

'When people say that, they usually mean it's something they don't generally wear. They refuse to believe there are several facets to their appearance or their personality. You look wonderful in black.'

'Oh.'

'Yes, "oh".' Suddenly more moved than he could bear, he pulled his chair round next to hers and put his arm round her, leaning his forehead against her hair. 'I love you. Is there anywhere we can go?'

'No. You know there isn't.'

'Let's be brazen and go to a hotel.'

'I couldn't.'

'Don't be prim. You could. You wouldn't have to do a thing except stand next to me while I tell the lies. Please let's do it.'

'Can we walk for a while?'

'If you want.'

'I do. I shall cry if we sit about any more.'

They left the carpeted twilight of the NFT and began to walk slowly along the terrace in front of the Festival Hall. It was a mild, changeable day, the river's surface was riffled in a light breeze, a man in a grey suit was flying a kite. Secretaries

157

with lunch boxes sat on the benches chatting, a tramp sold clockwork mice near the steps of Charing Cross Bridge.

'Let's watch the boats,' said Callum, and they went over and leaned on the wall. A pleasure boat back from Greenwich bustled by, and some people waved. Callum waved back. 'See? Everyone wishes us well.'

'You'll be saying next: "Everybody loves a lover".'

'And why not?'

She squeezed his arm. ' 'Tain't true.'

'Tell me,' he said, 'what will you do to improve the shining hour while I'm away? I utterly forbid you to sit and mope.'

'I shan't do that. I'm back at the nursery school – and I'm going to try and get into college for September.'

'That's terrific! You never told me.'

'It was you who suggested it.'

'Was it? Anyway, I'm entirely for it, it'll keep you off the streets.' He glanced down at her profile, looking out over the river. There were tears on her cheeks but her face was still, in repose.

'You know,' he said, 'if you meet anyone else – God it sounds so corny! But if you *do* come across anyone else, you will let yourself be happy, won't you?'

'Don't say it. It won't happen.'

'Do you think I *want* it to? I just want you to know that I don't expect you to sacrifice yourself on the altar of True Love or anything like that.'

'You're being flippant, but what use is anything if one doesn't made some *effort* for it?'

'I'm not making much.'

'You're doing your job.'

'Ah yes. I forgot, we lords of the earth must boost our egos at all costs.'

'It's your job.'

'What about going to a hotel?'

'I'd rather not. It's nothing to do with—'

'Okay, okay, don't say it, I understand. I'm sorry if I was pushy about it.'

She turned quickly to face him and he clasped her in his arms, tightly so that they stood like one person, with the great coloured kite, fluttering, tugging and swooping over their heads like some strange bird.

The Major was sitting in his chair on the lawn when Elvi got back. He turned his head as he heard her open the front door, but he no longer expected her to run straight through the house and out to greet him. She rarely did that any more. She was more secretive and self-possessed – there were more things on her mind. He heard her go into the kitchen and open the fridge. When she did eventually come out, she was walking slowly and she carried a glass of orange juice bobbing with ice. She kissed him quietly on the cheek and sat down on the grass. He did not ask about her day in town. She had told him she was meeting a friend for lunch and though he accepted it as only partly the truth he knew better now than to try and prise more out of her. He put out his hand and touched the top of her head. He thought she had hardly changed since she was thirteen – she was still slim and slight, her long red hair worn just the same, over her shoulders. But when she turned to look at him there was that new awareness in her eyes: they had lost that shiny, youthful look of optimism, they now met his with a steady, understanding gaze that both impressed and saddened him.

'What are you going to do?' he asked.

'How do you mean?'

'Now that you're no longer to be married.'

'Well – I'll carry on at the nursery school. And I'll try to get into teacher training college.'

'You're serious about that.'

'Yes.'

'Have you done anything about it?'

'I've discussed it with Mrs Maynard – I know *what* to do, but I haven't been able to summon up the energy to do it.'

She did, he thought, look bone-weary. And now she lay back on the grass, eyes closed, arms at her sides, entirely vulnerable to his loving scrutiny.

'May I tell you something?' he asked gently.

'Please.' Her lips formed a small, grim smile. 'Anything.'

'It's very much better – more honourable – to retreat, than to continue with a pretence. However sad and disappointed you, and others, may be now, it's nothing to the sadness you'd cause later by embarking on something that isn't right. You've done the right thing, Elvi.'

There was a pause, during which he held his breath. Then she reached out her hand and touched his leg with her fingers.

'I hope so. Now may I tell *you* something?'

'Of course.' He looked across at his roses. When she spoke there was a quiet, wondering surprise in her voice.

'I'm in love. I've fallen in love with someone.'

'I had guessed something of the sort.' He realized as he said it that it was true.

'Was it so obvious?'

'Not obvious. But now I think about it—'

'Ah, hindsight.'

'Not entirely. It was unlikely not to be the case.'

'Do you want to know all about it?' Her eyes were still closed and that made it easier for him to answer truthfully.

'Not really. I don't know why. I was fond of Alan, you see . . .'

'Yes, I see,' she said softly. 'I understand.'

'But if you want to talk – I don't mean to be selfish—'

'Why ever not? Everyone else is. I'll tell you one thing. He's going away soon, to Italy – for months. Ironic, isn't it?'

'I'm sorry, darling.'

'As far as I know you had nothing to do with it.' The brittleness of her tone hurt him.

'What will you do?' he asked.

'That's the second time you've said that this evening, you know.' She sat up, linking her hands round her knees, and stared across the lawn. There were bits of dry grass clinging to her hair at the back. Dick Beecham longed to brush them off but she was totally unapproachable.

'I'm sorry if I'm tedious,' he said quietly.

'You're not.' She reached out a hand and touched his, still without looking at him. 'The fact is I don't know what I shall do. This college thing . . . I know everyone thinks it's a good idea. *He* thinks it's a good idea. And yet, without him . . .' she paused for a moment, he knew she was fighting off tears, then went on: 'I just don't think I have the mental energy, the faith in the future, to do it.'

'Then don't.' It seemed to be all that he could do, to reflect her own mood, to go along with her. He couldn't hug her and kiss it better, not any more. She went on as though he hadn't spoken.

'I feel as if by starting something like that I should be providing myself with some kind of insurance in case he didn't come back. And I can't bear to do that. I can't bear to recognize even the possibility.'

'Is that how he sees it? As an insurance?'

'No. I don't know.'

'I mean, if that *is* how he sees it you might be best advised to invest in it.'

'Yes.'

'But if he means so much to you – I don't know what to say. You must do as you feel.'

'I know. And I feel I want to wait, very quietly and determinedly.'

'Try and stop time?'

'Yes.' She glanced at him, suddenly grateful. 'That's exactly it. If I could reduce myself to a tiny black dot, I would.'

'But you can't. I should go for the training course, create some continuity.'

'I'll see.' She had closed door again. 'I'm going to pick some roses.'

'Use the secateurs,' he advised automatically. 'Make a clean cut, otherwise you're hurting the plant.'

She did not reply and he watched her walk away from him in silence.

Twelve

Callum received a letter from Paul Donati.

Dear Callum Sheil,
  You certainly have a strong nerve and a long memory, I congratulate you on both of them. The answer is yes, you may, provided you understand that I shall make no concessions to your presence. This is a large apartment, you may stay here, you may observe and make notes and generally 'do your thing'. But please understand that I shall be working and that is something *I* do extremely hard. It's a form of cowardice really – I feel that if I let up I may grind to a halt. Impetus is all. I have an extraordinary American lady who organizes things for me, her name is Dawn Oppenshaw. Contact her at the above address with details re: your arrival, distinguishing features etc. This is the first, last and only part I shall play in attending to you. Yours respectfully, Donati.

Callum found the letter most gratifying. It was exactly what he had expected and hoped for. He at once booked a flight out at the end of the month, and went to see Max Myers.

'My dear Callum, I'm delighted!' Max was a tall, bony man, with a physique like a horse. His vague manner and air of physically clumsiness hid an iron determination and a dogged strength of will. Once he had decided on a course of action he was never deterred, though his apparently bumbling geniality sometimes led others to suppose that he had been. Now he rose from his desk and bounded round to wring

Callum's hand, sweeping several sheaves of paper off on to the floor as he did so. He had a tiny separate office, no more than a partitioned-off cubicle in which he crashed about like a heavy hunter in a horse-box.

'It's great news. Of course I shall be inordinately sorry to lose you and you've got a nerve going off and organizing things on the side like this, but nonetheless . . .'

'I realize it must look underhand. Actually, I sent the idea off to them months ago and I'd pretty well given it up when they finally wrote. Then of course I didn't want to hand in my notice without having something definite.' He produced Donati's letter and handed it to Max.

'I see the great man regards you as a cheeky chappie as well.'

'Only myself to blame.'

'And you've met him before, I gather?'

'That's right. We got on extremely well. I asked him then and there if he'd let me write such a piece if the chance came up.'

'So there you go. You'll be hard to replace.'

'Would you like me to advertise now, see if I can get someone soon enough to show them the ropes?'

'You've got enough on your plate. In fact we should try and phase you out as gently as we can. When do you plan on leaving?'

'I've booked a flight at the end of the month.'

'Have you indeed?'

'A month's notice is right, I take it.'

'Yes, yes, you're within your rights. Just.'

'But you hadn't expected me to stand on them . . .'

'Perhaps I didn't, but then – this is your big break. I don't suppose you'd like your job held for you, would you . . . ?'

'No, Max. It's kind of you, but no. If I'm taking a chance it's one that has to be taken and I'm not interested in hedging my bets. As you'll appreciate, I'm not investing in long-term security. A flash in the pan will be fine.'

'Yes, I'd better get back to the coalface. Shall we have a drink on the strength of all this later on?'

'Why not?'

The interview had not been as awkward as Callum had feared. He had been unsure whether Max would see his departure as some kind of betrayal. He himself believed fiercely in the importance and value of local papers and Callum had always genuinely supported him in his view. He had never made any secret of the fact that if the opportunity came he would move on, but still . . . As he sat down at his desk, Eddie remarked:

'Well laddie, what's new? You're looking bright-eyed and bushy-tailed today.'

'Cut out the "laddie", Ed, it doesn't suit you.'

'Don't you recognize biting sarcasm when you hear it?'

'I'm thick-skinned.'

'You're also late. And you've been with the Editor, which makes you later. I trust that we can now rely on your presence for a moment or two?'

'For the next four weeks, Eddie. I just handed in my notice.'

This remark had the desired effect – that of silencing Eddie, who, to do him justice, could see the funny side of the situation, and Callum was able to get through the day with the minimum of hassle. After a pint with Max in the evening he walked up the hill to the Andersons'.

Jean came to the door. 'Callum! Come in.'

'I'm afraid I'm out to make use of you. Can I borrow your phone?'

'Certainly.'

'Reverse charges, of course.'

'Of course. Help yourself.' Casually tactful, she waved him to the phone and retired into the kitchen, closing the door behind her. Callum dialled Elvi's number. The Major answered.

'May I speak to Elvi, please?'

'I should think so. Who is it?'

'My name's Sheil.'

'Oh yes. I'll get her.' What did 'oh yes' mean, wondered Callum. Was his presence at last officially recognized, and if so with what reaction? Elvi came to the phone a little breathless.

'Hallo, I was in the garden.'

'Does your father know of my existence?'

'Yes. Of your existence, but not your name.'

'He knows it now. He guessed.'

'Am I going to see you?'

'At the airport, I should think. I'm booked to leave at the end of the month, my notice is handed in.'

'I see.' Her voice was very distant and toneless.

'Elvi?'

'I'm here.'

'I shall be pretty busy this end, I don't want to leave the *Chronicle* with any loose ends to tie up. I suggest we arrange to meet the day I go.'

'No.'

'You don't want to.' It was a statement, not a question.

'That's right. Let's make this goodbye. Let's say it, and ring off, and that will be that.'

'Au revoir.'

'Whatever you like.'

'You don't want to meet again at all before I go?'

'It's not a case of what I want. I *want* – oh, everything. But I can't have it so I'd rather make a clean cut.'

'Okay.' This is awful, he thought. We're miles apart and we're both drifting, alone. We ought to be clinging close, giving ourselves some love, some hope for the future.

'Elvi—'

'Don't say it. Write to me when you get there. I'd like that.'

'Of course I will.'

'I'll look forward to your letter. Say it all then.'

'I shall, don't worry.'

'Goodbye, Callum.'

'Au revoir.'

He put the phone down and sat there, the silence humming in his ears. He was shocked. Was that really to be their last contact for months? It had been so distant, so unsatisfactory, so cold. He tried to remember how Elvi had felt in his arms the last time they had met, but it seemed an age ago. He had to admit to himself that the excitement of organizing the trip, of handing in his notice, had partially helped to distance them. It was easier for him. He was the one moving on, breaking new ground. She was the one who waited. He was also conscious of a certain urge in himself to push her from him. He half-wanted her to forget, to drift away, to meet someone else, because that would relieve him of the dreadful responsibility of her love. Perhaps while he was away, she would forget, or stop caring . . . but he knew they would not. Elvi would wait, loving him, and he would go back to her still a traitor, with a divided heart. He rubbed his hand over his face as if to erase the turmoil inside his head. Jean opened the kitchen door.

'Finished? Want to stay for supper?'

'Well, I didn't really come—'

'I know you didn't, but now you're here. Ian's out on call, I'll fix us both a bacon and egg, I'd like the company.'

'Put like that . . .'

He followed her into the kitchen. The room was untidy and homely, the children's drawing things still strewn over the table, and some racks of small buns set to cool at the other. They smelt superb.

'Have one.' Jean had caught him looking.

'They smell great.'

'Fresh cakes, you can't beat it. Go on.'

He helped himself and watched Jean as she prepared supper. He remembered Elvi in the same kitchen the first time he'd called. He'd been enchanted by her domesticity, her grace, the daffodils on the table . . . Jean was different, the way women with children were different. Hers was a cavalier style, a prac- tised slap-dashery, apparently hasty but warmly effective.

'Do you want a drink?' she asked, putting bacon in the pan with a sizzle like a hot spring.

'No, thanks, I just came from the local. I'm leaving the *Chronicle*.'

'Go on!'

'Honest injun. I'm going to make my fortune in Italy.'

'What, for ever?'

'No, I'm going to do one important article.'

Typically Jean asked no more about the work but concerned herself with the practical details. 'Are you all organized to go? When do you go? Where will you stay? You are a dark horse and no mistake.'

'It's all fixed.'

'Is that what the urgent phone call was all about?'

'Yes – there was someone I had to tell.'

'Well I never . . .' Jean got two plates from the cupboard and expertly slid an egg and rashers on to each. 'There you are. Bread?'

He ate, feeling cosseted and approved of, like a good child who has done something to make his parents proud.

The feeling prompted him to say: 'It was Elvi I rang.'

'I see.'

'Do you?'

'What do you want me to say?' She looked at him keenly. He saw that she was serious, but her eyes were kind.

'I want you to say that's all right with you.'

'It's all right with me.'

'You know what I mean.'

'You want my approval.'

'I think Elvi does, more than me. That's why she hasn't told you, she's afraid you won't give it.'

'If you want to know what I really think –' Jean got up and fetched a half-full bottle of supermarket rosé off the side – 'and I think I need some wine to get me through this – I think Elvi did right to break it off with Alan.'

'You knew him?'

'No, never met him, but I could see from the way she was when she came to stay that she wasn't happy. Nothing to do with him, probably, she just wasn't feeling the way she should have been. And that's no way to go into marriage.'

'She didn't love him?'

'I think she may have done, in a way, after all love is a lot of different things, isn't it? But it wasn't the right way. And she didn't want him physically.'

'No. She told me that.'

'So there you are. I've said my piece. I'm sure you've given it all due consideration.'

'Plenty of consideration.' He ran his fingers through his hair. 'I'm no further forward.'

'You're hoping that Italy may sort you out.'

'Maybe.'

'It might not.'

Callum got up and walked over to the window. Outside the summer evening was soft and clear, the mountainside a protective arm flung round the house. The little footpath wound away through the heather like a promise for the future.

'I do love her,' he said. 'Otherwise I'd never be in this deep. It sounds corny, but I never thought it could happen to me. It scares me a bit.'

'I think you should be straight with her.' Jean's voice was gentle, she came over to him and put her hand on his shoulder. 'She deserves that much.'

'I know.' He covered her hand with his own, still gazing out of the window, as if to concentrate his thoughts. 'I know, but I just haven't been able to find the right moment.'

'In my experience most people are a lot more sensible and selfish than we give them credit for. I should think she wants to feel that you can speak to her openly. Alan is a good man, but I suspect he was overprotective of Elvi. Treat her like a grown woman, Callum.'

'I may not see her before I go.'

'Then tell her when you write. You must.'

'Yes. I expect I will.'

He turned and smiled at her, a bright, final smile, closing the subject.

Sometimes he wondered if it was not so much conscience he suffered from, as a lack of conscience. He had retrained his sensibilities to deal with the past, and now the present, in the way that most suited him.

He hoped that Jude had forgiven, if not forgotten him. They could never forget each other after what they had been through, though God knows he for one had tried hard enough. Ruthlessly, he had never permitted himself to speculate on what might have been, on the future they might have had, the adventures undertaken, the films seen, the jokes shared, the relationship maturing with time . . . had never imagined what their child would have looked like.

She'd been a little older than him, but still only in her late twenties – gutsy and gallant, a force of nature. In a way, her spirit had been their undoing. Jude had helped him to grow up, to know who he was and what he wanted, and in the end that had not been her.

She'd always been someone in charge of her life, so it had come as a thunderbolt when she'd discovered she was pregnant.

'Something must have slipped under my radar,' she joked. 'Trust you.'

Much as he loathed the idea of any alternative, he was naïve, and it came as a shock to realize that Jude had every intention of keeping the baby. Once she had regrouped she went forward with her pregnancy with fearsome self-possession. She made it clear that this was her decision, that she asked nothing of him – her courage and determination were rock solid. Though he was scared half to death, it was probably this self-reliance of hers that kept him from fleeing anyway. And her enthusiasm had got to him – he began to look at the books with her, to feel the bump and its hidden, urgent movements, to consider what it might be like to be a father. Neither of them had any family to speak of – the Andersons were the closest thing to his – so they had only each other, and the baby of course, to worry about.

But when at six months the baby stopped moving and, they were told, had stopped living, too, he had been aware of a slippery worm of relief. While Jude had been devastated. He had never seen her that way before and it was an unimaginable shock.

He did his poor best. He sat with her during the ordeal of the forced labour, gazed with her at their tiny perfect daughter, and played his part in the wretched formalities that followed. From raging storms of uncontrolled grief Jude became even more terrifyingly withdrawn and silent. He took this as a sign of the iron entering his soul.

But the day after the ghastly, miniature funeral she said to him: 'Callum, if there's one good thing to come of this, it's that I know I love you.'

The word had never been said between them. They'd been partners, musketeers, brothers-in-arms. Now love had been thrown down, like a gauntlet. One he could not pick up.

It was no comfort to either of them that, at last, he behaved as she would have done. He told her the truth, and not long after that, he left. Or at least, did not go back, for they had not been living together. Fled like a coward from her grief, and her passion and her tough integrity, knowing that she would never, ever, call him back. Knowing she'd shed blood and tears in private but never speak ill of him to another. They'd exchanged a couple of respectful, carefully-worded letters and that had been that.

He knew that Jude, of all people, would not have wanted his pity. Let alone his dutifulness. But he also sensed in himself a smallness of heart compared with her, and was ashamed of it. There had been no turning point, no single moment when he'd said: from here on I'm in charge. It had simply happened.

And now, Elvi had happened. As different from Jude as it was possible to be, but changing by the day. And with whom, he feared, he was in love. All the good he'd learned from Jude he was bringing to this new love, but the bad things, the shame and guilt, were fellow travellers, whispering in the shadows, telling him to beware.

So he was going to Florence. To further his career. To give both of them time to think. To distance himself from Elvi. That way, maybe, the love would die.

*   *   *

Alan was touched and surprised to find that Alec's dinner party was a strictly conventional affair. In spite of Alec's promise he had imagined the sort of evening at which he would spectate rather than participate.

Instead, he arrived at the mews cottage in Bayswater to find the other guests sipping white wine and conversing in a perfectly orderly manner.

The house was two knocked into one, with the sitting and dining area on the first floor. Alec had opened glass doors on to a little balcony and the warm dusty London evening was gold and grey outside, the roofs and chimneys assuming a Mary Poppins glow in the long low shafts of the invisibly sinking sun. The room was elegantly furnished and decorated, green with plants, and there were evidences of Alec's impeccable taste on every side – pictures, books, elegant art nouveau pieces. There was a delicious smell of cooking. Alec welcomed him warmly, looking handsome and relaxed in a batik shirt and white trousers – Alan felt hot and overdressed in his light suit. The other guests comprised a young married couple and a slightly older, single woman, introduced as Chloe Miller.

'And this is Simon and Rachel.' It was obvious that the older woman was intended as Alan's opposite number. However, before the meal, while Alec was in the kitchen, it was Rachel who engaged him in conversation.

'Do you work on Alec's paper?'

'No, I'm in industry.'

'Goodness, so it's you we look to for the nation's wealth!' She had a forthright, vivacious manner, a mass of frizzy hair and big round eyes made up with spiky painted lashes. Alan smiled.

'I wouldn't, if I were you, we might not be able to deliver.'

'What is your business?'

'We make plastic containers and tubing.'

'Heavens!' She batted her eyelids, eager to react but not quite sure how. Then something occurred to her. 'Do you export them?'

'Certainly. As a company, we've been doing very well recently, but then we're only a small concern, so we don't have many labour problems.'

'That must be a relief.' She was trying hard. Alan decided to rescue her. 'How about you? Do you have a family?'

'Goodness no, time enough for that. I work on the paper – Simon's a freelance cartoonist. So you see we're here to butter up the boss.'

She cast a look over her shoulder at Alex who was emerging from the kitchen with a tray.

'Talking about me?'

'I said Simon and I are on our best behaviour tonight so that you'll be nice to us and give me a rise and commission work from him.'

'That's right. We're a corrupt lot in publishing.'

'Still, it's not many bosses who'll entertain their junior editorial staff to dinner, and we love him for it.'

'Well!' Alec turned from the table and beamed. 'Now you can prove how much you love me by eating everything that's put in front of you.'

At the dining table, Alan was between Simon and Chloe, and since Alec seemed to be dominating the attentions of the other two he turned to the latter.

'Are you in the world of letters?'

'No, I'm a doctor.'

'General practice or hospital?'

'Hospital. I'm an obstetrician.' She had a pleasant, quiet manner, with the sort of well-cared-for, healthy good looks that were increasingly rare in London. She wore trousers and a long shirt of unbleached cotton, with a lace inset at the neck, and smooth wooden earrings. Her face was un-made-up, and had a calm beauty, her smooth brown hair pulled back into a thick coil on her neck. Her hands, which lay on her lap with the fingers loosely linked, were bony and strong-looking, but well-formed, with long, capable fingers. She wore no wedding ring. Her quiet and composure were striking. Alan glanced across at Rachel, so lively and effusive, her hands fluttering constantly, her head bobbing: and then back at the woman beside him. He found that she returned his look directly, and with a hint of a smile.

'You're wondering how I know Alec?'

'Something like that.'

'I might ask the same of you.'

'Your turn first,' he said.

'I met him at a publisher's party and he asked me to do a piece on antenatal care, which I was especially involved with at the time. We don't know each other well but we like each other. We're so opposite.'

'I can see that.'

'And you?'

'I've known him for donkey's years, but we hadn't seen each other for some time until recently.'

'What brought you together again?'

'I suppose you could call it idle curiosity. And, as you say, we like each other. It's a waste to let a friendship go.'

'You're right – oh my, look at that!' Alec had removed the pâté and placed on the table a moussaka, its golden crust crisp and bubbling, and a green salad gleaming and aromatic in a glass bowl. Alan was delighted at his friend's cleverness.

'Alec, this is a talent I never suspected.'

'No? I'm thinking of going into it full time! I enjoy it.'

'Actually,' said Rachel, 'I can see you as the proprietor of one of those chic bistros, with a rustic decor and inflated prices.'

'How nicely you put it, my love.' Alan noticed that the husband, Simon, had a Zapata moustache, surrounded by a baby-smooth, pink and white face and blue eyes as clear as a summer sky. Something about the pair of them touched him. He himself was so vulnerable, so emotional at the moment. The slightest thing, and he was felled by a rush of sentiment. At that instant he could have put a fatherly arm round each of them and given them his blessing and begged them to take care of each other.

Instead he remarked, watching Alec dish up steaming plate-fuls: 'You're serious about it?'

'Never more so. I'd adore to run a restaurant and do all the cooking myself. I like to entertain, I like to be surrounded by people, I like to be my own boss. What better?'

'I think it's a terrific idea,' said Simon. 'We seem to go to so many places these days that have lights, and music and ambience, but where the food's lousy.' This provoked another spasm of animated discussion on the other side of the table. Chloe Miller said to Alan: 'I don't know about you but I hardly ever eat out.'

'I do too much of it,' said Alan ruefully. 'I disapprove of expense-account lunches, but they're too firmly built in to the system to dislodge. The result is, I've turned into one of those boring men who go to a restaurant and pick at a plain omelette with spinach.'

'I think you're very wise.'

'Of course, you're a doctor, you're on my side.'

'Absolutely. But other people can't bear to see someone abstain while they're filling themselves full of all the wrong things. It makes them feel uncomfortable, so they jeer.'

'You've comforted me. I thought I was becoming a bit of an old woman about it.'

'Not at all. You keep up the good work. Alec, this is superb.' She ate with obvious gusto and enjoyment for a couple of minutes, and then said to Alan: 'You're not married, then?'

'No.'

'Interesting, isn't it,' she went on, in her matter-of-fact way, 'here we are, the five of us round this table, a fair cross-section wouldn't you say?'

'Positively motley.'

'And yet three of the five – the older ones – are not married. That must tell us something. Now I was ahead of my time, I never wanted to or I never met anyone with whom I could possibly have lived for the rest of my life. Alec's not in the game. And you – are you a bachelor by choice?'

'No.'

'I'm sorry, I was intrusive. It was thoughtless of me, let's drop it.'

'That's all right. But no, I've been married once and was recently about to try again. I have tried twice and failed. That must tell us something, too.'

'Only how terribly hard marriage is. It's not a convenience for the conventional but a challenge for the exceptional. I admire you. It's all right –' her hand touched his arm – 'don't tell me about it.'

'I must have "Bore" written all over me.'

'I didn't mean that.' She looked across the table at Simon. 'Simon, we were just saying what brave souls you and Rachel are to be launching into marriage.'

'Either that or foolhardy!' Simon laughed heartily.

'Do you think that?' She did not reflect his laugh.

'I don't know, do I? If people believed the statistics, no one would get married. It's the confidence that's born of ignorance which enables you to do it. Right?' His bright blue eyes flicked from Rachel to Alan and back. Alan nodded.

'Possibly.'

'You're *full* of confidence,' said Chloe.

'It's all done with mirrors!' He laughed.

'And we have one whole year's happy marriage to prove it!'

'What's all this about marriage?' Alec passed the wine bottle. 'I won't have loose talk in this house.'

'Tell me,' Alan said, 'Chloe tells me you met at a publisher's party. Was it your book?'

'Bless you no, I've never written a book in my life. And it wasn't hers either, though she has written them in her time.'

'Have you?' He turned to her. 'What, medical treatises?'

'Socio-medical, I think you'd call them.' She smiled self-deprecatingly. 'They weren't very startling.'

'But it must be satisfying to see yourself between hard covers,' said Alec, 'it must be like having a baby, producing something that's all your own. It's how I feel about the perfect soufflé . . .'

The conversation drifted on to a more general and frivolous plane, with Alec holding the floor. He was in his element, thought Alan, he needs people to respond, to reflect his brilliance, to laugh at his jokes, and then he's incomparable. But what's he like when he's on his own? Quiet, methodical, even rather prim, maintaining his ordered and elegant household, sustaining himself on his own image as reflected in his surroundings. How could he possibly understand about Elvi? Suddenly Alan's mind was crowded with images of her, her face filled his vision, and her voice was in his ears.

'Don't go quiet on us, Alan.' It was Alec. 'It's not allowed.'

'Sorry.'

Surprisingly, Rachel said: 'People should be quiet if they want to be. If they've got nothing to say, I mean. I consider it one of my big failings that I can't do it!' She giggled but her remark had been so obviously well-intentioned that Alan smiled at her.

Chloe said: 'Yes, Alec, don't be bossy. You won't be able to tell people in your restaurant to be vivacious to order, you know. You'll have to put up with sulking wives and bad-tempered husbands, and tongue-tied lovers.'

'Never!' Alec was determined not to be serious. 'My restaurant will be crammed with beautiful, witty, voluble people.'

'Like paid mourners at a gangster funeral,' said Rachel.

'Not at all, the glitterati will be drawn to my establishment like moths to a flame.'

When dinner – which finished with sorbet and a ripe brie – was over, Alec put on Miles Davis and they sat in the darkening room, half-listening, half-conversing. The atmosphere grew calmer, even tranquil, talk was desultory and Alan relapsed into silence, content to sit and watch the bruise of evening spread across the city skyline. The music was haunting – Alan felt for the first time relaxed, but the sadness in the music called to the sadness in him and he found himself wondering what Elvi was doing at this moment. Was she alone – asleep, perhaps, in that child's room of hers? Or was she with him? He pictured again the young man he had seen – the thin, angular frame, the dark face with something intense about it; that brilliant gift of a smile. His youth and his independence frightened Alan. He himself had offered Elvi all his love, all his ability and support and protection, because he desired so much to keep her. This young man had won her easily, as of right. What if he hurt her, deserted her?

Alan put his hands over his eyes and pressed, trying to clear his mind of the painful images.

'Tired?' Chloe asked.

'Not really, lost in thought.'

'It's good to do that sometimes.'

'Yes.' He smiled at her. Her face was a pale blur in the gathering dusk of the room. Alec had lit no lamps and only the few remaining floating candles on the table gave off their small firefly light.

'I think I must be going,' he said flatly, without moving.

'Please don't,' said Alec. 'Why do you have to?'

'It's time . . .' He shrugged and smiled apologetically, better to be honest.

'Very well.' Alec got up, and as he did so Chloe rose too.

'Which way are you going?'

'Kensington. It doesn't matter which way, there won't be much traffic at this time of night.'

'Could I beg a lift to Holland Park?'

'Of course.' Alan made his farewells to Rachel and Simon and went downstairs accompanied by Alec. Chloe joined them, having collected a bright fringed silk shawl from the bedroom. The three of them stood by the front door. Alan was conscious of a little frisson of expectancy.

'Well, thank you for a delightful evening.' Chloe stepped forward and laid her cheek momentarily against Alec's. 'You're a wonderful host.'

'I second that,' said Alan. 'Many thanks. I couldn't possibly offer to reciprocate, but perhaps you'll let me buy you a meal some time?'

'I might. Good night, be good children.' Alec stood in the doorway and watched as they got into the Mercedes. With the light behind him he looks like a boy of eighteen, thought Alan, not without envy, and he has won by sheer spirit and effort his unassailable right to be himself and live his life in his own way. As they moved off he raised his hand in a wave that was like a salute.

'Alec's so great.' Chloe seemed to have read his thoughts. 'People like him are an ornament to life.'

'Yes – and more than that.'

'He means a lot to you?' She was looking straight ahead, wrapped close in her shawl, but her quiet question seemed to carry an extra dimension.

'There's no sexual attachment, if that's what you mean.'

'Emotional?'

'I'm old-fashioned, in my case the two have to go together. He's a good friend. I'm involved with him to that extent, I admire him and respect him. But when I didn't see him for years I didn't miss him.'

'You were busy working at marriage.'

'That's right.' Her remark had been without sarcasm. He felt at that moment as though he could have told her anything, her calmness and quiet were like an empty slate that invited writing. He glanced at her. Her profile had the passive regularity of a coin against the fleeting lights and movements of the Bayswater Road.

'Drop me opposite the tube station,' she said, and he looked away quickly, embarrassed that she had felt his eyes on her, They drove on in silence until he pulled the car in to the kerb opposite Holland Park station. She put her hand on the handle and said: 'I live right here in Holland Park Avenue. Can I persuade you to come in for a while?'

'Thank you, no. I think I've had enough to eat and drink for one night.'

'That's not what I was offering.' Her voice was perfectly even and matter of fact. Alan was taken aback.

'I'm sorry . . . I didn't realize. No, I think I must get back.'

'Why? It would be nice. I should like you to come.'

'It's not that I wouldn't—'

'Then why not? Accept the hospitality.'

'I just don't think I could. My heart, if you like, would not be in it.'

'I don't ask for your heart. Just you. For one night. As a friendly gesture.' Quietly and deliberately she leaned across and kissed him on the mouth. No other part of her touched him and yet the directness of her kiss was like the most rapacious of sexual assaults. She lifted her mouth from his and laid her cheek against his face. Her skin was cool and she smelt clean and fresh, like new bread. He could sense the slight tilt and weight of her body leaning towards and just over his but no touching. He could just feel the brush of her eyelash on his cheek bone. When he lifted his hand slightly it met the smooth cradle of her left breast and yielded minutely, her body coming fractionally towards him, her nipple starting into his palm like a bud in spring. At the same moment he felt a touch, light but firm between his legs, but with his complete arousal came a violent revulsion. He struck at her hand and leaned forward, knocking her sharply to one side, leaning his head on the steering wheel. He was trembling with excitement and nausea.

'Please don't,' he said and his voice didn't sound like his own but shamingly hoarse and pleading. 'Don't.'

'I'm sorry.' There was no anger or bitterness in her voice. 'I'll go now. Perhaps we'll meet again.'

He listened to the rustle of her clothes, the click of the car door as it opened and the thud as it closed. He did not speak, he could not look at her. But the window was open, and she leaned down to it.

'Why are you so guilty?' she asked coolly.

He shook his head, rolling it against his clasped hands on the wheel. 'I don't have to tell you,' he said, knowing what he meant but realizing it sounded childish.

'No, you don't. But I'd like to be your friend, so that you would.'

'No.'

'I said, your friend.' She waited for a moment, her words hung in the air between them, but he did not answer. Finally

179

she straightened up and walked away, quite quickly, her head held high. Not until she had rounded the corner and disappeared from view did Alan sit back, and the face he saw in the car mirror was like a caricature of his own, the lines scored in harshly, the eyes deep-set and staring. God knows how much he had wanted her and yet his gorge had risen at the directness of her invitation.

'Oh Elvi,' he whispered, 'Elvi, why did you go?'

Thirteen

Callum stood on the Ponte Vecchio and felt the heat lying over him like a shimmering golden net under which he and the others thronging the bridge were like so many teeming, suffocating small fish. He had never experienced heat like it, and yet they said it would grow hotter still in the next two months.

He moved to walk between the small shops to the parapet and the few steps made sweat burst out all over him. The River Arno had shrunk to an oily stream slithering down the centre of the broad, yellow riverbed, moist in the middle, cracked and dusty towards the edges. On either side Florence lay, sunbaked and lethargic, trembling in the heat, all its colours bleached ochre, yellow and dust-white in the sun. And like one great procession the people moved round it, shuffling endlessly through its art galleries and churches and museums, meandering through the streets. How many of them, Callum wondered, were dying to get to the beach and the sea, or to the countryside? Go out of the city a little way and you began to climb up tall tawny hills, barred by the cool black shadows of cypresses. There, you were above the worst of the heat, you could look down on the domes and spires of Florence with a warm wind blowing in your face and see how low-lying it was, how trapped in its valley, sweltering and airless.

Callum moved back from the parapet and began, very slowly, to make his way back towards Donati's apartment on the hillside south of the river. As he came off the bridge and halted at the busy road he bought himself a craggy pink *gelato* from a stall on the corner, strategically placed to catch pedestrians at the traffic lights. The ice cream was superb.

Callum experienced again the sheer childish bliss of that coldness melting on his tongue, the knowledge that, even for a few minutes, he could keep the heat at bay. His whole attention was concentrated on the *gelato*, he looked neither to right nor left but licked rapturously and then munched the crisp cone. At once, as soon as it was finished, he was hotter than ever and his fingers felt unpleasantly sticky. He thought, I'll have a cool wash when I get back. He began to walk fast and by the time he reached the side road leading to Donati's address he was wet with sweat. He let himself in and went up the black and white flecked tile staircase to the first floor.

Inside the apartment it was dark and cool, blissfully cool. Since arriving there a week before Callum had felt most keenly the difference in the approaches of the Englishman and the Italian to the sun. In England, where intense sunshine was a real bonus, people exposed themselves to it with ruthless determination, flying their doors and windows wide and allowing it to permeate every corner of their lives. Here, where the heat was a daily, inescapable, humdrum fact, indoors was a place of shade and enclosure, of heavy shutters and green plants and cold stone floors. Donati's apartment was like a grotto or oasis, with an air of womb-like secrecy. In the hallway, a fan on the ceiling turned steadily, brushing the air into soft eddies that cooled the perspiration on Callum's face.

Dawn, Donati's American girl Friday, appeared in the doorway of the drawing room. From her name, and from something in Donati's reference to her in his letter, Callum had pictured her as a smart, middle-aged matron, a product of the American matriarchal society. In fact, she had turned out to be a divorcee of about thirty, slim, gamine and attractive, with that kind of frighteningly intense intelligence that Americans often had. She flitted about Donati's apartment like a nymph, barefooted, her long, straight, rather wispy hair floating about her face in the breeze from the fans. Her working uniform consisted of bleached and frayed Bermudas and a skimpy halter top that barely covered her boyish torso. But her waif-like appearance and vague manner hid a steely competence. She

182

protected Donati like a tigress and nursed him and his novel like a midwife cosseting an expectant mother. Now she leaned the point of her shoulder on the door jam and crossed one leg over the other.

'You've been at it again, haven't you?' she said.

'At what?'

'Running around in the midday sun.'

'Yes . . .' he smiled ruefully. 'It's ridiculous. I can't shake off my British habit of taking constitutionals. All that sun out there, and I can't seem to get used to it.'

'You'll settle down. Here, come and have a drink.' She led the way to the kitchen. It was big and old-fashioned, with an absolute minimum of furnishings – an old three-ring gas cooker, a couple of cupboards, a hideous formica-topped table and chairs. The floor was littered with piles of old papers, boxes of books, baskets of fruit and vegetables and various other impedimenta, most of which had no rightful place in a kitchen. Dawn went to the small fridge which rattled restlessly in one corner. Donati's cat, Portia, was sitting on top of it, her paws curled beneath her breast. She was a long-haired tabby of arrogant and voluptuous beauty, but Dawn swept her off unceremoniously. The cat walked away stiffly, stretching each hind leg behind it in turn as if to prove that it was not to be hurried.

'Damn cat,' Dawn observed in her soft voice. She brought forth a bottle of iced water and poured Callum a drink. She leaned on her hands on the table, watching him.

'Is it how you expected it to be?' she asked.

'What, precisely?'

'Everything. Us. Him.' She jerked her head in the general direction of Donati's study.

'I don't think I expected anything. I had no preconceptions. He certainly works hard.'

'Sure does. You're very privileged, you know.'

'I realize that.'

'I've never known him so much as answer a question on the telephone before. You must have made one hell of an impression on him.'

183

Callum shrugged. 'I suppose so. I hope to God I can live up to it. Do him justice.'

'So do we all.' She grinned broadly to take any sting out of her words.

'How do you think I'm doing?' He genuinely wanted to know, he felt desperately unconfident and insecure.

'He likes you. He doesn't mind having you around. And believe me that's one hundred per cent better than anyone else has done. I'd call it a great start.'

'Any tips? Do I ask him too much?'

'He'd tell you if you did. He's perfectly straightforward, you know, there's no side to him whatsoever. Accept him at his face value and you'll do great.'

'I can't get over this feeling of being in the presence of a Great Man. It does nothing for my confidence.'

'Don't go under. Hey –' she got up, brushing her palms together busily – 'I have work to do. He'll be out in a minute, it's almost four o'clock.'

Dawn always seemed to know the time, though she never wore a watch. She left the room and Callum found himself alone save for Portia, who had taken up a position on the broad window sill between the Venetian blind and the glass, so that her tiger-striped silhouette appeared to be suspended in space.

Right on cue he heard the door of the study open and Donati crossed the corridor and went in to the drawing room. He always went first to Dawn when he finished work in the afternoon, gave her the pages to type and conferred with her on the answering of any mail that had arrived since lunch. Then he customarily drifted in to the kitchen in search of cheese, fruit, cold meat, even dry bread if there was nothing else, to satisfy the colossal appetite he'd worked up.

As he entered, Portia slithered round the side of the blind and ran across to him with a 'prroop!' of recognition.

'Hallo there,' he said to Callum, with that faint note of surprise in his voice which had not diminished in the seven days since he had been there. He opened one of the cupboards and discovered a chunk of salami on a saucer. This he peeled, taking care to keep the skin in one piece like a ringlet, and then tucked in with gusto, standing with the saucer held beneath his chin as if to catch crumbs.

He was a chunky, sturdily built man in his forties, with the powerful torso and short legs of a rugby player. His thick, frizzy brown hair stuck out all over his head as though galvanized by some permanent electric shock. His face was square-jawed and rugged. His blue eyes were set wide apart and, lizard-like, seldom blinked.

He did not speak again until he had finished the salami.

'Shall we have our talk now?' He was always scrupulously correct, never forgot their agreed routine. Indeed it was one of the things Callum found most disconcerting in their relationship. It was as though by adhering so rigorously to a pattern, Donati was excluding him from the rest of the day, saying: 'This is your portion, take it, and leave me with mine.' But he could not complain, the man was being more than generous. He followed him into the drawing room. This was where Donati preferred to sit, although their conversation had to compete with the rapid, intermittent fire of Dawn's typing. Callum suspected that Dawn had made herself so indispensable to the writer that he actually felt safer in her presence.

Their evolved pattern was for Donati to say what he had been doing that day – Callum read the work when Dawn had typed it – and then to enlarge on any problems or revelations that had sprung from it. He was always explicit, frank, voluble. But again his very forthrightness seemed to rob Callum of initiative. His voice, which was deep and resonant, rolled mesmerically on and Callum dutifully took notes. The writing had gone reasonably well, the characters had looked after themselves as he put it, the pages had got filled and the required development of the plot had been managed. He was a systematic writer, sometimes amazing Callum with his workaday approach. He began with a detailed synopsis, broken up into sections and chapters, and stuck rigidly to this while writing. What he put before Dawn at four o'clock each afternoon was the finished product – he re-read it in its typed form, and then again in galleys and page proofs, but rarely made any but the minutest alterations.

Callum had asked him about this: 'You must have tremendous confidence in your ability to get things right first time – don't you feel the need to rewrite?'

'I don't let myself. I don't like writing. I like ideas, playing with words and concepts in my mind, conjuring up scenes. But covering the paper is a chore and nothing more. If I wasn't rigidly disciplined about it I'd never do it at all. As it is, I do the best I can on the day – by "best" I mean closest to what I had in mind – and say goodbye to it thankfully.'

'And have you ever been dissatisfied later on?'

'Not really. I seldom read my books once they're out, and until then I'm still seeing them as I want to. I may be arrogant and vain. I prefer to think of myself as a realist.'

Donati always sat in the same white-painted wicker armchair, with legs crossed, and his hands linked behind his head, gazing at the ceiling. He was unfailingly accurate and honest in his replies, but try as he might Callum could not alter what was basically an interview and make it a conversation.

At about five Donati would disappear and take a shower and Callum would read the pages he'd written that day. This exercise filled him with an unfailing sense of excitement, it was like witnessing a birth to hold those fresh, crisp, newly written pages in his hands, and to compare them with the handwritten ones of an hour before. The latter were written on narrow-lined foolscap in the sort of immaculate, tiny handwriting he associated with accountants. So neat were they that Callum had felt prompted on one occasion to ask Dawn whether they actually needed typing.

'Two reasons,' she'd replied. 'One, we need copies and there's no machine here. Two, he doesn't spell very well.'

'Away with you.'

'No, really, he has blind spots about certain letters and formations. It's not a problem I have, so I correct as I go along.'

'Does he realize he makes spelling mistakes?'

'No, I don't think so.'

Callum was amazed. 'But he could go his whole life not being able to spell! It's ridiculous, he's not a child.'

Dawn had shrugged. 'You tell him.'

Callum saw what she meant.

It was in the evenings that he thought most of Elvi. Donati, ever a creature of habit and not one to allow visitors to break those habits, would go out for his evening meal. On the first night, he had asked Callum along, since then he had not done so. Dawn usually went at the same time – she shared a small modern apartment with another American girl on the other side of the city. Sometimes she walked, sometimes she hitched a lift part of the way on the back of Donati's yellow Lambretta. This machine was his pride and joy and some of the most relaxed conversation between Callum and himself had taken place over and about it. It was, he claimed, his concession to the male menopause. On it he felt like one of the Italian youths who scooted about the city, bare-chested and tight-jeaned, with the obligatory cool girlfriend, perched with dangerous languor, side-saddle on the back. The Lambretta was ridden with a maximum of sang froid and the minimum of due care and attention, one of its chief purposes being to impress upon both passenger and pedestrian the devil-may-care attitude of its driver. Thus they would speed away from the kerb at a sickening angle, Dawn's mermaid hair flying and whipping in the slipstream, one thin brown arm hooked around Donati's waist. Their attitude to each other, Callum observed, was one of totally asexual professional regard. Donati was one of the few men he had met who actually was able to treat a woman like a man, or at least no differently from anyone else.

Callum would be deserted for a couple of hours. Sometimes it was much less, never longer. It was the only time of the day when he had absolutely no access to the writer. He was allowed at all times to wander in and out of the study when Donati was at work, to watch, make notes, listen to comments and even ask questions. But this period between seven and nine was sacrosanct. It had never been officially declared so, and yet Donati might have departed to another planet for all Callum knew of his whereabouts. At nine o'clock he would reappear, always in expansive form, and from then until he chose to go to bed he would be excellent company. But there was no more talk of writing. He had a schoolboy sense of humour which, according to his own mood, Callum found either hilarious or exhausting.

But between seven and nine Callum thought of Elvi. Her memory persisted and grew clearer and more alluring. Each day that he spent without her made her image more distinct, it was there in the back of his mind all the time, like a cool, pale lily in a dark place amid the heat and dust of Florence in the summer. He had only to close his eyes to feel the smooth freshness of her skin against his, to picture her face as he had last seen it, pale and sad and beautiful. All the things she had said, the things they had done, came flooding back with an agonizing pathos. He felt her absence, the distance between them, more keenly than he would have imagined possible.

The story on Donati was progressing, he was collecting material, and in other circumstances and in other times he would have found it wholly absorbing, fascinating. But, he had to admit, his heart was not in it. He watched Donati from a distance, he observed his behaviour and his work as though looking in through a closed window. He felt uninvolved, and this frightened and depressed him. The article would be no good unless it had something of himself in it – it would just be a hollow, empty catalogue of observations and facts, with no life or colour. Simply, he missed Elvi. She had, with his barely noticing, become an indispensable part of his life. He was crippled without her.

He wrote to her, but the things he wanted to say remained unsaid. After all, hadn't he wanted to put distance between them, to play for time, to postpone commitment? He had to give it time, to let things ride, at least for a while. He was bound to miss her most to begin with, and he had barely started on the work yet. It would come.

When Callum's first letter arrived, about ten days after his departure, Elvi kept it all day in her bag and did not read it until she was able to sit down on the lawn in the evening sunshine and do so at leisure. She hoped, by this massive exercise in self-control, to dampen and suppress any expectations she might have concerning the letter. As it was, her hands shook as she tore open the envelope and she read the first page so fast that she had to go back to the beginning to take it in.

My love – Here I am then, and there you are, are we quite mad? But I don't want to go all over that ground again, it will make us both hurt. I'll tell you what it's like here. First of all, it's unbelievably hot, the city swelters in a yellow haze all day and it's in a kind of basin so there's no relief unless you climb the hills that are all round, which I do sometimes, just to feel a wind on my face. But Florence is beautiful and so packed with superb architecture and sculpture and pictures that you simply can't take it in. I went to the Uffizi gallery but you have to trail round with a long crocodile of sightseers and it was so unbearably airless I couldn't enjoy the paintings. I have realized how much I am adapted to those soft Scottish mists, and those gentle, grey-blue days when the rain just hangs in the air like a fine curtain. Never complain about the British climate, Elvi, you can have no idea how I crave its infinite variety! Anyway, I am beginning to understand how to live with the heat: I stay in in the middle of the day, I don't worry about getting a tan or seeing the sights, or anything in fact except doing what I have to do. On that score, things seem to be going fairly well. It's a strange *ménage* here, I can tell you. There's the Great Man, who looks and behaves more like a professional sportsman, but I must say he's being extremely accommodating. There's Dawn Oppenshaw,

189

his assistant, who corrects his spelling mistakes and has generally made herself indispensable. And yours truly, trying to discover a niche for myself and feeling a bit self-conscious. And Portia, who's a cat but who deserves a mention by virtue of her beauty. The apartment is dark and mercifully cool, but not at all smart or luxurious. The kitchen is barely furnished at all and has an unused and unappreciated feel which you would hate. Those are his priorities, I suppose. His eating habits are more like refuelling operations, I don't think he cares in the least about food except to stoke up. He grabs a bit at about ten in the morning and then again at about four – and I do mean 'grabs' – and then he eats out every evening. That's when I creep into the kitchen and cook spaghetti and eat too many fresh peaches – the fruit here is like something out of one of those Rubens Bacchanals.

I was frankly homesick to begin with, I never realized I was so lacking in a spirit of adventure. But then there is no you here, and that is the worst part of it. I sometimes worry that you're miserable and lonely and then I curse myself for being conceited, so I hope you're carefree and happy. But really I hope you're lonely and miserable.

I don't know how much time I shall have to write letters, all my spare time and energy goes into writing up my notes, and I found even this letter strangely difficult and unsatisfactory which is why it's so short. I cannot say how things will turn out. Miss me but don't wait around, Elvi. We men always say, 'I'm not worth it', but in my case it's true. Callum.

Elvi read the letter twice, the second time with tears trickling down her face. It was the thin end of the wedge, then. He using this trip as an escape, but if so, why? She felt the sudden change of mood and style in the final paragraph like a body blow. It was clear he had braced himself, squared his shoulders and written it in that way quite deliberately. It had been added later than the rest, it was in darker ink. Whatever had passed through his mind between the end of the previous paragraph and the writing of that?

His evasions hurt her more than anything. She would have valued directness and the truth, no matter how painful. But he seemed hell bent on shutting her out and locking the door. She recalled his occasional odd moods of bitterness and harshness, apparently so uncharacteristic. The shadow of something unspoken had fallen across them then but she had not had the courage to lay hold of it and bring it into the open. Or he had not had the courage. She could not understand this in him – that he made such a virtue of directness, of truthfulness, of not being wasteful in his day-to-day dealings, and yet there was something in his life with such power over him that it reduced him to panic and deceit, even cruelty, she reflected looking back on those other occasions.

She tore the letter up and threw it away, but the words of that final paragraph were stamped on her memory – she could not restore her peace of mind.

She did not answer the letter, but a few days later tried to phone him. She was amazed at her own bravado, but it seemed the only feasible course of action. The speed and clarity with which she received an answer unnerved her slightly, it had not given her time to compose her thoughts. The voice on the other end of the line was clear, young, female and American.

'Hallo?'

'Hallo? Is that Paul Donati's apartment?'

'Who is that speaking, please?' Whoever it was was instantly on the defensive.

'Oh, he doesn't know me. Actually, I wondered if I could speak to Callum Sheil, who I believe is staying there at the moment.'

'Hold the line a moment, please.' There was a sudden hush as the American girl put her hand over the receiver. A full minute elapsed before she spoke again.

'I'm sorry – who did you say it was calling?'

191

Elvi felt a tide of panic rising inside her. 'I didn't – my name's Elvi Beecham.'

'One more moment, please.' There was another stifled hush. Elvi could have screamed with frustration and annoyance. 'Hallo? Hallo?' she snapped impatiently, but the silence was heavy on the other end.

At last: 'Hallo? Miss Beecham? Sorry to keep you. No, I'm sorry Mr Sheil is not available at the moment.'

'Why not?'

'He's with Mr Donati just now.'

'Look, I am calling from England. Couldn't he come to the phone for one minute?'

'I'm afraid not.' The girl's cool was unshakeable, there was a note of practised, polite regret in her voice which incensed Elvi still more.

'This is ludicrous,' she said. 'I wouldn't have called unless I most particularly wanted to speak to him.'

'Of course not. I'm sorry.'

It was clearly hopeless to expect any change on this front. Elvi took a deep breath and enquired: 'Can he call me back, then?'

'I'll give him a message, certainly.'

'And ask him to call back,' Elvi insisted. Something evasive in the girl's manner bothered her.

'I'll tell him you called.'

'Very well.' Elvi rang off, and sat by the phone shaking with anger and anxiety. In that moment she seriously contemplated ringing the airport and booking herself a flight out to Italy. But this impulse was followed by a draining of the adrenalin which left her desolate. She felt as though she had run headlong into what she had thought would be a welcoming room, only to find it protected by a sheet of thick, invisible glass.

She went out to the kitchen where the Major was sitting at the table looking at some estate agents' leaflets which had arrived that morning. He had begun in rather a desultory way to organize the sale of the house. Elvi knew it was part of his self-education towards a life without her, and she found it at once heart-rending and irritating. He had been painfully discreet about the whole thing and yet she was always coming upon evidences of it and she saw them as a reproach and a mockery.

After all, where was she to go? The future looked uncertain and unfriendly, the supreme happiness of the past few weeks had taken on the over-lit quality of things remembered.

'Well?' she asked, almost briskly. 'Anything there?'

'Oh, I'm only looking, you know.' He smiled up at her and spread his well-shaped, old man's hands over the papers on the table.

'Yes, but is there anything nice?' She did not want to be fobbed off by him as well. 'There's no point in just looking.'

'I don't know . . .' He moved the leaflets about with his finger tips. 'I suppose I'm not altogether sure what I'm looking for.'

'No.' She sat down opposite him, and peremptorily pulled the sheets over, glancing over them unseeingly. 'That's because the sort of house you really want is here.'

'I think it's time to move on,' he said gently, gazing out of the window. 'This is far too big, especially now.'

'When I go, you mean?'

'Not entirely, it's really too big for the two of us, as things are. I should have wanted to move anyway, when you got married.'

'Yes.' She realized she had been cruel, but self-dislike prevented her from backing down. Her father rose painfully from his chair and went over to the window. He stood there, looking out over the garden, his hands resting on the curve of his stick, one on top of the other in a prayerful attitude.

'I shall miss the garden, of course,' he said, and Elvi realized that he was talking to himself as much as to her. 'But then if I had a smaller garden I could do it all myself, and that would be more satisfying.'

'*Could* you do it all yourself?'

'I think so. It does us old sticks good to keep moving, you know. This –' he patted his hip – 'is always better in the summer when I'm out more, doing things about the place and walking. The same goes for the house. It's quite ridiculous to have to get Mrs Dix to come here when you're away. If the house was compact and manageable there'd be no need.'

'We asked her to come the last time because your hip was bad,' Elvi reminded him. 'Living in a matchbox isn't going to alter that.'

'Elvi –' he turned and looked at her directly, and there was something of his old natural authority in his face – 'what are you trying to do?' She shrugged, miserable and discomforted. 'Exactly. All this –' he indicated the paper on the table – 'it's something that has to happen. It's the practical, economical, intelligent thing to do. So please stop trying to dissuade me. You have your life to think of. Busy yourself with it, attack your problems. I should be much happier to think that you were doing that.'

'I'm sorry.' She covered her face with her hands, pressing her fingers over her eyeballs. 'I just hope it's not hurting you too much.'

'I think,' he said and she felt his hand on her shoulder, 'I think it's you who is hurting, my dear. And, to be purely practical, you must remember that I haven't always lived at the Beeches. I was a career soldier for all those years. I am not, as you appear to think, going to shrivel up and die if I have to live in a more confined space. In fact I think I should rather like to have one of those pin-neat bungalows, with flowerbeds at the front and lawn at the back, it would appeal to my sense of order.'

'Perhaps.'

'Just now – were you trying to ring your young man?' She nodded.

'And you couldn't get through?'

'He was busy . . . he couldn't talk.'

'I see. Don't worry. Don't let so much depend on him. Get on with your life.'

'He is my life, everything depends on him.'

As she said it she realized for the first time how true she had let it become. But at the same time she knew how she sounded to her father – young, blind, pigheaded. But all he said was: 'Better luck next time.'

That night when she went to bed she took out Alan's photograph and studied it. She was unsentimental, detached. It was as though she were searching for something that she might have missed. It was odd, she reflected, how soon a face that had once been familiar – and beloved too – became the face of a stranger. She tried to recall his voice, but that was hard. And yet Callum was so clear in her mind as to be almost with her – not just the sight and sound of him, but the feel, the texture, even the smell of his hair, the look of his eyes. She bent her head on to the photograph, her face twisted as though crying, but dry-eyed.

The effort of attending the nursery school the following morning was tremendous, but as always the children drew her out of herself, and the need to respond to them, answer their questions, stimulate their interest, effectively prevented her from brooding. Also as usual, Mrs Maynard quizzed her about her arrangements for the autumn, and tut-tutted over her apathy in that department.

'You realize you're probably too late to begin in September now?'

'Yes, I realize that.'

'It's such a *waste*, what are you going to do with yourself?'

'There are more important things I have to sort out.'

'Oh!' Mrs Maynard made an impatient gesture. 'In my opinion those things are better left to sort themselves, and they're more likely to if you get on with the job.'

'What's the matter with this job?' Elvi smiled at her.

'Trick question. You know I'm delighted to have you here, you're worth your weight in gold, but I'm not so selfish as to want you to doddle along here for ever.'

'Not for ever.'

'Even another year. Apart from anything else, no one could call it well-paid. Look at us –' they were sitting over cheese rolls and coffee preparing collage material for the afternoon session – 'slogging away like long-term prisoners, and for what?'

'For love?'

'Peanuts.'

'Well.' Elvi got up and went to pour herself more coffee. 'I think I might go abroad in the summer, how's that for initiative?'

'I'm told lots of people do.'

'Ah, but not me. I must be the only twenty-year-old in Britain who's never been out of these islands. I thought I'd try Italy.' As she spoke she realized that it was a possibility, though one that she had never seriously entertained until that moment.

'By yourself?' asked Mrs Maynard dubiously.

'I know one or two people out there,' replied Elvi airily.

About a week later, though she had not written herself, she received another letter from Callum. It was newsy, amusing – impersonal. It was only in the last paragraph that he wrote:

> . . . By the way, why did you ring up? Please don't, I can't chat on the phone here, there's too much to do and I can't ditch Donati if he's in the middle of something really interesting. Please understand. How are your arrangements going? I do so hope you're not neglecting your plans . . .

This time, there was no doubt. The handwriting was swift, sure, legible, the message as irrefutable as a legal document. Elvi felt her spirit flinch and shrink from the harshness of the blow. She wrote back, one black paragraph on the plain white sheet:

> . . . I shall not write again, I see what you are trying to

say. But whether you like it or not I shall be here when you get back. More than anything I wish you hadn't tricked me. I love you. Elvi.

Fourteen

'So what's the next move? asked Cavendish, in his most annoying, thrusting manner.

'The next move,' Alan said, 'is for you to persuade that shiftless lot of yours to meet the orders.'

'I'm afraid the backlog—'

'Must be cleared,' said Alan tersely, and rose from his desk. Cavendish delayed a split second before rising too, it was to show that he was not a fawner.

'I'll do my best,' he said, 'but I think we need some leeway on this.'

'Look.' Alan felt his impatience growing dangerously – Cavendish always brought out the worst in him. 'We've *had* leeway. Always looking for an extension is simply the primrose path. I've spoken to David Conway and he's in an extremely embarrassing and invidious position – he's worked his guts out getting the orders, trailing round the country drumming up business. How do you think he feels when he can't deliver? My sympathies are with him. This company has a good record, let's keep it like that.'

'Certainly, of course . . .'

'Thank you.' Alan opened the door for him. Cavendish swept out, past someone who was waiting in the outer office. Alan was so choked with irritation that he shut the door again at once, although his secretary was half-rising from her desk to attract his attention. Then, realizing he had been rude, he opened the door again.

'I'm sorry—'

It was Elvi. He stood back to let her enter and they faced each other.

'You were the last person I expected to see. I'm sorry.'

'That's all right. When you shut the door again so firmly I thought for a moment—'

'Good heavens, no. Please forgive me. Sit down.'

He sounds stiff and formal, thought Elvi. It occurred to her that he was actually shy of her.

'I hope you'll forgive me for turning up like this,' she said.

'Forgive? I should think so.' He pulled a chair up for her and went and picked up cigarettes and lighter off his desk. For the first time, as she watched him light a cigarette and draw deeply, she saw it as a defence activity, a play for time.

'I wish you'd give that up,' she said.

'I should, I know. It's difficult.'

'Easy for me to say, eh?'

'No, you're quite right, it's a dirty, dangerous habit. One of these days I will. Till then . . .' He shrugged and came round to perch on the edge of his desk. He was studiously avoiding meeting her eyes.

'Why did you come?' he asked, studying the carpet.

'I wanted to see you. You said you'd be there if I needed you.'

'Yes.'

'I need you now,' she said simply.

'Tell me.'

'I'm afraid you'll think I'm using you. And, I suppose, I am in a way.'

'If I can be of use, go ahead and use me.'

'I need a friend. Someone to talk to, who won't criticize or judge me. Somebody who loves me enough to understand what I really want.'

'You're asking a lot.' There was pain in his eyes as he rose and went over to stand with his back to her at the window.

'Am I?'

'If you think that I'm saintly enough to act as agony aunt—'

'Friend was the word I used.'

'All right, all right, but we both know what you mean. Things are sticky between you and Mr Wonderful, so it's back to good old Alan.'

'If that's how you want to put it.' Her voice was quiet and composed. Alan turned to look at her in amazement. She had changed utterly. She had found the confidence to demand his help and attention, she had weighed the pros and cons and come to him quite openly, risking his bitterness and anger, relying on his love. Now she sat there, calm and still, looking back at him with a kind of challenge in her eyes. But there was tenderness, too, she was testing what she knew to be his strength, his loyalty and honesty. She was asking him to prove it to her.

'Very well,' he said.

She told him about Callum, about his departure and the subsequent letters. She spoke in a soft monotone, merely recounting events, her fingers playing always with a copper necklace she wore, one Alan did not remember. He listened, and tried to picture the young man he had seen. What sort of person was he? Why would he – how could he – be so casual towards Elvi?

She finished with her first and only comment on her own feelings: 'I just wish there was no mystery.'

'You feel there is one?'

'He's scared of something.'

'Of over-committing himself, probably. I'm told it's quite common.'

'He's not like that. He's a person who is very much in control of his life, his behaviour . . . he sets great store by giving things their proper value. But there is one thing in his life which causes him to be evasive and selfish. And as I don't know what it is I have to suffer the consequences without the means of reply.'

'A secret is a useful weapon.'

She ignored this. 'I don't know . . . I can't help feeling that it's his reaction rather than the thing itself which is the weakness.'

At this moment there was a knock at the door and Alan's secretary entered with a handful of mail. She glanced at Elvi and asked: 'Would you like to me to send Sandra out for some sandwiches, Mr Neilson?'

'Elvi, what were your plans? I was going to stay in this lunch hour, but we can go out if you'd like.'

'Thank you. Count me in on the sandwiches.'

'A few rounds of this and that. Sandra knows.'

'Very well, sir.'

When the secretary had left, Elvi said: 'I'm keeping you from your work.'

'Yes, you are, but I've weighed that up. I have to go out at two, anyway. Are you staying in town?'

'No.'

'Could you come up at the weekend and we could have some dinner?'

'Yes, I'd like to.' She hesitated, and then said: 'It must have been strange – seeing us together.'

'It was, like watching someone through a two-way mirror.'

'And?'

'What?'

'And what did you think? Did you hate him very much?' Alan sensed in her question a quite irrational desire for his approval, coupled with the fear that it could never be given. He tried hard to be truthful, yet not to hurt.

'You must understand he's a stranger to me. And a stranger who robbed me of what I cared for most in life. That said, he looked – personable, young, he had a pleasant smile. But none of those are qualifications in themselves for so easily winning you. I rest my case.'

'Thank you.'

'For what?'

'For being reasonable – and honest. You can't know how much that means to me.'

'I don't suppose –' he put his hand on to the window in front of him and spread the fingers like a star – 'that it means enough.'

201

'No.' Her voice was very quiet. 'Not now. Not yet.'

Sandra, the typist, appeared with the sandwiches. She looked awkward and embarrassed. It was obvious to both Alan and Elvi that Miss Brierly had taken the opportunity to sketch in a few biographical details. When the girl had left Alan smiled ruefully.

'Who was more uncomfortable – her or us?'

'I don't know. Horrible, isn't it? I'm afraid I've been very clumsy.'

'Nonsense. Help yourself. By the way, I've only got Scotch. Will you have one?'

'You know I won't.' He poured himself one and sat down in the one other easy chair. His eyes took her in. She seemed to know that he was studying her, but with a cat-like calm and composure she did not fidget or return his gaze.

'You look marvellous,' he said. 'You've changed.'

'Yes, I have. I'm sadder and wiser.'

'You should be happier. You were happy with me.'

'I was, in a way. But then I was hardly a person.'

'I don't know so much about that . . .' His voice broke a little and for one sickening moment she thought he was going to break down, then he remarked conversationally: 'I like your dress, and the necklace.'

She was wearing a cream cheesecloth smock, ruched at the yoke and cuffs, then loose to the knee. Her legs below the hem were slim and lightly tanned, the bare skin smooth and shiny. She had got thinner; the bones at her ankle had a pronounced, schoolgirlish look, and there were hollows on either side of her collarbones where the copper necklace cast a shadow. Her face, unmade-up, was gently freckled, the summer sun had given it the colour of a pale brown eggshell, but the eyes looked bigger, darker. The transparent clarity and sparkle had been replaced by something gentler and deeper. Alan found her unbearably desirable.

He held out his hand, and she took it. It felt quiet, still and thin in his like a small bird that knows its only chance lies in passivity and trust.

'I still adore you,' he said.

She smiled, and softly pulled her hand away. 'Do you?'

'I can hardly bear to have you here and not hold you in my arms. I can hardly bear it, it's real physical pain. Can you believe that?'

'Oh yes.'

'Yes, of course.' Stupid question, he thought – this was how she felt about the other man. Almost rudely, Alan asked: 'So what part am I to play in all this?'

'I never asked you to play a part, Alan. It's the real you I want – I *need* – to tell me what to do for the best.'

'Come back to me.'

There was a pause. She seemed to be giving this suggestion her full attention. 'I don't think so,' she said.

It was ironic, she thought, that she could now value Alan's qualities at their true worth, that she was prepared to exploit them, only when she needed to draw off strength for herself. She found it easy to be with him. There was no difficulty in adjusting her behaviour. Far from having to be devious she found that simplicity and directness were the natural approaches. There seemed no point in apology. On the way home that afternoon she felt a sense of relief, the proof, she reflected of that old saying 'a trouble shared is a trouble halved'. She felt confident in Alan's ability to help her, to be reasonable and sane. She wanted nothing from him but his attention as a listener, and she felt no shame in asking for it.

When she got back, she wrote to Callum. She felt calm and rational. She would write exactly what she meant.

. . . I rang because I love you, and I don't understand your attitude. I wanted to clarify things but you wouldn't let me. I don't know why, so I assume that you will explain in your own good time. I simply want us to work things out. For now I won't be in touch again till

I hear from you, the ball's in your court. I miss you, I'm
dull and lonely . . . Elvi.

She posted the letter with a feeling of finality. She had said
her say, done all she could. Now she could only wait.

On Saturday she met Alan at the Boulestin for lunch. The
restaurant's rich, clubby atmosphere awed her a little.

'This is a very grand place.'

'Not really, just a good, old-fashioned one.' They chose
a corner table. It occurred to Elvi as she hid behind the
enormous menu that they must appear like a pair of lovers.
She had on a brown cotton sundress and orange espadrilles,
summery and casual.

'I'm afraid I'm not dressed for this,' she whispered.

'You look lovely.'

'Yes, but not *right*.'

'Don't worry about it.' They ordered and sipped Pimms
while they waited.

'Tell me,' said Alan, 'would you consider coming back
to me?'

'No, Alan, I can't. Whatever I say is going to sound selfish,
but I can't help it. At the moment, I have no choice. It's not
simply a question of having chosen him – or even of love. I
really crave him, like an addiction, I feel all the time not quite
myself without him. Do you see?' She looked anxiously across
the table at him. She was wearing the copper necklace again.

'I see.'

'Is that – do you feel like that?'

'No.' She looked crestfallen so he added: 'I'm more deliberate than that. I had it all worked out.'

'I'm so sorry.'

'Don't be. And anyway, we're here to talk about you and
– Callum.' It was an effort to speak his name. 'Tell me what
sort of person he is.' She did. As she talked, Alan thought
she seemed more of her old, carefree, light-hearted self. She
seemed to delight in every remembered detail, and sometimes
it was as though the man himself was standing there. Halfway

through she put her hand across the table to touch Alan's arm and asked: 'I want you to realize why it had to be him, I want you to understand because I *care* about you . . .' and he had nodded cut to the quick.

When she had finished, he remarked, 'But now you're not sure if he feels the same.'

'He *did*, I know he did. And I think he still does. Except for this – whatever it is.'

'You can't do a thing about that. If it's something that affects him as deeply as you think, he'll only tell you when he's ready. Or he may simply choose to run away.'

'I don't think I could bear that . . .'

'You might have to. Don't think I'm saying that because I want you back. What I want is your happiness, however trite that sounds.'

'I believe you. You're the only person I know who seems to be able to love unselfishly.' She smiled ruefully. 'I certainly can't.'

'You've never tried.' He gazed at her curiously. 'Who knows what you might be capable of?'

'As you say.' When they had finished, she leant back in her chair with a stretching movement like a cat. 'That was a good lunch.'

'I'm glad you enjoyed it. Shall we do it again?'

'I'd like to. It was so good to talk to you. But I don't want to cause any – problems, shall we say.'

'No problem. And anyway, I live in hope.'

She looked down at her fingers, flexing and stretching them thoughtfully. 'I suppose if Callum were to come back tomorrow I should go straight to him, I couldn't see you any more.'

'I suppose that, too. I understand.'

On the day Elvi and Alan had lunch together, Callum saw Jude.

It was in the early afternoon, when most Italians, and all sensible people, were taking a nap, but when Paul Donati was writing flat out. The heat was intense. Even Dawn lay flat on the couch, an electric fan on the coffee table stirring the air with its blurred, spinning face. The apartment was heavy with silent industry, and torpor . . .

He had to get out. As he emerged from the cool, stuccoed darkness of the hall into the street the sunlight was like sheet metal, the heat smacked his face and made him blink.

The street was on a hill, and at the foot of the hill was a little *piazza* with a stone fountain like an upended dolphin and a couple of poky, no-frills cafés. According to some system known only to the proprietors, one or other of these cafés contrived to be open in the heat of the day, with one or two elderly locals sitting in the furthest recesses, escaping not just the temperature but whatever ailed them at home.

Callum walked slowly down the hill, keeping to the narrow band of shade beside the buildings. Within a minute his T-shirt was damp beneath the arms and between the shoulder blades. The street was silent, the windows of the houses shuttered, the shopfronts blinded. The heat lent the silence a density, it stunned all living things, like a gas. It pressed on his eardrums.

At the foot of the hill he turned into a café that was open. There were the two old men sitting at the back, hands on their knees, staring out, waiting for the day to go by. At the bar, a younger man in work overalls was reading a folded newspaper. Callum ordered a beer and went to sit at a table, away from the window but with a view of the square.

It was a slow-motion world at this time of day. Those people who had to be out trudged, heads down, through the early after-noon white-out. A fat old woman swayed with massive dignity to her door, let herself in, dissolved into the interior blackness. Mangy cats lay on the steps of the fountain like dirty rags. A man unaccountably taking a bicycle up the hill pushed past, his cap pulled down over a black fringe damp with sweat.

When the young woman appeared she was no different. She walked with a slow, swinging gait, like someone carrying water, from the far corner of the square, where there was no through road, and crossed uphill, towards the opposite corner to the right of where Callum sat. The moment he saw her he caught his breath. There was no doubt in his mind. The walk, the carriage, the straight mouse-brown hair, half pinned up – even the clothes were hers, what she'd always liked – patched jeans and an embroidered shirt, sandals, the gleam of a ring on her foot.

Jude . . . ? He was transfixed. She was crossing on the far side of the stone dolphin, and must have paused by the water tumbling from its mouth. Leaving his beer, he left the café and went over to the fountain, half dazzled by the sudden glare. On the far side the woman was bent over the basin, her hair lifted in one hand, the other sluicing her neck with water. The hands, strong and spatulate, were hers, he was sure he recognized a silver ring in the shape of a buckle.

'Jude . . . ?'

She straightened up, sweeping her hair back from her face, water running over her shoulders; gave him a blank, irritable look.

'I'm sorry. *Scusi.* I didn't mean to . . .'

It wasn't her.

As he returned, sweating, to the café, it seemed impossible that he could ever have made the mistake. This woman, though handsome, had a heavy, sallow face, pocked with acne scars, and deep-set eyes beneath straight brows. Not a trace of Jude – nothing like her.

When he got back to the apartment, he wrote a letter to her. He didn't allow himself to think too much, he simply took pen and paper and began, describing the incident in the piazza. Then, for the first time, he wrote his thoughts and feelings. He didn't have to strive after honesty, or the truth, because that was all there was, his reason for writing. When Donati's tea-break time was imminent. Dawn emerged from her room.

'Hey, Callum . . . don't tell me you're at it too?'

'What?'

'The great novel?'

'No. Just writing a letter.'

207

She smiled, scrunching up her hair with one hand. 'To your lady back home?'

'No.' He didn't hesitate, or need to. 'To a dear friend.' He caught Dawn's sweetly sceptical smile. 'Long overdue.'

He didn't know whether he had Jude's address right, or even her name – she could be married, moved, anything. But the act of posting the letter unlocked something in him. That evening he told Paul Donati he had to try and get back to England for a couple of days, soon.

'Fine where I'm concerned,' said Donati. 'You don't work for me.'

'That's true.'

'On the other hand you don't want me either to get writer's block, finish the book, or bin the whole thing while you're away.'

Callum laughed. 'I confess it would be helpful if you could avoid those things.'

'I'll do my best but I promise nothing. The creative process, you know . . .'

They fixed on a date in a few days time. The night before Callum left, he and Donati had dinner together in a restaurant in the hills above the city. There was a security for him in the writer's company, he appreciated the older man's non-judgemental and dispassionate interest.

'So why the rush to get back,' he asked over the second bottle, 'all of a sudden?'

'There's someone I need to see.'

'Female someone?' Callum nodded. 'All well, or is this a rescue dash?'

'Neither. I think it's time I put her first – I want to put her first – and time she knew it.'

'It'll be appreciated, I'm sure.'

It was late, and still warm. The lanterns were lit among the vines at the edge of the terrace. Florence was a broad river of lights below them. In between was the soft, buzzing dark of the hills.

Callum said, 'May I ask you something?' Donati opened a hand acceptingly. 'Have you ever felt there were emotions that you couldn't – or wouldn't allow yourself to express?'

'In life, or on the page?'

'Life.'

'Why do you think I became a writer?' He refilled Callum's glass. 'Writing thrives on repression, so everyone's happy, including my publisher.'

'That's not a course open to all of us. Unfortunately.'

'It's certainly open to you,' pointed out Donati. 'You haven't written a novel yet, thank God. But you and I are in the same line of work.'

'I suppose so.'

'All is copy, and all copy is therapy. Either that or revenge.'

'That's an outrageous assertion!'

'It's second-bottle talk, I grant you. Some truth in it though. Write it out, man.'

'I think,' said Callum, 'I may have done that.'

'Excellent.'

'But where does that leave the real life part? Putting it in writing is one thing, but not the whole thing.'

'I suspect it is for me. Which is probably why in the second half of my life I'm a lonely bachelor. Not for you though. The writing clears the crap out of the way, helps you see the pattern, makes a story of it. After that, if you want to, all you have to do is say it.'

All he had to do. Open-heart surgery. Swimming the Atlantic. The desert marathon. Everest.

Say it.

Fifteen

D onati was only half right. Saying it may have been simple, but it wasn't easy.

Jean – not for the first time – was entirely right. He had underestimated Elvi.

Feeling that it would be easier for both of them if they met on neutral ground, he called her from the airport. To his dismay it was her father who answered the phone. He was well-spoken, measured, courteous.

'I believe she's just got in . . . Would you be so kind as to hang on a minute?'

Callum heard him call: 'Elvi – Elvi, there's a young man on the phone for you! I do apologize, I didn't quite catch your name.'

'Callum Sheil.'

'A Mr Sheil! She's coming – no, she's going to pick it up in the study.'

'Thank you.'

'My pleasure.'

There was a pause, then: 'Callum! Where are you?'

'At Gatwick Airport.'

'You're here!'

'To see you, Elvi. Do you think you could meet me somewhere?'

'But why don't you come down here, I could meet you at the station—'

'It's a nice idea, but what I want is to talk to you in private.'

'We could be—' she began, and then added, 'no, I know what you mean. I'll come anywhere you say.'

They arranged to meet for dinner in a town that was equidistant between them, which she could get to directly by train. He would pick up a hire car and meet her at the station. She ordered a taxi. As she replaced the phone her father appeared in the hall.

'Are you going to see him?'

'Yes.'

'Good.' He was so discreet, she could see him searching for the right thing to say, something that would convey his care, his love, his concern for her happiness. But all that he did say was: 'It's a beautiful evening. Enjoy yourselves.'

Elvi hadn't known what to expect. Their parting, the tone of his few letters, had made her wary. But the moment she saw him she knew that nothing had changed. Her heart seemed to balloon, her feet not to touch the ground, and when their arms went round each other she knew she had come home.

'Let's drive out and find somewhere quiet,' he said. And then: 'I love you, Elvi.'

'And I love you,' she replied. Firmly, clearly.

They drove out of the town in silence and found a country pub with tables in the garden. He went to the bar to get their drinks, and she sat alone, content to wait in the summer evening. In the pub garden there were apple trees, beyond it was farmland, the acres of late summer corn standing upright like a silent, golden army. There were huge, blowsy poppies among the stooks, their heads too big for their spindly stems. When she was little she used to pick the poppies and put them in jam jars on the kitchen window sill but they had always proved a disappointment, the petals falling within a day and the stalks leaving a sticky, bitter juice on her fingers.

Callum returned with their drinks. 'It's nice here,' she said.

He took her hand and buried his mouth in the palm, eyes closed. 'I hope I'm not about to spoil it.'

'You're here,' she said, 'that's what matters. I've missed you so much.'

'I've come back because there are things I need to tell you. Things you deserve to know.'

'Yes,' she said, 'I believe there are. And you're right, I do deserve to know.'

'The reason I haven't told you before is that it's complicated, and I've been ashamed to – and most of all I didn't want to admit that our love was that important.'

'Tell me now.'

He did. He told her about Jude, and how much she had meant to him; of her spirit and passion; of his own less certain youthful feelings; about the influence and inspiration she had been. He told her about their baby daughter, christened Faith, born in the deep secrecy of death. He told her about Jude's overwhelming, raging grief that put his ambivalence to shame. He told her about their parting, that had been without recrimination of any kind, but which had been cutting his heart ever since, so that the only way to stop the pain was to bind the heart tight, and keep it close.

When he'd finished, he found he was trembling. She didn't touch him, but said: 'Callum, I am so sorry. What you and she went through. I can hardly bear to imagine it.'

'She went through it, Elvi. Not me.'

'Of course you did. It wasn't a crime for you not to be like her. She sounds like an extraordinary person – but you are too.'

'I ran away.'

'No, you were there when it mattered. You wanted different things. She loved you more. You were both wise, and you cared about each other enough to let it end.'

Elvi, too, was being wise. Callum wiped his eyes, which stung with tears. 'I never again wanted to have that much asked of me, so I could fail again. Elvi, I wanted our love to go away.'

'I know.'

'But it wouldn't.'

'I'm glad.'

'There's something else,' he said. 'Not long ago, I thought I saw Jude.'

For the first time, there was a stain of anxiety behind her eyes. 'Oh?'

'It wasn't her. But it turned me over. Really shocked me. I went up to the woman, I spoke to her before I saw she wasn't Jude. The point is that afterwards I realized that what I felt when I believed it *was* Jude wasn't the same as – what I felt when I saw you coming out of that station. Not – joy, elation, total love. I thought, there's Jude, I can speak to her and apologize, and ask for her forgiveness, and put the past behind me. And then, of course, I couldn't.'

She was silent, waiting for him to go on. Perhaps, not trusting herself to speak.

'So I wrote to her. Put on paper everything I should have said before. Acknowledged all she'd meant to me, my own inadequacy, my feelings about Faith – everything. And told her about you, Elvi.'

She glanced away for a moment. 'Have you heard from her?'

'Not yet. And I may never. I had her old address, she could be anywhere in the world, knowing her. Married . . . who knows? My guess is that I will hear from her, eventually. I feel it in my bones. But it doesn't matter. That letter needed to be written. It helped me make sense of things, to see that I had to be straight with you, too. Most of all with you, because I love you so much. I couldn't bear to lose you because I'd allowed myself to become closed and twisted.'

'That's not how you appear to me.'

'I'm good at disguising it. But just the same I *was* twisted. And straightening out is painful. I'm going to need your help, Elvi.'

She laid both her hands, palm uppermost, on the table to receive his. 'You have it. I may not be yours, any more than you're mine, but I'm yours to call on. You can never ask too much of me. I love you.'

'Elvi . . .' He could scarcely speak for the fullness of his heart.

'There's something I want to tell you, too.'

'Please.'

'My name is Elvira. It was my mother's second name and she wanted me to have it. I think my father found it difficult, after she died, so he called his little girl Elvi, and it stuck. No one's ever called me by my full name; I didn't used to like it. But I think you should know it.'

'And do you like it now?'

'Yes,' she said. 'Things are different, now.'

At the station, in the sweet agony of goodbyes, he said impulsively: 'Come back with me!'

'No,' she said. 'Everything you said before is true. I need to organize my course, sort myself out, think about what I'm going to do.'

'How am I going to work? It's been so hard without you!'

'But you have been working, just the same, and that's how it should be. Make it brilliant, Callum. For me. For us. And I'll come and visit in a few weeks' time.'

'Promise?'

In reply she simply gave him a grown-up, challenging look that chastized him for his doubts.

Still, when the train drew in she clung to him. 'My darling, darling, Callum . . .'

'*Au revoir*,' he said against her hair. '*Au revoir*, Elvira.'

She told her father. Not everything, but enough for him to know how important Callum was to her.

'Do you want to marry him?' he asked.

'He hasn't asked me.'

'Would you, Elvi, if he did?'

'I know I want to be with him. But we have a long way to go.'

Dick Beecham took his daughter in his arms. 'It's good to travel forward. *Bon voyage*, Elvi.'

*   *   *

On the weekend of her visit to Italy, Alan drove her to the airport.

'Indulge me,' he'd said. 'Allow me my last-ditch stand. Who knows? I might persuade you not to get on that plane and I'll be driving you back again.'

In the event, they behaved like old friends – courteous, amiable, exchanging news of a general nature, touching on nothing that was sensitive. When they were within a couple of miles of the airport, he said: 'You needn't have worried. I've finally got the message.'

She wanted to ask how, but without her having uttered a word he added: 'It was nothing you said. It's the way you are.'

She knew this was true. 'I've changed.'

'You have. Out of all recognition. Grown, and blossomed. The Elvi I fell in love with is still part of you but you've gone on and left me behind.'

The sadness in his voice touched her deeply. 'We'll always be close, you know that.'

'Maybe. But not necessarily. Enough to know that we have been, don't you think?'

At the barrier they embraced, standing still in each other's arms for a minute, an embrace complex with all that had been between them. Then he pushed her gently away.

'Have a wonderful time,' he said. 'And an even better future, whatever it holds.'

'Thank you.'

'And give him my congratulations.' He lifted a hand and began moving away. 'He's a clever, lucky bastard.'

Callum had booked them a room for two nights in a *pensione* in a village further up the hill, a little place of warm stone that caught whatever breeze there was above the furnace of the city.

He was working – writing up and ordering his notes. For the first time in months he was enfolded by that special pleasure and contentment that came from immersion in what he did best.

For once it was Donati who came in to him, and who said: 'Leave that, why don't you? You want to be there when she arrives. It's not polite to keep a lady waiting, especially one who's been waiting this long already.'

Callum glanced up.

'It's all right,' he said. 'Don't worry. There's plenty of time.'

It had been raining in England, but now they were above the clouds, droning through the blue towards Italy.

Elvi reached into her flight bag for her book. Her passport came out with it, and she flipped it open idly, always surprised and amused by that image of her three-years-younger self, staring back with a wild and nervous surmise.

Elvira Rose Beecham. Not so young now, nor so nervous. Going forward with trust in love, into the wonders of an uncertain future.